MW00909051

Quest
For The
Holy Shroud

The CAUL - Part V

To Tom Higgins,

Best regards

James A Matte

James Allan Matte

Published and Distributed throughout the World by

J. A. M. PUBLICATIONS
43 Brookside Drive
Williamsville, New York 14221-6915
Tel: (716) 634-6645 – Fax: (716) 634-7204
E-Mail: editor@jampublications.com
Website: URL: http://www.jampublications.com

To Order: http://www.createspace.com/3447582

ISBN: 1452814473
ISBN-13: 9781452814476
Library of Congress Control Number: 2010905544

Edited by J. A. Petruskie

Quest
For The
Holy Shroud

The CAUL - Part V

James Allan Matte

J. A. M. Publications

2010

CONTENTS

Quest
For The
Holy Shroud

This book is dedicated to
Father Donald Higgins of the Stigmatine Fathers
For his unyielding faith in Humanity.

INTRODUCTION

Although the story, characters and events in this novel are ficti-
tious, this author made every effort to present the evidence con-
cerning the authenticity of the Shroud of Turin in an accurate
and factual manner. The references listed at the end of this novel
provide a significant body of research and literature that offers a
compelling argument that the Shroud of Turin covered the body
of Jesus Christ and the imprint of his figure into the Shroud was
caused by a burst of radiation during his resurrection. Hence,
this author feels rightly justified in referring to the Shroud of
Turin as the Holy Shroud.

PROLOGUE

The CAUL trilogy was followed by The Divine Executioner, wherein the protagonist James Markham was again placed in the inescapable position of defending and rescuing victims of the most sinister villains he had ever encountered at a time when he believed that his ultimate destiny and *raison d'etre* had been fulfilled. Then fate reintroduced him to a former victim he had once rescued, and learned that she had a terminal illness with less than a year to live. She elected to spend this time with the man she loved, James Markham, and whom she married regardless of his advanced age. At her request, he buried her at sea where her parents had died at the hands of pirates, and as he sailed away from her watery grave, his overwhelming grief lashed out with a cry to the heavens that was heard miles across the sea. Markham had become a man in despair, without a purpose or destination.

In this book, we learn of Markham's destination following the sea burial of his wife and his escape from the painful agony of his loss. When all seems hopeless for this desolate man in despair, providence comes to his rescue, but not without a heavy price.

CHAPTER I

Search for the Truth-Seeker

The tall figure of a man whose blond hair had turned gray with his advanced age stared out of the large window of the office of the Director of Clandestine Operations at the Central Intelligence Agency. His icy blue eyes saw beyond the advancing storm with its lightning show and threatening winds, and it reminded him of his longtime friend sailing the world alone on his 41-foot cutter-rigged yacht. He wondered what had happened to him. The last time he'd heard from James Markham was in Paris, France shortly after he had married a young, terminally ill American woman, Claire Perkins, and their plans of a honeymoon to Venice, Italy aboard their yacht The Caul. That was a month ago, and the satellite transmitter that had been secretly planted by the CIA on the vessel and had been tracking Markham's travels for the past three years, had shown that he had cut short his voyage off the coast of Spain and returned to the Port of Saint Nazaire, France. It was unlike Markham not to return electronic mail messages from his friend Alex Petrov with whom he had shared many an adventure, and Petrov was now worried that his seemingly invincible friend may have finally become the victim of foul play. Petrov's reverie was suddenly interrupted by a knock on his large office door, and one of his two assistants entered with a look on his face that spelled mission failure.

"Well, Scott...what did you find out?" asked Petrov, hoping for good news.

"Sir," replied Scott, "our Paris agent checked out Markham's sailboat docked at the Port of Saint-Nazaire. Apparently, the marina manager knows Markham real well from his previous visit to the marina, and this time when he sailed into port, he noted that Markham looked like he hadn't slept for a week. He just handed him the boat keys and his credit card number and told the manager that he would be gone for an undetermined amount of time. The last time he saw Markham was when he boarded a taxi, hearing him tell the driver to take him to the train station. He suspects that Markham was headed for Paris."

"Who's the agent that checked him out?" asked Alex Petrov, knowing the names of every CIA agent in Europe.

"Special Agent Roy Palmer," replied Scott.

"Did he check out those people in Paris whom we know had previous contact with Markham?"

"Yes Sir," replied Scott. "I provided him with the names of his previous landlord, the two O.S.I. Agents assigned to the Paris office, and even his favorite restaurants, to no avail. It's as if he just dropped off the face of the earth."

"Scott…there's something you must understand. James Markham may not be on the Agency's payroll, but he is one of our most valuable assets but I don't need to tell you, you've seen first hand the major contributions he's made to this agency and this country," replied Petrov whose friendship with Markham dated back more than four decades.

"We could send that new agent Tom Breckinridge over to Paris to search for him. He hasn't been assigned any cases yet and this would not be a particularly difficult assignment for a new agent," said Scott, wishing he could be selected for the job, but knew that Petrov wouldn't think of it. "He could probably complete the assignment within a couple of weeks and it would be good experience for him learning his way around France."

"No. We need someone who speaks fluent French, who's familiar with Paris, and I think I've got just the person for this job," said Petrov, with a smile returning to his face.

"Who would that be, Sir?" asked Scott.

"Theresa Brenner," replied Petrov. "She'll be retiring from the agency in twelve months, so she's been relieved from active cases and is working in the case review center. She has twenty-four years of experience as an agent, is fluent in French, Italian, Spanish, and served three years in our Paris office. She also studied Arabic at the Army's Foreign Language School in Monterey, California, not that it would be useful for this mission."

"Sounds like she's perfect for this job," replied Scott, impressed with Brenner's resume.

"Yeah," replied Alex, "but she first must review and study Markham's file, so you'd better advise her of her new assignment and the need for her to be ready to leave for Paris a week from tomorrow. That'll give her time to settle her immediate affairs."

"Will Ms. Brenner be using her cover name on this mission?" asked Scott.

"She shouldn't have to," said Alex pondering the question. "It's her last assignment before retirement and this mission is a straight forward search and hopefully not a rescue operation."

"Excuse me, sir," replied Scott, "but considering Markham's past adventures and the unlikelihood of him disappearing this long, there's a distinct possibility that he may be in serious trouble requiring maximum measures to liberate him."

"You've raised a good point, Scott," said Alex. "If Ms. Brenner has to use maximum measures, then she needs to be traveling under her assumed name to protect her identity and relationship with this agency."

"So if I understand you correctly, sir, Ms. Brenner will be given authority to use maximum measures and will be traveling under her assumed name," said Scott confirming Alex Petrov's orders.

"That's correct, Scott. Have her report to me when she's completed her study of Markham's file," said Alex who had another thought. "Remember Father O'Malley?"

"Yes, I met him at your house last Thanksgiving Day," replied Scott. "As I recall, he baptized your children."

"And my grandchildren too," said Alex. "He's with the Stigmatine order of priests of the Roman Catholic Church, and has recently been transferred from Saint Joseph Hall in Waltham, Massachusetts to the Basilique de St. Denis in the northern section of Paris, France."

"Why did they transfer him to France?" asked Scott incredulously.

"For one thing, he's fluent in French and the Stigmatine Fathers is a missionary order," replied Alex. "You know...this could be a blessing in disguise."

"Why's that?" asked Scott.

"Because in the past, whenever Markham reached a point of despair, he always sought refuge in a nearby church. I'll have Father O'Malley pass the word around to the other pastors to be on the lookout for him," said Alex, pleased with the cleverness of his idea.

The narrow sidewalk glistened from the light drizzle reflecting the amber glow of the street lamp a few feet from the entrance to Le Petit Bistro, a small pub, in the northern section of Paris frequented mostly by the French residents and its low-rent prostitutes. The area is also well known for the renowned 12th century Basilique de St. Denis. Inside the small tavern, at a table for two against the north wall, sat a strapping curly gray-haired man, sporting a white beard. The wall lamp emitted an eerie shadow over that lone man whose gaze seemed to be focused on the half empty glass of Scotch resting on the table in front of him. Picking up the glass with his right hand, he downed the contents, and then raised the empty glass to signal the waitress for more Scotch. There were few customers in the place, being a weeknight, and this particular customer had been a regular for weeks. He ordered the same drink night after night, usually finishing an entire bottle of Scotch at each visit, yet no one knew his name, not even the owner, Jean Batiste, a Vietnam Veteran who luckily had completed his French military term of service before the massacre of the French Army at Dien Bien Phu. He expressed his curiosity of this mysterious man to his waitress who had only managed to get the words *Scotch whisky* from him.

"Save yourself a trip, Madeleine, bring the bottle to him," said Batiste in his Parisian French.

Madeleine approached the man who now raised his head towards her with liquid eyes that begged for an end to his sorrow.

"Would you like another drink of Scotch, mister?" she asked in French with an empathy she had seldom felt.

"Just leave the bottle," he replied in French, which were the most words he had uttered in all of the many nights he had spent at this tavern.

Upon returning to the bar, Madeleine reported to owner Jean Batiste. "I think he's Canadian. His accent is unmistakable. I tell you, Jean, I've never seen such agony in a man's eyes."

"Ten to one, it's over a woman," said Batiste.

"And she probably doesn't know or care," replied Madeleine.

The heart wrenching voice of the late Edith Piaf, France's most famous vocalist, could be heard over the strategically placed speakers in the small, poorly lit bistro. The song of misery and lost love penetrated the inebriated mind and suffering heart of the gray bearded man, who knew of Piaf's early squalid life and personal anguish that permeated most of her songs with a melancholy that could drive a depressed man to drink himself to oblivion.

The big man poured himself another drink from the bottle of Scotch to dull the painful memory of his loss, but the haunting face of his recently deceased wife kept appearing on the screen of his mind, alternating from the tenderness of her loving smile to the visage of her death in his arms and burial at sea. *Oh! God*, he thought, *put me through the fires of hell but spare me the agony her loss.* He downed his drink, then poured himself another, and as the night wore on, his lone presence became the topic of conversation at the bar between a prostitute and her kept man.

"I heard Madeleine tell Jean that he's Canadian and he comes here every night. Must have money, hen!" said the French wiseguy.

"Probably, but I don't think he's interested in female company, Gaston," said Giselle, who was dressed in a tight skirt and form fitting shirt that accentuated her slim but well developed figure.

"You'll never know unless you try, Giselle," replied Gaston.

"I don't know, Gaston. He's a big man, looks strong. You think you can handle him?" she asked with some concern for her own safety, and her feelings of guilt about victimizing a man already downtrodden by life's misfortunes, of which she herself had much experience.

"The guy's an old man and he drinks like a fish. He'll be no problem, and besides, I've got my equalizer," said Gaston, patting the blackjack in his pocket. "Wait 'till he's had a few more drinks then make your play."

"Alright, Gaston, but I have this strange feeling that this guy's no easy mark," replied Giselle.

"Stop worrying. We could use a few euros," said Gaston now watching his prey pour himself another drink. At last, Giselle made her move and walked up to the beleaguered man. "Would you like some company, Mister?"

The gray haired man slowly raised his head and peered at Giselle through the slit of his eyes. "No thanks," he replied in French.

"You sure, Mister?" she asked. "You look lonely and I could use a drink."

"If it's a drink you want, go ahead and pour yourself one," he replied.

Giselle sat down at the small table facing him and the waitress brought her an empty glass with a knowing look. Giselle poured herself a drink from the bottle of Scotch.

"I'm Giselle. What's your name?" she asked in French.

The bearded man raised his head again and after a long look lowered his gaze without answering her question.

"I can see that you're the strong silent type. I like that. Your bottle of Scotch is nearly empty. How about coming over to my place for a drink," she said in a sultry, seductive voice that promised a good time.

"You're wasting your time, mademoiselle," replied the seasoned man in French, pouring himself the last drink left in the bottle. He stood up, all six feet and 220 pounds of muscle, gulped down the drink of Scotch, and then walked away from Giselle, still sitting at the table, past the bar of customers including a disappointed Gaston, and out the door onto the street. He flipped up the collar of his blazer jacket against the still drizzling rain and started walking slowly down the deserted street towards the Place du Caquet, unaware that Gaston had followed him out of the Bistro with the intent to slug him with his blackjack and rob him of his money. However, Giselle's empathetic conscience urged her to stop Gaston, running after him in her high heel shoes which clattered on the sidewalk alerting the big man that he was being followed. As he turned to see who it was, he instinctively raised his right forearm to block Gaston's hand wielding blackjack that was aimed at his head. In spite of his large consumption of alcohol, the big man's past training in martial arts and superior physical strength made short work of this robber, who ended up with a dislocated shoulder and a broken collar bone, when the big man came down hard with a rabbit punch to the side of his neck that caused him to crash to the ground like a broken mannequin. Giselle stood a few feet from the fight scene nearly paralyzed with fear at the sight of this fierce tiger of a man, waiting for his next move, before she dared go to Gaston's aid. The big man gazed at her with glassy eyes that conveyed no emotion, then silently turned around and resumed his walk towards the Place du Caquet. At that moment, Giselle's empathy had turned to admiration for this powerful man. She felt the sudden urge to join him but her friend Gaston's immediate need of assistance prevailed. *Besides,* she thought, *he rejected me once, and he probably thinks I was in league with Gaston, thus would reject me again, and not so kindly.*

The big man walked north on the Place du Caquet, crossed the Rue Edouard Vaillant without a thought about the previous incident as he was no stranger to violence. The near deserted street, due to the late hour and poor weather, accentuated his loneliness. He felt like a rudderless boat alone on the sea without destination or purpose. *A man without the love of a woman,* he thought, *was a mere robot. Was he destined to be alone for the rest of his life?* That thought was more menacing than any physical threat he had ever encountered. The thought of abandonment resurrected his fear of desertion by the God whom he had served so well. *Oh! God,* he pleaded silently, *have you forsaken me?* As he walked, he came upon the sight of a most magnificent basilica which he recognized as the Basilique de St. Denis with its large rose window in the church's façade and the crenellated parapet on the top reminiscent of a castle's fortifications. Markham's heart and soul compelled him to mount the stairs to the entrance of this 12th Century basilica that seemed like an oasis to a dehydrated desert Legionnaire. To his relief, the door was still unlocked, allowing him inside the cavernous building adorned with lighted candles that were placed before statues of Jesus, the Virgin Mary and various saints. The weathered man, desperate for God's creation of a soul mate to soothe his pain, chose a pew in one of the last rows to his left, and after dipping his right hand in the bowl of holy water and making the sign of the cross, he knelt on the hard wood kneeler joining both hands in prayer.

At first he didn't know what to say and reflected on his life which revealed that the happiest times were during his short-lived marriages to Suzanne who died of cancer and Claire who had re-cently succumbed to heart disease. He had such an abundance of love to give and equally as great a need for the love of a woman, so that life seemed worthless without it. But the distinguishing mark of this man was the fact that he was an idealistic romantic with a poetic heart, and could be an adoring and tenderly passionate lover who would rather sacrifice his life than be unfaithful. There he knelt before the statue of Mary, Mother of Jesus Christ, with her arms outstretched as if inviting the bearded man to join her in prayer. As he recited the Lord's Prayer, a priest dressed in a black robe and roman collar appeared at the rear of the church and si-lently advanced towards the praying man. Markham's words were now audible to the priest and he realized that this man was an American with a recognizable New York accent. Unaware of the priest's presence and unable to contain his overwhelming emo-tions in the face of his creator, the man raised both hands to his face as he sobbed uncontrollably. Father O'Malley moved into the pew and knelt next to him. He suspected from the man's unique physical appearance and New York accent that he was none other than James Markham whom he had met once at Alex Petrov's residence a few years ago, but he couldn't see his covered face. O'Malley decided to recite a prayer he himself had composed and had given to Markham at the time of their meeting, and it would be a good way of re-establishing their acquaintance.

> "Through the intercession of Our Lady of Hope and Peace, Queen of Apostles and Mother of Jesus Christ, Crucified and Risen, and our Mother, may the blessings of Almighty God, Father, Son and Holy Spirit descend upon you. May she embrace you in her Immaculate Heart and share with you her peace, love, joy, and strength. In the shield of her Immaculate Conception may she protect you from all spiritual, physical, and emotional harm. May Jesus Christ The King, her Son, Our Risen Lord, the Light of the world, grant you perfect health of body, mind and soul and oneness in Christ, and God's peace, joy, and wisdom. Amen."

Father O'Malley's prayer penetrated the sorrowful man's mind with a familiar ring that suddenly made him lower his hands and turn towards the priest whose face he recognized.

"Father O'Malley?" said the distraught man in his low baritone voice.

"Yes, Jim, it's me," he replied, recognizing Markham's distinctive voice leaving no doubt of his identity. "It looks as if I've come at an opportune time."

Markham was speechless with embarrassment and turned his gaze back to the statue of Mary.

"The Lord moves in mysterious ways, Jim," said Father O'Malley. "I was transferred to Paris at this Basilica a few weeks ago. Alex told me to be on the lookout for you, Jim. He's very worried about you."

"He needn't worry, Father. I'm just going through a period of grieving that's taking longer than I expected," said Markham, trying to minimize the severity of his grief.

"Where are you staying, Jim?" asked Father O'Malley.

"At a small apartment nearby," he replied without looking at the priest.

"Listen, Jim. I want to help you. Whatever you need, God will provide," said Father O'Malley. "Don't go away. I've just got to lock the side doors, and then I'll be back so we can discuss your situation."

Markham watched Father O'Malley as he walked briskly to the front of the basilica then to the church's right wing where he disappeared from view. A short time later, Father O'Malley returned to the rear of the basilica to discover that Markham had left without disclosing the location of his apartment.

Early the following morning, Father O'Malley telephoned Alex Petrov to inform him of his brief meeting with Jim Markham.

"Where do you think he's staying?" asked Petrov.

"I don't know but he said in an apartment nearby. This parish is fairly large though. The rector took ill and there are only two of us priests to manage the church, so I'm unable to canvas the parish, Alex. But should he come in again, this time I won't let him go without finding out exactly where he lives," said Father O'Malley.

"I'm sending one of my agents over there to find him. She'll be contacting you. Her name is Teri Flanigan. Ask to see her credentials, Father. We can't be too careful," said Alex.

"Can you give me a brief description of her, Alex?" said Father O'Malley.

"She's 49 years old, has long dark curly hair, green eyes, about five feet seven inches tall with the build of a ballerina," said Alex recalling her distinct attractiveness. "She could easily pass for thirty," he added.

"I don't want to tell you your business, Alex, but do you think it wise to send this attractive woman to find Markham in his current emotional condition?" said Father O'Malley. He was concerned about the corporal temptation she may present to this man starving for the affection of a woman, not realizing that Markham was vulnerable only to a woman ordained to be his life mate.

"She's man-proof since the death of her first and only husband some twenty-five years ago. I know Jim Markham like my own brother," said Alex Petrov. "She's exactly what he needs to get out of this slump. She has the tenderness of a woman and the emotional and physical strength required of a special agent whose chastity has never been in question."

"Then I'm looking forward to meeting her, Alex," replied a reassured Father O'Malley. "In the meantime, I'll keep my eyes and ears open."

"Teri will be leaving for Paris in three days," said Alex. "Keep me posted Father, and God Bless."

On the day before her departure for Paris, Teri Flanigan appeared before her boss Alex Petrov at C.I.A. Headquarters.

She sat in one of the two large chairs in front of Petrov's massive wooden desk, which made her feel smaller than her slim five foot seven inch frame. *Probably designed to make the visitor feel physically inferior to his host,* she thought. She had met Petrov only once before during her tenure at the C.I.A., and it was at a general reception for the newly appointed director of the agency which did not provide an opportunity for any inquisitive type conversation. However, now at the end of her career, she finally gets the chance to meet this legendary figure on a one to one basis, with some trepidation about her professional presentation.

"Well, Mrs. Brenner, or shall I call you by your code name Miss Flanigan, are you ready for your trip to Paris?" asked Alex Petrov with a sincere smile of approval at her unaffected attractiveness.

"Yes, sir, I have read Doctor James Markham's entire file and started on his autobiographical novel which I expect to finish by the time I arrive in Paris," she replied modestly.

"Well, what do you think of this man you're about to rescue?" asked a most curious Petrov.

"Judging from his past exploits, I don't know that he needs me to rescue him, sir. I thought my assignment was to locate him and provide any needed assistance," she replied.

"Even the strongest man has his weakness, Theresa. May I call you by your first name?"

"Yes, sir, that's my real first name, sir," she replied.

"I've known Jim Markham for more than four decades. He's been through hell the past three years, and the loss of his second wife Claire just might have been the straw that broke the camel's back. His disappearance without as much as a reply to my e-mails is of great concern to me as well as the agency. Your job is to find him and give him whatever support he needs to return to unofficial active service," said Petrov, looking intently into Theresa's eyes.

"I understand, sir. I will do my very best, sir," she replied.

"I personally selected you for this mission. I don't mind telling you, Theresa, that Jim Markham is a very close, personal friend of mine and anything you do to help him recover will be most sincerely appreciated by me personally," said Petrov. "You have been given authorization to employ maximum measures if needed. I'm sure that you will use it judiciously."

"Yes, sir, I will," she replied, knowing that the likelihood of its use was quite remote.

"Do you have any questions?" said Petrov looking at his watch which did not go unnoticed by Theresa who knew that it was a signal he had another appointment waiting.

"Yes, sir, I do have one question," she replied. "Does the Paris office know the details of my mission?"

"No, they do not. They only know that you are authorized to operate in Europe including France and they are to provide you with whatever assistance you require without questioning your need or details of your mission," replied Petrov. "Our Paris office has been notified of your impending arrival."

"Thank you, sir," she replied politely.

Alex Petrov came around his desk and extended his right hand. "I think I've made the right choice, Theresa. Bonne chance and bonne chasse (Good luck and good hunting)," he said in French, as he shook her hand.

CHAPTER II

Mission of Love

Teri Flanigan, dressed in a navy blue tailored suit, with her long dark hair pulled straight back into a bun, giving her a serious business appearance, landed at the Charles de Gaulle Airport in Paris and immediately rented a metallic gray Peugeot convertible automobile with a satellite navigation system. She then drove to a nondescript four-story house in the eastern sector of Paris. Once in the vestibule, she entered her security code on a wall-mounted keypad electronically unlocking the door that led to the entrance hallway where she was greeted by a middle aged blond haired woman also dressed in a conservative suit.

"May I see your identity card, please?" said the blonde haired woman.

Flanigan pulled out her C.I.A. identification card which she dutifully relinquished.

The woman slid the card through an electronic code identification box on her desk. "Welcome to Paris, Miss Flanigan," said the woman, returning the identification card. "Would you please follow me? Mister LaMotte wishes to speak to you."

Flanigan was led into a small elevator that took them to the third floor.

"Mister LaMotte's office is straight ahead," said the escort. "Just go right in, he's expecting you."

"Thank you," replied Flanigan who anticipated the usual briefing by the Special Agent in Charge upon arrival in France as in any other foreign country. However, she had been advised by Alex Petrov at C.I.A., Headquarters not to discuss her mission in Paris with other C.I.A. agents unless an emergency situation arose that required it on a need-to-know basis.

"How was your flight?" asked a slim, mustached man whose died hair camouflaged his middle age.

"Fine, thank you," replied Flanigan who surmised that all of the Paris office personnel she had known during her assignment there several years ago must have been rotated back to the United States or reassigned to another foreign country. But then, she may not have met all of the personnel there.

"My name is Henri Lachaise. I'm the first assistant to Mister Charles LaMotte, the Special Agent in Charge of the Paris office," he said without extending his hand accurately reflecting a chauvinism regarding female agents.

"A pleasure to meet you, Mister Lachaise," she replied, purposely withholding the word 'Sir' as being underserved.

"You must have an important assignment, Miss Flanigan, to warrant the issuance of this tool kit," he said, pointing to a black bag sitting prominently on the corner of his desk.

Teri Flanigan knew that she had to get used to her assigned cover name but did not have to respond to the baited question.

"I will need your signature on this receipt for the contents of this tool kit, Miss Flanigan," said Lachaise in an official manner, that reflected his disappointment at Flanigan for not sharing details of her assignment.

Teri had instantly sized up Lachaise as a womanizer who felt superior to all women, and that they existed only for his pleasure. Teri unzipped the top of the black bag and removed the contents of the bag onto the desk.

"One 9 millimeter plastic semi-automatic handgun with two clips of composite ammunition and a shoulder-waist combination holster," she said in a low voice. "One stiletto knife, one cyanide capsule, one mace cartridge, three GPS transmitter capsules, one rechargeable mini stun gun, one mini directional microphone recorder, and two micro listening devices with wireless recorder."

Teri checked each item on the receipt, then signed and dated it. She then replaced each of the items in the black bag, zipped it closed, and pulled it off the desk.

"Thank you for the tool kit, Mister Lachaise," she said, turning slowly, giving him a chance to add his goodbye salutation.

"Where will you be staying, Miss Flanigan?" he asked.

"I haven't decided which YWCA yet," she replied sarcastically.

"Well, good luck Miss Flanigan," he said, as she opened the door and left the office.

Teri locked the tool bag inside the small trunk of her convertible automobile along with her other luggage consisting of one suitcase and one carry-on airplane bag. She drove to the InterContinental Paris-le-Grand Hotel located on Rue Scribe near the Opera House in the center of Paris, where she had made reservations for a suite before departing the States. Teri Flanigan was a self-disciplined woman who left nothing to chance, partially the result of her espionage training, and the fact that she and her sister were taught at an early age to rely on themselves in a man's world. She assumed the possibility that she may find Markham in a condition and location that would require immediate relocation under her around-the-clock supervision, hence the large suite at the InterContinental Hotel. She showered and changed into an olive green dress, then placed her 9 millimeter handgun into her purse along with the mace cartridge. She then went downstairs into the hotel's elaborate restaurant for something light to eat prior to paying a visit to Father Donald O'Malley at the Basilique de St. Denis.

Even though Teri Flanigan was a Catholic and had previously been assigned to Paris for a number of years, the Basilique de St. Denis had somehow escaped her notice. The grandiosity of this basilica was simply awe inspiring and she wondered how she could have missed such a wonderful 12th century gothic structure. It was late afternoon when she entered this great house of worship which had a surprising number of worshipers occupying pews and a few waiting to be heard at the Confessional. As known in the Catholic Church, the confessional is a large boxed area where Catholics can confess their sins to God in the presence of the priest who has authority to absolve them of their repented transgressions. Having been told by Alex Petrov that Father O'Malley had only one priest to assist him, she surmised that he was probably the minister inside the confession booth; hence she decided to kill two birds with one stone. She walked over to the confession line and stood behind the one man and two women that were waiting their turn to confess their sins and receive absolution. Her turn finally came and she knelt facing the square screen that prevented the priest from identifying the sinner. She waited more than a minute while the priest conferred with the person on the other side of him, then the wooden panel behind the screen opened and she heard the priest blessing her and asking her to confess her sins.

"Are you Father Donald O'Malley?" she asked in a friendly, respectful voice betraying a Long Island accent.

There was a moment's hesitation, and then came the answer. "Yes, I am," he replied in his New York accent, rather perplexed by the directness of her question.

"I am Teri Flanigan, Father. I believe you've been expecting me?" she said, purposely omitting the name of her sponsor.

"Yes, I've been expecting you, but not in a confessional," he replied, remembering Petrov's cautionary measure, he added. "Would you slip your identification card through the slot on the side of the screen, please?"

After examining the CIA identification card, Father O'Malley returned the card to Flanigan. "Is Alex still taking wooden nickels?" he asked jokingly.

"I don't think so, Father. He graduated to electronic transfers. Have you discovered the whereabouts of James Markham, Father?" she said, returning to official business.

"No, unfortunately, this parish has kept me too busy to venture out. I would recommend that you visit the various taverns within the St. Denis district after 2200 hours. You'll find a list of them in the telephone directory," said a disappointed Father O'Malley who would not get to see Petrov's femme fatale.

Teri than confessed an indiscretion she had three years ago with a man she had been dating. It was just of a sexual nature and not the requited love she had had with her husband so she had broken it off. Father O'Malley listened intently without interruption and assured her that God would forgive her sins. He understood the pain of her loss and her feelings of despair. *What she needed,* he thought, *was renewed hope in a God who is all merciful.* Then Father O'Malley said to her, "You must never give up hope. Everything comes to he who waits, so be patient. What you are seeking may be just around the corner."

Teri Flanigan left the Basilique de St. Denis feeling renewed, and her mission was now in gear as she began frequenting the various taverns in the St. Denis district of Paris. On occasion she would wear a casual evening dress with her curly black hair loose around her shoulders. She didn't feel at all uncomfortable without a male escort as Paris was a most liberated *ville* and she was no stranger to the city of lights and its *boite de nuit*. She felt an air of excitement because this was a city with an aura of mystery that never sleeps and promotes love in all of its forms, giving one the subtle promise that what you are seeking is waiting for you at your next destination. She didn't stay long in any of the establishments she visited and managed to restrict her alcoholic intake to one glass of Pernod. In the meantime, James Markham found himself back at the Petit Bistro drinking his Scotch Whisky at the same table for two he'd been occupying for the past several weeks. He was oblivious to the talk about him at the bar between Jean Batiste the bar owner, his waitress Madeleine, and Giselle who was telling them about the night when her friend Gaston got himself a broken collar bone and dislocated shoulder in his attempt to rob the Scotch drinking Canadian. She related her story, in French, how the Canadian had shook off Gaston like a fly on an elephant.

"And where is Gaston now," asked Batiste.

"Home with his neck in a cast and his right arm in a sling," she replied. "That man," she said in French, looking in the direction of Markham whose name was as yet unknown to them, "is nobody to mess with, I tell you."

"It's the quiet ones you have to watch out for," said Batiste. "I learned that in the Army, especially with war veterans. You never know what will trigger a violent reaction."

"He didn't seem a bad sort," said Giselle. "He just reacted when Gaston tried to hurt him. Honestly, he could have killed Gaston, but he just walked away."

"Well look what we've got here," announced Madeleine, looking in the direction of the entrance to the bistro.

"Looks like someone from the gentry class is slumming," said Giselle.

"Hey! Watch it," replied Batiste. This is a first class drinking establishment, I'll have you know."

There stood Teri Flanigan in her two inch heel shoes and dark green dress contouring her ballerina figure, surveying the tavern from the entrance with large green eyes that suddenly stopped at the sight of the gray bearded man pouring himself a drink from a bottle of Scotch. His gray hair was long and so was his beard. *Probably hasn't shaved in several weeks,* she thought. *Then maybe it wasn't Markham.*

Flanigan's presence had gathered the attention of nearly everyone at the bar as she slowly walked past them to the section where the bearded man was sitting at his small table. She stood before him but he never looked up. Not until she called his name.

"Are you James Markham?" she asked softly.

The glassy eyed man took his eyes off his glass of Scotch and looked up briefly at this strange woman who seemed to know his identity. "Indeed I am. What do you want?"

"I'm Teri Flanigan, Mister Markham. May I sit down?"

"Suit yourself lady," he replied carelessly.

At that moment Madeleine the waitress came over and attempted to rescue Markham from this apparently uninvited guest. "Look Lady, no solicitation in this establishment, so be off with you," she said in French.

"I find your remark insulting. He's a friend of mine, so get lost?" replied Teri in French vernacular that the waitress clearly understood.

Teri sat down facing Markham whose appearance, aside from his long hair and unkempt beard, still resembled the photographs she had seen in the file at CIA headquarters. She felt magnetism in his presence that drew her to his eyes for insight into this man of mystery whom she was about to rescue. "Alex Petrov sent me to find you, Mister Markham. He's very worried about you. He hasn't heard from you in nearly two months."

Finally, Markham looked up at her and fixed his gaze into her almond shaped green eyes that contrasted her pale face and black curly hair completing the image of an awaited angel. "He finally answered my call," said Markham whose inebriation had slowed his speech, referring to God.

"What call?" she replied, puzzled. "We don't have any record of you calling us, Mister Markham. In fact, that's why I'm here… to find you."

"Never mind, now that you've found me, you can report back to Alex that I'm OK," replied Markham who then picked up the bottle of Scotch and poured himself another drink.

"You're not OK, Mister Markham, you're drunk and I've been assigned the task of sobering you up and getting you back to your old self again so that you can be useful to yourself and your country."

"If you're going to look after me, then you can drop that 'Mister Markham' and just call me Jim," replied Markham slurring his speech.

"Alright, Jim, that's your last drink. Let's get you home, wherever that is," she said with the assertiveness of a sister addressing her long lost brother.

As they were leaving the bistro, Madeleine looked at Batiste, "We'll never see him again."

"Why not?" he replied.

"Because she'll make him forget his reason for drinking," said a knowing Madeleine.

"I agree with Madeleine," said Giselle. "He seemed simply captivated by her beauty. I think he'll follow her anywhere, lucky her."

"It's the old story of Samson and Delilah," said Batiste with implied wisdom.

Markham, accompanied by Teri Flanigan, exited the bistro and she steered him towards her automobile parked at the curb. She remotely unlocked the passenger door, which she then opened, and Markham obediently sat himself inside the small convertible immediately falling asleep before she could obtain the address to his apartment. *Great*, she thought. Now she had no choice but to take him to her hotel where she fortunately had a large suite with a separate room for her guest. Upon arrival at the InterContinental Paris-le-Grand Hotel Flanigan parked her rented car in front of the marquis, and as she opened the passenger door to her car, the uniformed doorman stood wondering if he should ask if she needed assistance as Markham was having trouble awakening from his slumber.

Remembering Markham's lengthy military training and the fact that he was a retired Chief Warrant Officer, officially referred to as *Mister*, she summoned it to gain his attention. "Mister Markham, general alarm, report for duty immediately," she said in a most officious voice.

Markham's eyes instantly flashed open and he almost hit his head on the auto's canopy as he exited the small car, wondering where he was, but felt relief at the sight of Flanigan, his newly found angel.

"At ease, Mister Markham, you're under my care now," she said grabbing his arm as she led her groggy and acquiescent companion into the foyer of the hotel with the staff looking on, not without reluctance at voicing their disapproval of her choice of companion to bring into their high class hotel. Once in the elevator, Markham momentarily came to life when he uttered "Where are you taking me, angel?"

Amused, Flanigan replied, "I'm not your angel, Mister Markham, I'm your nurse."

"Well do me a favor, nurse. Find me a bed quick, before I fall asleep standing," said Markham who felt his body weighed a ton.

At that moment the elevator door opened on the fourth floor and Flanigan announced they had arrived, but she had to hold the door open for Markham whose sleep deprived body moved lethargically in search for a place to rest.

She didn't have far to walk with her sleepy hulk. The entrance to her suite was only a dozen feet from the elevators.

"Upon entering the lightly lit suite of rooms, she immediately led Markham to the guest room where upon seeing the double bed, he wasted no time in removing his jacket, shirt, shoes, socks and pants, oblivious to Flanigan's presence. Standing only in his boxer shorts and white undershirt, he pulled the sheet covered blanket from the bed where he flopped, face down, instantly falling asleep to the amazement of Flanigan. She just stood over him, wondering what to do next, now that she had captured him.

She picked up his strewn clothes and placed them all on a nearby sofa. She then picked up the telephone and called the hotel desk clerk for someone to collect Markham's clothes to be cleaned. She also ordered men's toilet articles including shaving gear. *Heaven knows,* she thought, *he also needs a haircut.*

Now that Flanigan's first part of her mission had been accomplished, she had to figure out the best avenue for his recovery and decided to call her boss Alex Petrov in Langley, Virginia to deliver a progress report and seek his guidance. However it was 7:00a.m. in Virginia, and she hesitated to call him at this early hour, nevertheless, she suspected that he was an early riser and would want to hear about Markham without delay.

Using her cell phone, she dialed Petrov's number and he immediately answered "Petrov!"

"Sir, this is Flanigan," she said, using her cover name in case the line leaked.

"Teri. Top of the morning to you lass," he said jubilantly. "I hope you are the bearer of good news."

"Well, sir, I did find our subject and he's now at my hotel suite fast asleep."

"Asleep in your hotel suite!" he replied in a voice that demanded an explanation.

"Yes, sir, I found him in a very intoxicated condition and not knowing where he lived, it was necessary to bring him back to my hotel suite which has two bedrooms, sir," she said, and before Petrov could comment, she quickly continued, "as soon as I directed him to the spare room, he flopped onto the bed and passed out like a light. My plan is to let him sleep it off and when he wakes up, I'll have brunch served and then a hairdresser will come up and give him a haircut and trim his beard so that he will recognize himself as the man he used to be."

"He looked that bad, huh!" said Petrov incredulously.

"Yes, but nothing that a good haircut, shave and shower won't cure," she replied.

"Good," said Petrov somewhat relieved. "But that's no guarantee that he won't fall off the wagon again. Listen, Teri, as soon as you get him cleaned up, get him back to the Caul at St. Nazaire."

"You mean, get him back to his sailboat?" she asked for confirmation.

"If you read his file, you would know that's the name of his sailboat," he said impatiently, and then remembering the delicacy of her mission, he added, "his sailboat is his home, Teri."

"I know, sir, but won't that boat bring back a flood of memories of his deceased wife whose funeral at sea was launched from the Caul," she replied in the softest tone that begged the question, "Isn't that what pushed him over the edge?"

"That is true, Teri. However that's where Jim Markham safeguards the Caul of his birth; in a safe on his boat, his only home and sanctuary, and that's where he gets his strength and inspiration," said Petrov. "He must face the truth sooner or later…that Claire is dead, and the Caul will help him come to terms with that fact, and I have had the strange feeling from the moment I chose you for this mission that you were the one ordained to assist him in his recovery and beyond."

Beyond, she thought, *what does he mean by that? Strange enough that Markham called her 'Angel,' is there such a thing as destiny she asked herself? We'll see,* she concluded.

"I will do my best, sir to get him back to his sailboat," she said, but she felt like telling him that she had not been trained as a CIA agent to be a client's nursemaid, even though this client was of special importance to the agency.

It was nearly noon when Markham awakened from his deep slumber. As he looked at his grand surroundings, he experienced a vague recollection of a beautiful, dark haired woman who must have brought him to this unfamiliar port. Seeing the open door to the adjoining bathroom, he stood up, stretched, and then went inside the bathroom, closing the door behind him. Looking into the large bathroom mirror he became horrified at the sight of a disheveled man whom he hardly recognized. He suddenly realized the depths to which he had fallen and his strong survival instinct, and some of the self esteem he had left, triggered an immediate desire to clean up his act. To his surprise he found a new safety razor and shaving cream on the sink counter which Flanigan had provided from the hotel. After showering, he shaved around the contours of his beard and mustache, but needed a beard trimmer and most certainly a haircut. Stepping out of the bathroom with a towel wrapped tightly around his waist, he noticed a clear plastic package contained three sets of boxer shorts and T-shirts and next to it sat three pairs of over-the-calf black socks which he preferred. *No doubt,* he thought, *this mysterious woman acquired those personal details from the clothes I wore and shed. Nevertheless, it shows a thoughtful person.* Then he noticed his pants, shirt and jacket hanging in the closet in preen condition, which brought a smile of appreciation.

As Markham was dressing, Teri Flanigan, who had heard the quiet commotion of Markham's resurrection from his long slumber, sat at the small dining table sipping a cup of tea and reading the Paris morning newspaper. She was awaiting Markham's grand entrance which he finally made with a such a quiet appearance, he caught Flanigan by surprise as she was engrossed in an article in the newspaper that had caught her attention. Markham saw a look of approval from Flanigan that brought a smile to his face and he slowly approached her when she stood up to greet him.

Looking at his visage she saw nature's work at its very best. His long curly gray hair speckled with dark strands would be the envy of any *coiffeur.* A thick gray beard over pure skin accentuated his masculinity, and his vivid liquid eyes conveying kindness on a large muscular body, portrayed unmistakable strength. *This was a man to be reckoned with,* she thought. *Amazing what a shower and shave did for him. This mission is turning out to be better than I thought.*

"I'm Teri Flanigan, Mister Markham, in case you don't remember last night."

"You do have a face that's hard to forget, Miss Flanigan," said Markham noticing an absence of a wedding band on her left ring ringer. "And I remember you introducing yourself as one of

Alex Petrov's agents, but how I got here is rather foggy. You do work for Alex?" he asked for confirmation.

"Yes, Mister Markham. I've been sent here by Mister Petrov to find you. He hasn't heard from you in several months and he was very worried that something horrible might have happened to you," she said.

"I want to thank you for having my clothes cleaned. That was very thoughtful of you," said Markham looking into her beautiful green eyes. Then seeing a table covered with a white table cloth, a pot of tea with two cups and a platter of croissants, Markham slowly moved towards the table famished for some food. "Well, you can tell Alex that I'm OK now, and if you don't mind, Miss Flanigan, I'm most anxious to taste these croissants with a cup of that tea."

"Please have a seat, Mister Markham and I'll order whatever you like. I'm sure those croissants won't be enough for a bulky man like you."

Looking at his watch showing it was a bit past noon, "I guess I'll have a late breakfast of steak and four eggs, hash browns if they have it, and rye toast well done but not burnt. Oh! and a glass of orange juice, a large glass of regular milk and a banana."

"Are you sure that's all you want, Mister Markham?" she asked with friendly sarcasm.

"Just call me Jim, and I'll call you Teri, if that's alright with you?" said Markham, who disliked formalities.

"I suppose it's alright," she replied, a bit unsure of herself.

"Good, I'm famished, Teri. How good is the service here at the InterContinental?" he asked.

"So you discovered where you are from the name on the towels and the bathroom accessories," she replied, impressed with his powers of observation. She also noticed that he didn't suffer from any apparent hangover which she fully expected, considering his heavy and prolonged consumption of alcohol. But she failed to recognize that Markham's recovery secret was his long ten to eleven hours of uninterrupted sleep.

"The service here at the InterContinental is excellent. As a matter of fact, James, after you've eaten your brunch, I've arranged

26

to have a coiffeur come here to give you a haircut and trim your beard, if you don't mind," she said, hoping he wouldn't be offended.

"Seems that you thought of everything, and I do have to agree with you, after seeing myself in the mirror as I was shaving," said Markham. He had thought to himself Teri Flanigan was a worthy reason for cleaning up. While he sat at the table pouring himself a cup of tea and munching on one of the croissants, he watched Teri standing by the telephone ordering his brunch. He noticed an elegant and cultured manner about her. She appeared to be a woman of depth and after looking into her face, he was convinced she was also a woman of unbridled passion. But the right man would be hard to find for a disciplined CIA agent who must not allow her emotions to control her intellect. She certainly had the necessary attributes to distract Markham from his melancholic state of depression over the loss of his wife, and he realized that's exactly the reason that Alex Petrov chose her. It was her mission to locate and rescue him from his prolonged depression; and make him realize that life is for the living to love and be loved. Those we love and lost will meet again in the after life as one big family.

"How do you like your steak, Jim?" she asked while holding the telephone receiver.

"Thick, lean, and medium," he replied.

Flanigan returned to the small dining room table to join Markham as he devoured his croissant and sipped his hot tea. "Alex thought it would be a good idea if you left Paris and returned to your sailboat which he believes would be the best therapy for your grieving."

Markham raised his eyes from his cup of tea looking straight into hers for a tense moment. "I'm not ready to go back to The Caul," he replied firmly, which left no room for discussion.

"What will you do then…remain in Paris?" she asked.

"Sure, why not. I love Paris and there's a lot I haven't seen as yet," he replied.

"Do you mind if I keep you company…that is…to watch over you until you return to The Caul?" she asked, attempting to hide her anxiety about his reaction to this invasion of his privacy.

"Is this Alex's idea or yours...to be my nursemaid?" he asked.

"It's Mister Petrov's orders and my sincere desire to be of assistance in your recovery from your loss, Jim," she replied with an earnestness that deeply touched him. As he looked at her, he felt a pleasurable chemistry that he had not anticipated nor sought.

There was a knock on the door to the suite and Flanigan quickly allowed the bellboy to wheel in his cart containing Markham's brunch. Markham stood up to search his pants pockets for money to tip the bellboy, but Flanigan beat him to the punch and gave the bellboy a couple of euros which he graciously accepted and left the suite.

"You shouldn't have done that, Teri. I'm not a vagrant...I do have money."

"I know your financial status, James. I read your file at the agency and your autobiographical novel. In fact, James, I know you better than anyone except Mister Petrov. And I'm not destitute either, you know. Besides, the agency is picking up the tab. So relax and enjoy your brunch," she said with an unmistakable smile of friendship.

Markham cut into his steak which he found pink and to his liking, all the while digesting Flanigan's remark about her knowledge of his life, and deduced that she was indeed a remarkable woman whom destiny had perhaps reserved for this critical moment in his life. *You're getting ahead of yourself, Jim,* he thought, *one step at a time.*

"Listen, Jim. There's plenty of room for you to stay here, and it would certainly make it easier for me to be your nursemaid as you put it," she said invitingly.

"Well, it sure would be an improvement over my dingy apartment," he replied, but then added, "but it wouldn't do your reputation any good."

"This is Paris, James, the most liberal city in the world. Are you kidding me?" she chuckled. "Besides, you have the agency's stamp of approval as official business."

"You offer a most persuasive argument, Teri," he replied with a smile. "Official business it is."

After eating brunch, Teri drove Markham to his rented residence at 41 Rue Berne, northwest of the Basilique de Saint Denis. They climbed the creaky stairs to the second floor and entered his small apartment.

"Well, James," said Teri, "I can see where living in this place would drive a man to depression and booze."

"Frankly I didn't care much where I stayed. That was probably the lowest point in my life," replied Markham, still feeling morose over Claire's death.

"Do you have the landlord's telephone number?" asked Teri.

"Yeah, I'll call him when we get to your hotel," replied Markham. "He owes me a deposit."

Teri looked inside the closet and saw one dark blue suit, a beige sailor's windbreaker, a pair of light blue slacks and three sport shirts, all hanging neatly on a horizontal metal bar. "You certainly travel light, James."

"He who travels light travels fast," he replied. "I'll hand carry those clothes, Teri," said Markham who thought they'd be too heavy and burdensome for her to carry. He started packing his underwear and other clothing in his lone suitcase, and inserted his toilet articles in a leather bag which he placed in his AWOL bag.

"OK!" exclaimed Markham. "I'm all packed and ready to go. You can carry my AWOL bag and I'll carry the suitcase and the hanging clothes down to the car. I'm leaving the key on the dresser." Looking back at the apartment one more time as he stepped into the doorway, he remarked to Teri, "This apartment wasn't so bad...it protected me from the foul weather, same as a boat would."

He has such small wants...that's what makes him so rich, she thought smiling to herself.

Upon arrival at the InterContinental Hotel, Teri summoned the bellman to get a cart to carry all of the clothes up to her fourth floor suite. As Markham accompanied Teri to her suite, clean shaven, hair cut, beard trimmed and pressed clothes, he felt as if he had rejoined the world of the living and was most thankful for Teri's intervention and his friend Petrov's active concern for his welfare. This truly touched his sensitive mind and heart. *True friends are so hard to find*, he thought. *You can choose your friends, but you can't choose your family for sometimes a relative can be your worst enemy.* He quickly dismissed the thought of calling his two OSI friends stationed in Paris. He needed some quiet time to recuperate, and Teri seemed like the perfect companion for visiting the various fine museums of art and exploring Paris. Markham had always delighted in all that Paris has to offer, and museums particularly, that invite the quiet appreciation of its viewers as they attempt to interpret the painting or sculpture and thoughts of the artists who magnificently execute these works of art.

"I know that you've been to the Louvres, since you've been to Paris before, so how about going to the Museum of Modern Art?" asked Markham.

"You're right, James. I have been to the Louvres, although I could spend another month or two there. But I'd love to visit the Museum of Modern Art," replied Teri.

"Afterwards, I know of a quaint little restaurant on the West Bank," said Markham. "They have a most agreeable accordionist who plays all of the old French songs that made Paris famous."

"Sounds nostalgic," said Teri. "You lead the way, but remember, James. I'm just your dutiful nurse whose mission is to keep you out of trouble."

Markham looked at Teri discernibly. "I believe you could take care of yourself quite well in a pinch. Hopefully you won't have to prove it."

The Museum of Modern Art was not especially crowded that afternoon as they strolled down the hallways and rooms whose walls were decorated by some of the world's most precocious paintings, when Markham suddenly stopped before the painting of a fair-haired woman extending her hand towards a white swan at the edge of a small pond. Markham seemed transfixed by the painting which had apparently captured the memory of someone who had left a lasting impression.

"She reminds you of someone from the past, doesn't she?" said Teri as a statement more than a question which went unanswered.

The painting had resurrected the suppressed memory of a woman who had captured his heart but left his soul filled with guilt.

"Were you in love with her?" she asked unabashedly.

"I haven't seen her in several years," replied Markham, still staring at the painting.

"But you haven't answered my question," said Teri insistently.

"What is love but a fickle emotion whose durability depends almost entirely on the mutual blindness to human frailties with continued appreciation for the qualities that attracted them," said Markham with poetic evasiveness.

"You still haven't' answered my question, James," she said.

"I can't afford to be in love with her," replied Markham succinctly.

"Why not?" asked Teri, intrigued by his answer.

"Because she belongs to a very close friend and colleague," replied Markham. "She could have posed for this painting...it is so much like her. Her adorable face, her femininity and tender heart..." Markham didn't finish the sentence.

"You are in love with her, James, whether you care to admit it or not," said Teri. "And you've suppressed it all those years out of loyalty to your friend. That's most noble of you. Does she have a name?"

Markham looked at Teri before answering her question, wondering if it was wise to reveal her name, but then he rationalized that Teri would never meet her. "Her name is Michelle," he answered, remembering that a major attraction was the similarity of their roots dating back to their childhood, and on those infrequent friendly meetings when her native charm invaded his heart forever.

"Is she French?" asked Teri.

"She's of French ancestry," answered Markham, not wanting to answer any more of her questions. *Besides,* Markham thought, *the memory of Claire is still too fresh in my mind to be thinking about past emotions that could possibly be surfacing only to fill the void left by Claire's earthly departure.* "I'm thirsty. Why don't we go to that small bistro across the street?"

Teri smiled at Markham whose behavior had become quite transparent. She also realized that she would not be able to compete with such a profound memory of a woman who was unattainable therefore flawless in Markham's mind. *Claire didn't have to compete,* she thought, *since she was married to Markham a total of eleven heart wrenching months awaiting her predicted ill-fated death.* But Teri then realized that she also had a memory hurdle to overcome in the person of her deceased husband, Jeffery, who had died in the prime of their youthful marriage leaving her with a near faultless image of a husband who could never be replaced. *Here,* she thought, *were two people of sound mind but with hearts imprisoned by unrequited love. With time, their close proximity might change that,* she hoped.

That evening, Markham was unusually pensive, leaving Teri with the burden of conversation. However, the following morning, Teri noticed a geniality in Markham that was most reassuring. *A good night's sleep can do wonders,* she thought.

"I think I'm now ready to return to my sailboat," announced Markham in a matter-of-fact tone of voice.

"Really? I'm glad to hear that," replied Teri. "I'm anxious to see your boat. I hope you'll take me sailing."

"Absolutely, but I hope you won't get seasick?" said Markham.

"No, I've never had that problem. I've done some sailing in small sailboats on lakes and bays but never in the open ocean," said Teri, wondering if she would measure up as a blue water sailor.

Teri didn't feel a need to check out of the InterContinental Paris-le-Grand Hotel as she packed only a few casual clothes for the trip to the Port of Saint Nazaire where the sailboat was moored.

"I guess I'd better buy myself a pair of deck shoes or sneakers, huh!" said Teri.

"Yes, you'll have to. Besides, they're also comfortable to wear around Paris when you're wearing jeans and other casuals," said Markham.

"I know just the store for that," replied Teri. "It's not far from here. We can stop there on the way."

"Great. You want me to drive?" asked Markham.

"No. I'll just program your Belle Place marina at Saint Nazaire into my satellite navigation system and it will direct us right to your boat," said Teri with confident pride. "Not bad, huh?"

"It's the first time I've had two women drive me around simultaneously," replied Markham.

"Oh, No! James. I elected to use a male voice on my nav system and his French accent is definitely Parisian," she said with good humor.

"In that case, we can definitely do without him. Haven't you heard…three is a crowd? I know the way…I'll be glad to direct you," said Markham.

"Why, James! If I didn't know you any better, I'd swear you were jealous," she replied with a big smile.

"Why should I be jealous? All he can do is talk," said Markham now laughing, although he had now looked upon her as his younger sister rather than a potential lover. He hadn't forgotten the painting that had brought back the memory of Michelle who had invaded his grieving heart.

Teri knew her way around Paris and Markham was more than happy to yield the driving to her while she made her way through the narrow streets eventually landing them in a parking spot at the curb that had just been vacated by a likely store customer.

"While we're in the store, I'm going to buy you a pair of white gloves and a chauffeur's hat," said Markham, impressed by her aggressive driving in a city whose occupants use only their horn and accelerator.

"Hey! If you can't beat 'em, join 'em," she said as she waltzed into the store before Markham could open the door for her. She was in an elated and tomboyish mood, in preparation for the forthcoming sailing adventure and Markham just went along for the ride. The store didn't have any deck shoes; hence she purchased a pair of white low quarter sneakers and a lightweight blue waist jacket. "Might come in handy on those windy days at sea," she commented as she paid for the merchandise.

"We should also stop at a deli for a couple of those French hero sandwiches and a drink, 'cause it's about 383 kilometers to the Port of Saint Nazaire which will take us several hours to get there," said Markham.

"That's about 237 miles, if my calculations are right," replied Teri.

"That's about right," said Markham, "and the roads being what they are, it'll take us about 5 to 6 hours."

On the way out of Paris, they stopped at an *epicerie* also known as a grocery store where Markham added a bottle of table red wine to their two long French ham and cheese sandwiches.

"Oh, no! James," said Teri, as she removed the bottle of wine from the counter. "You're not going to fall off the wagon; not after all the progress you've made." "Do you have any lemonade?" she asked the sales woman.

"Oui, Madame," she replied. "It's freshly made, right over there on the second shelf in the cooler."

Leaving the grocery store, Markham couldn't help remarking, "You're getting to be more of a Mother Theresa than a sister Teri. It's just not French to have a picnic without wine."

"Listen, James. I'd like for you to drive, 'cause I'm feeling tired and I will feel safer if I know you're sober," she said in a voice that pleaded for understanding.

Markham laughed as they got into the Peugeot after placing the groceries and two bottles of lemonade in the back seat. Markham didn't bother turning on the satellite navigation system as he was quite familiar with the route to the Port of Saint Nazaire. "It would take a lot more than a bottle of wine to affect my driving, but if it'll make you feel safer, I'll yield to your wishes, Mother," he replied teasing.

Teri punched him on the shoulder. "You're making fun of me, and you are a brute."

With the top down and Teri at his side, Markham drove the convertible southwest for the long ride that turned from highway to country roads, some of which were a panoply of overhanging tree branches whose leaves gave the illusion of traveling through a long tunnel of green and orange vegetation. The charm of France rested not only in its capital city of Paris, but in its beautiful countryside made famous by such artists as Van Gogh and Jean Baptiste Corot. Teri turned on the car radio and found a station that played familiar French songs of yesteryear transporting them into an era of gaiety and melancholy.

"Were you ever able to visit France with your husband?" asked Markham.

"Unfortunately, no, we were married only a year when he was shot down in Vietnam. We never got a chance to really celebrate our wedding," replied Teri.

"He was a fighter pilot, wasn't he?" said Markham.

"Yes. You would have liked Jeffery," she replied. "He was an idealist and very patriotic. I'm sure he would have like you, Jim. In many ways, you're very much alike, yet so different."

"Different? In what way?" asked Markham out of curiosity.

"Well," she hesitated. "He didn't drink alcohol, ever, and even though he was a fighter pilot, he hated physical violence. You might say he was the brainy type who didn't excel in sports."

"I see the dichotomy," said Markham. "We have similar philosophies, but different physiological attributes."

"It's the philosophies that really matter," she replied. "You two would have become good friends if fate had arranged for you to meet."

"That wasn't in the cards, Teri," said Markham. "We have to play the cards that are dealt to us the best way we can, and some of us don't recognize a winning hand."

"Sounds like you'd be good at poker," said Teri with a chuckle.

"I can hold my own," he replied, recalling some of his experiences at cards.

"Yes. I've seen your poker face, James," she retorted.

"Oh, yeah! When?" asked Markham, stopping the car to allow a bunch of ducks to cross the road in their single file.

"At that boite de nuit in Paris when I first met you," she said, recalling the event.

"Oh, that! I was inebriated. That doesn't count," he replied.

"Well in any event, let's just say that you've had a lot more experience in games of chance," she said with finality.

"My dear Teri, I am sure that if you were trained by a professional gambler, you'd be very adept at the game."

"But I would never want to play against you," she replied.

"Why not? I think you'd be good at it," he said.

"That's just it, Jim. I wouldn't want to take all your money?" she said laughing.

Markham joined her in laughter. He so enjoyed her company.

"You don't mind if I dose off a bit," she said, inclining her seat a few inches.

"No, go right ahead, sister," he replied with a grin.

Markham enjoyed driving while listening to the French music and in the company of Teri whom he had found to be a most attractively pleasant but platonic companion, which under the circumstances suited him perfectly. After driving more than 180 kilometers, Markham spotted a clearing and parked the car off the road that overlooked a corn field in full bloom.

"Teri," he said, placing his right hand gently on her shoulder. "It's time to wake up and smell the corn."

Teri opened her big green eyes. "Where are we?" she asked.

About half-way to our destination," said Markham. "I thought it was time to eat our lunch and this seemed the perfect place for it."

"Oh! It was such a peaceful rest," she said, "but you're right. I haven't been good company."

Teri climbed into the back seat and retrieved the sandwiches and bottles of lemonade which she brought up front. "If we had a blanket we could sit outside and have a picnic."

"Well, with the top down, we can make believe it is," replied Markham who took one of the sandwiches from Teri and started to devour it like a wolf who'd been starving.

"My goodness, Jim, you were hungry!" she said. "Maybe you should have gotten two sandwiches."

"No, that's enough for now. I guess I'm just anxious to get to the boat now to check it out," replied Markham.

"But you said that the marina manager is a good friend who takes good care of it. So you should have nothing to worry about, right?" said Teri.

"Yes, you're right, but no one really takes care of a boat like its owner, and it is my home you know," he replied, thinking about all of the things that can go wrong with a boat left unattended in the water off the ocean. "But I don't want you to rush your lunch. We have plenty of time left to get there before dark."

"You know, Jim. I can see why Claire married you. You're so nice and easy to get along with. It's a damn shame her dying at such an early age. Just when you think you've got the brass ring, it eludes you, forever," said Teri thinking of the loss of her own husband in less than a year after her marriage, about the same amount of time Markham was married to Claire before her demise.

"Yeah! But you know what they say; when one door closes, another one opens," said Markham with a ray of hope in his voice.

"After twenty-five years, I've given up on another door ever opening, Jim," she replied in an unconvincing negative tone.

"I say, leave it to providence, Teri. The French have a saying, 'Quest cera, cera'"

"What will be, will be. I know," replied Teri who noticed that Markham had already finished his sandwich and was now drinking his lemonade. "I guess I'd better stop talking and finish my sandwich or we'll be here all day. But aren't these corn fields beautiful. Almost like a painting."

"Yes, it is beautiful. But we have corn fields like that in the States too. I think it's a state of mind... it's because we are in France, and century old paintings of the French countryside hanging in the Louvre museum cause us to place a value on these particular fields that served the great French painters," said Markham.

"I didn't know you were so pragmatic, James," replied Teri.

"Well, now you know another side of me," said Markham. "I see that you're about finished eating your sandwich. If you don't mind, Teri, you could sip on your drink while I continue driving."

"No, I don't mind, Jim. I'm finished eating and it was simply delicious. Let's get this show on the road," she said with her usual cheerfulness.

Upon arrival at the Belle Place Marina, Markham drove right up to the one-story office building and parked the car. "You don't have to come in, Teri," said Markham. "I'm only going to get the boat keys from Philippe."

Philippe Cadieux was sitting behind his desk reading a newspaper when Markham walked in. "Hey bien, Jacques, I see you have found yourself a beautiful mademoiselle," said Philippe, glancing out the office window at Teri who had momentarily stepped out of the car to stretch her legs.

"Her name is Teri and she's a colleague of mine," replied Markham who wanted to dispel any notion of romanticism.

"We French have a saying that a man and a woman cannot be friends, only lovers," said Philippe. "And you, my friend, have French blood."

"Give me the boat keys, Philippe, before you have us married," replied Markham with his winning smile.

As Markham stepped out of the marina office with boat keys in hand, Teri expressed her impression of the marina.

"It's such a lovely seascape. There's an air of adventure at the sight of all those boats on their moorings. Where's your sailboat?" she asked.

"It's docked at the far end of the marina," replied Markham stepping into the car as Teri joined him on the passenger side with obvious excitement in her eyes.

It was a short ride with few people on the docks as they approached the only sailboat tied to the dock's south end. They both exited the automobile and slowly walked up to the cutter-rigged sailboat resting against three large inflated fenders that protected its hull from the weathered wooden covered cement docks. A long yellow-colored power line connected the sailboat's electrical system to the power box on the dock. Teri watched as Markham walked on the dock the full 47 foot length of his boat examining its hull and deck. Apparently satisfied with his inspection, he looked up at the mast and its rigging.

"Is everything alright?" asked Teri walking up to Markham.

"So far so good," he replied. "We'll know more when I get onboard and inspect the interior and the electronics."

"Well, James...I've got my sneakers on. Shall we board her?" she asked cheerfully.

"I've just appointed you as my first mate," said Markham who unlatched the safety line then stepped on board the boat. He then invited Teri to come aboard, not offering his hand as he knew from experience that a sailor must learn to depend entirely on his own equilibrium and the vessel's stays and safety lines for balance.

"Wow! This is a big sailboat," she uttered. "I'm dying to see the inside."

Markham led the way towards the cockpit and using one of his keys, unlocked the companionway, then stepped down the fcw steps onto the teak cabin floor with Teri following in his footsteps. Markham went to the instrument panel and turned on the main switch that controlled all of the boat's lighting and electric accessories. The sun was resting on the horizon and soon it would be dark. There were only a few docked boat lights augmented by the marina's sparse lampposts along with the rotating light from the nearby lighthouse to illuminate the Belle Place Marina. Markham turned on all of the interior lights as well as the deck and mast lights.

"Make yourself comfortable, Teri," said Markham. "I've got to go up on deck and check out things before it gets dark. There's the fridge if you want something cold to drink."

"O.K. Captain," she replied.

Markham quickly checked the rigging and after unlocking the forward hatch, checked the contents that included fenders and an anchor line, then closed the hatch cover and went back to the cockpit where he checked the contents of its two lockers. Satisfied with his cursory deck inspection, he returned inside the cabin and checked the bilge for water which was pleasantly absent, indicating that his automatic bilge pump was working properly.

"Well Captain, is everything O.K.?" asked Teri.

"I'm glad to report that all is well, first mate," replied Markham with his disarming smile. "Let me fix us some dinner that we can eat in the cockpit under the stars which will be coming out shortly."

"You mean you still have edible food on board after all this time in storage?" she asked incredulously.

"Yes. The boat's been on shore power all this time and what is not in cans is in the freezer," said Markham.

"What a great boat you have," replied Teri, impressed with the boat's self-reliance.

"How about steaks and rice?" asked Markham.

"Sounds good to me, Captain," replied Teri. "If you show me how to operate this stove, I'll do the cooking."

"That won't be necessary, Teri. I'll throw the steaks on the propane grill that's fastened to the stern railing."

"What about the rice?" she asked.

Markham pulled out a small box and opened its top. Then he pulled out one of the five cellophane packs of rice which he handed to Teri. "Just put this bag of rice in a pot of boiling water for 10 minutes and it's done."

"Easy does it, huh!" said Teri. "You've got it down to a science of simplicity."

"On a boat, you've got to keep it simple because oftentimes you're cooking in foul weather," replied Markham who spoke from experience. He placed the two steaks he'd taken from the freezer into the microwave oven for several seconds to thaw them out.

While Teri heated the pot of water to a boil, Markham climbed the stairs to the cockpit and uncovered the propane grill extending over the water by a stainless steel arm attached to the port side railing at the stern. He turned on the grill to a high flame to disinfect the grill and to sear the two New York Strip steaks that were now sizzling from the extreme heat. He liked to seal in the blood until it coagulated and cooked to a pink rose color.

"How's the rice coming, Teri?" asked Markham.

"Seven more minutes and it'll be done, Captain," she replied in an exuberant voice.

"Perfect timing, the steaks will be done about that time," said Markham turning over the steaks while he observed some hungry seagulls circling his boat. Markham pulled down the grill cover, and left the cockpit to retrieve a bottle of red wine and two clear plastic stem glasses which he placed on the teak pedestal table. He then moved swiftly to the grill and opened the cover and tested one of the steaks with a knife.

"The steaks are done, Teri," exclaimed Markham. "You can bring up the rice."

Markham placed each steak on a rubber bottom nautical plate sitting on the teak table. Using a French bottle opener, he pulled the cork from the bottle of wine and half filled each glass, leaving the bottle open to breathe the salt air.

Teri climbed the few stairs into the cockpit carrying the bowl of rice and a bowl of heated string beans which she placed on the cockpit table then sat opposite Markham who picked up his half-filled glass of wine and proposed a toast.

"To lasting friendship," he said, clinking his wine glass against Teri's.

"To lasting memories," she replied, thinking of Jeffery, her deceased husband, not realizing that her toast revived Markham's earlier thoughts of Michelle, so vividly portrayed in the museum painting. The memory of her would not stay suppressed and he wondered if there was a divine reason for her resurrection, since everything in his life seemed preordained. He was suddenly jolted from his reverie by a low-flying seagull that nearly hit the overhead boom.

"Wow! That was close," said Teri, holding on to her glass of wine.

"That's most unusual," replied Markham. "They usually avoid people." However, Markham said nothing about the two large-wing white seagulls that had occasionally appeared to alert him of danger and had become mystical figures in his nautical life.

"Maybe he was hungry for a steak," she said laughing.

"Well, if he's that hungry, I'll give him mine, but I think he likes fish," said Markham.

"It is so peaceful out here," said Teri, admiring the seascape and the sound of the halyards clanking against the aluminum mast emitting the familiar sound of docked sailboats. The sun had transformed into an orange ball that sat on the darkened horizon, slowly sinking into the sea. Markham went below deck and returned with a lantern which he hung from the overhead boom spreading an amber glow over the cockpit. Teri grabbed the two empty plates and bowls and brought them below into the galley sink where she quickly washed them and left them on a plate holder to dry. She then returned to the cockpit and poured herself some wine into her now empty glass then sat on the stern's port seat facing Markham who was now leaning against the bulwark with his second glass of wine, assessing the circumstances of his environment.

"A penny for your thoughts, James," said Teri with a faint smile which elicited no verbal response.

"May I make a suggestion, James?" said Teri.

"What's that?" he asked, taking a sip of his wine.

"Why don't you find Michelle and tell her how you feel. Maybe she doesn't have those same feelings and that will end your fantasy about her," said Teri who felt that Markham might be the man who could end her own fantasy about her deceased husband.

Markham hesitated for a moment, and then decided to reveal his thoughts. "To declare my love for her would plant the seed of her own fantasy that would eventually alienate her affections for her husband who is a very close friend."

"But there are lots of people in loveless marriages, just waiting for the love of their life to come along, especially women, who are definitely more romantic than men," said Teri, pleading her own case.

"I'm well aware of that, Teri. But you must understand that a person with a conscience will eventually forfeit that happiness if it is attained at the expense of another, especially if it is a close friend," said Markham.

"If she is that unattainable, then perhaps you should direct your emotions towards someone whose love would make you happy," replied Teri.

"There's only room for one person in my heart, and if Michelle is in there, no one else can enter," replied Markham who suspected that Teri had an ulterior motive.

"I think your heart is much bigger than you think, Jim," said Teri, now smiling in an effort to trivialize the discussion while retaining her position as the leading suitress.

"I would be doing a terrible disservice to any woman who would entrust her heart to me at this time while the memory of Claire is still fresh in my mind," replied Markham. "I have a strong feeling that fate is in this game and I must allow it to play its hand."

"Yes, I do remember that you were born with the Caul of destiny and I believe that you have it secured on this boat," said Teri now somewhat excited. "Would it be possible for me to see it?"

"Of course," replied Markham. "Tomorrow, when it's daylight."

"Will I be sleeping in the aft cabin or in the forward salon?" asked Teri.

"Take your pick. It makes no difference to me," replied Markham.

"I'll take the aft cabin. I noticed that the bed is already made up and the cabin leads directly to the bathroom," said Teri.

"You might as well learn the nautical terms. A bed is known as a *berth* or bunk and the toilet or bathroom is known as the *head*," said Markham in an instructive but friendly voice.

"Thank you my captain. Actually I knew that but had forgotten. It's been a long time since I've been on a boat," replied Teri looking a bit fatigued. "I think I'm going to retire for the night, if you don't mind, Jim."

"No, I don't mind. It's been a long day for you. You'll find linen and blankets in the various drawers under the berth," said Markham. "As you've noticed when you washed the dishes… there's plenty of hot water on this boat, so you'll be able to take a shower whenever you wish."

"All the comforts of home, aren't you going to retire?" she asked.

"No, not right now, I'm nocturnal. I enjoy the sea at night with the moon's glow shimmering on the waves that enter the bay and crash against the rocks that protect this marina," said Markham in a nostalgic voice.

"Well, James, I'll say goodnight and leave you with your seagoing dreams," said Teri, who secretly wished that she would be the focus of his reverie.

Markham waited for Teri to settle in the aft cabin for the night; then he went down into the galley and retrieved a bottle of Irish Mist. He poured two jiggers of the liqueur into a snifter glass then placed the glass into the microwave oven that was built into the cabinetry and heated the beverage for 15 seconds. After removing the drink from the microwave he passed the glass under his nose and inhaled the intoxicating fumes with a smile of approval and great satisfaction. Sitting on the port side locker with his back against the bulwark and resting his right leg against the cowling, Markham slowly nurtured his smooth drink while observing nature's wondrous spectacle. In his relaxed mind the live figure of the museum painting appeared walking ever so closely towards him until her face was all he could see. Her blue eyes were mesmerizing bright as she leaned her head slightly to her right then to her left with a smile of approval. Her silence was at once deafening and heartbreaking as he wanted to reach and embrace her. The image of her adoring visage aroused his frustrated love to a climax that brought tears of melancholy in his eyes that were mercifully soothed by the compassionate sea's westerly wind. Markham gulped the remaining liquor in an effort to dull the agonizing pain of his distressed heart. He wondered if this apparition in his mind was a telepathic message of her unspoken love for him. But then a tremendous feeling of guilt engulfed him as he realized that he had no right to expect love from a married woman, especially the wife of a friend who trusted him. Markham stood up facing the oncoming wind with his fists clenched in anger, wanting to scream to the heavens for mercy and pity but to avoid awakening Teri, he cried through the silence of his mind, "Dear God, I cannot conquer these feelings that are in my heart. Please help me." And the tears in his eyes started to roll down his cheeks as he wept quietly in the night.

Markham never left the cockpit sleeping the night under the stars. It is where Teri found him the next morning when she got up to make breakfast. Stretched out on his back over the port side locker with his head propped against a floatation cushion, Markham's slow, heavy breathing suddenly stopped as he became aware of Teri's entrance into the cockpit.

"Good morning, Captain Jim," said Teri looking at Markham's windblown curly gray hair which gave him the appearance of a true rugged mariner. She felt a tinge of excitement at his presence and realized that her feelings for him were more than mere infatuation.

"What would you like for breakfast, my dear captain?"

Markham sat up rubbing his eyes, then took a good look at Teri dressed in light green shorts and pullover. "You look very sprite, this morning," he said. "Eggs and bacon would do the trick, but you'll have to defrost the bacon. That and a cup of tea will be a great start for a busy day."

"You just relax, James and I'll get the breakfast going," replied Teri with much exuberance.

Markham felt embarrassed at not having washed before breakfast. He stood up and went down below into the aft cabin where he stripped naked and took a shower, then brushed his teeth and dressed into white shorts and T-shirt. As he stepped out of the aft cabin into the galley, Teri announced that breakfast would be ready in a few minutes.

"Great. I'll go raise the pedestal table," replied Markham who climbed the steps into the cockpit. *Today,* he thought, looking at the near cloudless sky and brilliant sun, *would be a perfect day to do some minor repairs and clean the boat.*

Teri climbed the companionway stairs carrying the breakfast fare in both hands with the agility of a young panther, even though her life spanned a half a century. During breakfast, the topic of boat chores was raised by Teri who expressed an anxious desire to help.

"Are you by any chance afraid of heights?" asked Markham.

"No, I used to do much mountain climbing in my younger days," replied Teri. "Why do you ask?"

"I noticed last night that the masthead light was out," said Markham. "I have a chair that is designed to hoist a person up the mast using one of the mast halyards."

"For sure I wouldn't be able to haul you up to the top the mast, but you could haul me up, I'm sure, and that's nothing compared to some of the mountains I've climbed," said Teri with a great measure of self assurance.

"Great! All you have to do is unscrew the light cover, remove the existing light bulb, screw in the new bulb and replace the cover with a couple of screws," said Markham who was impressed by her willingness to perform a task that most women and many men would fear to undertake.

"The deck and cockpit will also need to be scrubbed and hosed down," said Markham. "But the weather is perfect for it."

"I might even get a tan," said Teri whose fair skin would be prone to sunburn.

"I would recommend that you change into a sleeved shirt and trousers after a half hour on deck, Teri," said Markham, discreetly admiring her ballerina figure. "Otherwise you're going to suffer severe sunburn."

While Markham found Teri most attractive, his past loves and love for Michelle although unrequited, left no room in his heart for Teri who, after twenty-four years, having found Markham, was now ready for her second and final love commitment. She knew only too well the surreal obstacle that stood in her way but she was not going to give Markham up without a fight. While her intelligence and self-assurance might have frightened some men, her beauty had never ceased to attract confident men of substance. *Markham*, she thought, *was a challenge worth the effort.*

Teri showed no fear as Markham cranked her up the tall mast to the top where she changed the light bulb without mishap then still perched at the top of the mast, she perused the surrounding area admiring the seascape, and imagined herself sailing the ocean escorted by seagulls with Markham at the helm. Her obvious seaworthy agility and apparent love of seafaring life did not go unobserved by Markham who nevertheless felt he could only offer her brotherly love.

By dinner time, the deck and cockpit had been completely scrubbed and cleaned. The cabin's interior woodwork had also been polished by Teri who found that the reflection of the amber lanterns against the teak cabinetry and flooring gave the cabin an aura of maritime romanticism that had great appeal to her.

After dinner, they sat in the cockpit facing each other across the teak pedestal table, each with a glass of red wine commenting on the beauty of the sun resting on the horizon and the serenity of their surroundings.

"I could easily settle for this lifestyle," said Teri, holding her glass of wine near her lips while staring into Markham's eyes for his reaction.

"Life at sea is quite different than life in port," replied Markham.

"I can imagine going through some storms, but that's what makes life exciting," said Teri trying to convince Markham of her seagoing attributes.

Markham didn't want to encourage that vein of conversation as he guessed only too well her motivation.

"My lower back is sore from all that cleaning exercise. I guess I'm out of shape," said Markham. "I'm going to rest my back against the bulwark."

"Why don't you let me massage it for you, Jim?"

"No, that might make it worse. Rest is all it needs," replied Markham, knowing it might lead to intimacy.

Without waiting for her comment, Markham moved himself to the port side locker where he placed a cushion against the bulwark and with glass of wine in hand, sat with his right leg bent at the knee resting against the cowling and his left foot on the cockpit floor.

Teri brought her glass of wine and sat at the end of the port side locker just a few inches from Markham's right foot, where she faced him for some serious talk.

"Would you mind terribly if I asked you to tell me about Michelle?" she asked softly.

Markham looked at Teri and saw an opportunity to tell someone who apparently cared about his dilemma. "What is it you want to know?"

"Where does she come from and how did you two meet?" she asked.

Markham took a sip of wine then looked out at the sea. "I first met her many years ago at an international polygraph seminar in Miami, Florida. She was with her husband who was a polygraph examiner from Montreal whom I had met some years earlier when he was with the Provincial Police of Quebec. We became friends almost instantly. He wanted to go partners with me in a polygraph business but at the time I had my hands full in Buffalo so I couldn't oblige him, but we remained steadfast friends ever since,"

"Do they have children?" asked Teri.

"They each have two children by a previous marriage. They're all grown now. Actually I learned sometime later that they're not legally married...probably because it would complicate things with their previous spousal arrangements. But for all intents and purposes, they're married," said Markham.

"So Michelle is French Canadian?" said Teri.

"Yes, and she's bilingual and so is her husband Jean," replied Markham, now looking directly at Teri to see her reaction to all of this personal information.

"If they're not legally married, Jim, then what is to stop you from telling her how you feel about her?" asked Teri with a puzzled look.

"Because whether they are legally married or not, they are both very special friends. I could never in good conscience interfere with their relationship which appears to be in a most harmonious state," replied Markham.

"Yes, but are they both in love with each other? That is the question, Jim," said Teri.

"From all appearances, I think they are," replied Markham, "and I'm not going to test it."

"That's most noble of you, James, but appearances are often fooling," said Teri, a bit frustrated at Markham's reluctance to press the issue. "I think you should at least tell her how you feel about her and then let her decide who she wishes to spend the rest of her life with."

"Don't you see, Teri? Even if she does love me, I don't want to gain it at his expense. He's an extraordinarily kind man whom I wish all the happiness he justly deserves and Michelle gives him that. What kind of a friend would I be to take that away from him? No Teri. I must accept the cards that fate handed me, and fold."

"Well, if I ever meet her, I will sure tell her," replied Teri who hoped she would get a negative answer from Michelle clearing the way for her to win Markham's heart.

"If you are indeed my friend, you will keep your silence," said Markham with finality. "The stars are out tonight which means clear skies and a good day for sailing tomorrow."

"Oh! Good. I'm looking forward to it," replied Teri with enthusiasm.

The following morning, Teri awakened to the sound of seagulls and after showering and dressing in her sailing attire, she entered the galley to fix herself a cup of tea. She noticed that Markham was still asleep in the main forward salon and decided not to wake him. She was fascinated by the navigation station with its small desk and electronics built into the cabinetry above it, including a monitor screen. She instinctively tried the desk's middle drawer and to her surprise it was unlocked. Inside the drawer she found a black cover notebook which she thought was the boat's log book and opened it.

The first page astonished her as she read 'Poems of the CAUL by James Markham.' She leafed through it quickly, fearful that Markham would awaken, and then suddenly stopped at a page that bore the title 'Michelle.' She sat down on the small navigation stool while she read the poem dedicated to her rival.

Whenever I hear the name Michelle
my mind falls under her spell
I see the aura of her golden hair
her vivid blue eyes and angelic stare
truly the visage of the goddess of love
with the majesty of a white dove.

Michelle is my secret mignone
My love for her must be forlorn
because she belongs to another
who is my best friend forever.

My heart cannot forget her
nor my soul able to release her
She invades my imagination
as lovers ice skating together
riding a snow sled in winter
decorating a Christmas tree
sharing heartfelt presents with glee
sailing under the dazzling sun
declaring you are the one
under the stars shining bright
we embrace till morning light.
If this wonderful dream ever came true
Life on earth would be heaven with you

But alas, my dear Michelle
I must suffer the agony of hell
perhaps for my soul to be pure
heaven will accept me for sure
But if this is my ultimate fate
may you be at heaven's gate.

Teri musingly closed the book of poems and placed it back in the drawer, then went up into the cockpit and on deck where she sat leaning against the mast staring out at the bay with a feeling of depression and defeat. *Maybe,* she thought, *I'm destined to love him like a sister and be his nurse. Oh! well, qu'est cera, cera.*

When Markham got up, she made no mention of the book of poems, fearful that he would feel that his privacy had been invaded, not to mention the intimacy of his poem to Michelle. *Besides,* she thought, *there was no date to this poem, hence it could have been written before he met her. No sense dwelling over it now.*

After a leisurely breakfast, Markham started the diesel engine and let it idle while he went on deck and removed the bolts from the furling mechanism of the genoa and staysail that would allow the drums to turn and unfurl the sails.

"OK, Teri, step out on the dock and untie the spring line and throw it on board," which she did with the agility of a young girl.

"Good! Now untie the fore and aft dock lines and throw them on the bow and stern," said Markham using the bow thruster to keep the bow from leaving the dock.

"Good show, Teri, climb aboard," said Markham who watched Teri adroitly jump from the dock to the stepping edge of the cockpit, then onto the portside locker.

She dutifully assembled the three dock lines and placed them inside the starboard locker while Markham piloted the boat out of the marina into the harbor and the open sea.

"The sails are still down. Do you mind if I go up on deck, Jim?"

"No, go right ahead. I won't be unfurling the sails until we get out a ways, then I'll let you know in plenty of time." said Markham who was inspecting the sky for the weather and the direction and strength of the wind for eventual tacking. The sea swells were moderate and the weather promised a pleasant even keel sail for Teri's first sailing experience with The Caul. Teri sat against the mast facing the bow that plowed through some of the irregular large swells sending a light spray of salt water over her lightly clad body, absorbing the sun's warm rays for a much desired sun tan. *This is the life,* she thought, *free as a bird, no stress.* She was near her retirement with the C.I.A., and had planned on purchasing a small house on the shores of Connecticut. Now she wondered whether that was what she really wanted. She thought of the old saying, *the best plans of mice and men.* Then she heard Markham calling to her that he was about to raise the sails. She immediately left the deck and sat under the Bimini in the cockpit to avoid further exposure to the sun. She now wore a large brim beige hat that formed a halo around her dark hair and fair skin. Markham was surely aware of her beauty but would not allow himself to appreciate it lest he felt disloyal to the memory of Claire.

After all, he thought, *she was one of Alex Petrov's agents on a mission that had now apparently been completed.*

"I guess you'll be returning to the states, now that I've recovered," said Markham.

Teri looked up at him by raising the brim of her hat. "Are you trying to get rid of me, James?"

"No. On the contrary, I enjoy your company, Teri. But I know Alex. He'll want you back at headquarters the moment he learns that I'm back on the wagon."

"Let's not tell him until he asks, shall we," she replied with a smile.

"Alright, a few days of sailing won't hurt his budget or my conscience," said Markham.

"I noticed that you have a couple of exterior speakers in your cockpit. Does that mean that you can play music in the cockpit while we're sailing?" she asked.

"Yes. Would you like me to turn on some nautical music?" asked Markham.

"What do you consider nautical music?"

"Piano music mostly," replied Markham. "I like to play classical music when I'm sailing. "Let me play you something that I think you'll like."

Markham turned on the autopilot, then went into the cabin below and activated the compact disk player that already contained several disks. He returned to the helm and deactivated the autopilot. In a few seconds the music enveloped the entire cockpit.

"Oh! I know that composition but I can't put my finger on it," exclaimed Teri.

"It's Clair de Lune by Debussy," said Markham. "It's one of my favorite pieces."

"After this you'll hear Tchaikovsky's Love Theme of Romeo and Juliette."

"You are a romantic, James," said Teri. "Now I recall from your file that you are a Pisces, a water sign and prone to the arts."

"So what's your astrological sign, Teri?" asked Markham.

"I'm a Libra, born on the first of October" she replied

"According to astrologers your positive qualities are intelligence, charm, gentleness, emotional balance and a search for justice, all desirable elements for an agent of the CIA," said Markham.

"You said nothing about our propensity for love," she said inquisitively.

"You understand that this is not my opinion, only what has been written by astrologers. Libra women are not overly passionate. They are infatuated with love's surface beauty and never question the basis or reason for that love," said Markham.

"Do you really believe that?" she asked.

"No. I don't think you can pigeon hole people into specific categories, but it is entertaining," replied Markham hoping he had not offended her.

"Well, I don't believe in astrology either, but as you said, it is amusing," she said relieved by Markham's absolving remark.

Tchaikovsky's love theme of Romeo and Juliette came through the cockpit speakers with a clarity that stopped their conversation, so they might appreciate the exquisite music surrounding them as the sailboat moved silently and carefree through the ocean without a destination.

Upon their return to the marina several hours later, Markham decided to take Teri out to dinner at a local French restaurant in Nantes as a change of pace and she agreed heartily.

They were attracted by the quaintness of a restaurant with a sign that simply stated 'Chez Nous." It was not sumptuous but very clean and traditionally decorated with lots of red and white colors. Naturally, Markham ordered a dozen escargots (snails) as an appetizer and Teri settled for half a dozen which made Markham happy that she shared his taste in French cuisine. She agreed to a steak chateaubriand, one of Markham's favorites and a bottle of red table wine completed the repas. After a couple of glasses of wine, Teri became less inhibited and what had been simmering now came to the surface.

"I'm going to be leaving soon for America, Jim," she said in a low voice. "I can't leave without knowing whether I have a chance with you?"

Markham felt uneasy at her question and remained silent, not knowing how to answer.

"I know how you feel about Michelle, but she's just a memory, Jim. I'm here, I'm real and I'm in love with you," she said holding back tears.

"You are very special to me, Teri, but right now I don't know how I feel. I haven't allowed myself to feel any emotions towards anyone, probably because of the recent loss of my wife Claire," said Markham apologetically.

"Oh, God! I'm so sorry. I forgot the reason for my being here in the first place. Please forgive me, Jim."

"That's alright, Teri. Please be patient with me and leave problems of the heart to providence."

"Don't say it, James. Qu'est cera, cera."

Markham laughed at her last comment and they each sipped their wine pensively looking into each other's eyes for a glimpse of their thoughts.

Upon return to The Caul, Teri reminded Markham that he had not yet shown her the Caul stored in his safe. Markham went into the aft cabin followed by Teri and opened a floor cabinet door revealing the safe. After turning the safe combination dial several times he opened the safe door and pulled out a black velour covered silver case and stood facing her.

"You may touch it but you must not remove it from the case," said Markham as he opened the lid.

Teri looked intently at the thin tanned amniotic sac. "So that's the membrane that covered and protected you at birth," she said, then carefully touched the Caul with the tip of her fingers. "It feels so smooth. Am I supposed to make a wish?"

"Not that I know of, but you may if you're so inclined," replied Markham.

Teri silently made a wish that she wouldn't have to return to the United States and leave Markham. "OK! I made my wish."

Markham closed the lid and returned the case to the safe and locked it.

"I understand that according to legend, having the Caul on the boat protects it from maritime disaster," said Teri.

"Yes, and I believe it," replied Markham.

"You are a fascinating man, James. I'm going to miss you," she said with a longing in her eyes.

"You know. We've been so preoccupied that I haven't checked my e-mail," said Markham now seated in front of his computer at the navigation station.

Markham deleted several junk e-mails then noticed the origin of one e-mail was from Alex Petrov. He immediately opened it and read the short message:

'Jim, I've been trying to contact you for several days to no avail. Flanigan has not been answering her cell phone. It's urgent that you both get back to me ASAP. Alex.'

Without turning his head, Markham asked Teri, standing behind him, if she had turned off her cell phone.

"Good grief," she exclaimed, looking at her cell phone. I must have forgotten to turn it back on. Mister Petrov is going to be furious with me."

"Call him now while I respond to his e-mail," said Markham.

CHAPTER III

Mystery of the Holy Shroud

Teri dialed Alex Petrov's telephone number and waited for an answer but received no response. She was about to leave a message when Markham interrupted her.

"Don't leave a message," said Markham. "Let me call him. We go back more than four decades. I'll apologize for the both of us and he'll readily accept it 'cause he wouldn't be so anxious to locate us unless he needed us for something important. I sent him an e-mail telling him we'd be on call."

Markham waited five minutes, then using Teri's cell phone, he called Alex who answered with his last name.

"Alex, this is Jim."

"Where the hell have you been? I've been going nuts trying to contact you. Is Flanigan with you?"

"Yes, she is. We're on my sailboat and she inadvertently turned off her cell phone and didn't realize it had been turned off until I received your e-mail. It's really my fault, Alex. Don't blame her. She did a remarkable job of getting me back on the wagon."

"Don't tell me her methods of persuasion. I don't want to know," replied Alex with a chuckle reminiscent of the old days when they were stationed together in France.

"I know what you're thinking, Alex. Teri has completely lived up to your expectations and she's been a wonderful nurse," said Markham in defense of her morals.

"Well, that's good. How long have you been on the wagon?" asked Alex.

"About a week, I'm fine, Alex. What's up?"

"You get to the point, as usual," replied Alex. "Jim, we've got a major crisis on our hands. I mean a world crisis and we need your help my friend."

"We! Who's we, Alex?"

"Me, the agency and the Vatican," replied Alex.

"The Vatican?" said Markham somewhat surprised.

"Yes, the Vatican," replied Alex with gravity in his voice.

"Is the Cardinal General involved in this?" asked Markham.

"Yes, and the Pope, my friend," said Alex. "This is such a serious matter that when I tell you the details, you won't be able to refuse your participation in the case."

"I'm waiting with bated breath," said Markham.

"I see that you're using Flanigan's cell phone," said Alex. "I presume that she's there with you."

"Yes, she is."

"Put your phone on speaker mode so that both of you can listen to my conversation," said Alex.

"OK, Alex! We're both listening," said Markham.

"Flanigan…I want to congratulate you for a job well done. Now I've got another, job for you. You will be working with Markham on this one, and before you say anything, Jim, please allow me to explain."

"We're listening, Alex," replied Markham.

"Three weeks ago, someone stole the Holy Shroud of Turin from the Royal Chapel of the Cathedral of Saint John the Baptist in Turin, Italy," said Alex with a pause. "The Italian authorities have been unable to develop any leads in the case and even invited the Defense Academy for Credibility Assessment out of Fort Jackson to send two polygraph examiners to Turin to polygraph suspects in the case."

"My God!" said Markham. "You weren't kidding when you said this was an important case. Apparently the polygraph tests didn't turn up anything or you wouldn't be calling me."

"That's correct, Jim. They didn't develop any useful information."

"So what's next, Alex?"

"You are on board then?" asked Alex.

"Did you have any doubts?" said Markham.

"I guess not. Effective immediately, you're on the payroll and Flanigan will be assisting you. Do you copy, Flanigan?"

"Yes sir," replied Teri who could hardly contain her joy at not having to leave Markham for the states.

"Jim...you've got carte blanche and special credentials will be given to you by one of our agents at the Charles de Gaulle airport where you will be boarding a plane with Flanigan to Turino. You will be met at the Turino airport by an aide to the Cardinal General who is overseeing the case for the Vatican."

"Are we flying by commercial airline?" asked Teri, thinking of the tool kit with special weaponry from the Paris office that is in her custody.

"I know what you're thinking, Flanigan. You'll be flying in one of our own private aircraft," replied Alex. "You are authorized to use maximum measures. I have a feeling that this case will take you all over the globe. I know, Flanigan that you're due for retirement in eight months, but I surely hope that this case will be solved before then."

"Yes, sir, I will do my best," replied Flanigan.

"Jim, when you arrive at the airport in Paris, our agent will provide you with a briefcase that will contain all available information developed so far and the Cardinal will fill you in on the rest when you get into Turino. I'm sure you'll be meeting with the Italian authorities as well."

"You sure are full of surprises, Alex," said Markham. "Never a dull moment."

"Like old times, my friend," replied Alex. "Good Luck, and keep me posted."

"Will do, take care," said Markham, turning off the phone.

"Well, James, I guess you're stuck with me," said Teri, pleased with the new assignment.

"Fortunately it's for a limited time," he replied, then realized the implication of his remark.

"You mean you don't like my company?" she asked.

"Of course I like your company, Teri. I meant that I'm used to traveling alone and a man of my age gets set in his ways. You know what I mean."

"I'll try not to be too much of a bother, Mister Markham."

"So now it's Mister Markham. C'mon Teri. Don't be oversensitive. I couldn't think of a better partner, but this case has all the earmarks of danger and I don't think you should be placed in harm's way being so close to retirement."

"Why don't you just say it, Jim? You think that as a woman I'll be a liability rather than an asset to your investigation."

"Not true. I have every faith in you, Teri. I'm just concerned for your safety."

"Damn it, Jim, would you be that concerned if I were a male agent?"

"You've got a point. I did sound like a male chauvinist. Present company accepted; will you accept my apology?"

Teri looked at Markham for signs of sincerity and noticing his sheepish appearance, smiled and walked up to him. "I'll accept your apology if you comfort me with a hug."

Markham wrapped his big arms around her gently and kissed the top of her head.

"Teri...forgive me for being so protective."

"That's alright. I feel the same way," she replied, leveling the gender scale which did not go unnoticed by Markham who preferred to let the issue rest.

"Let's pack our bags and button up this boat, Teri. Luckily, we've got your rented car. I expect that we'll have to stop by your hotel to change clothes and pick up some things, but for convenience's sake, why don't you keep that room. That way we can travel light."

"Good idea, Jim. Are you going to be carrying?"

"Yes. The Agency provided me with a non-metallic pistol some time ago."

"Good. I'll be bringing the usual tool kit as back-up," replied Teri.

Upon arrival at the Charles de Gaulle airport in Paris, Teri parked the rented car in the long-term parking lot and walked alongside Markham, each carrying a mid-size black shoulder bag. Inside the grand terminal, they walked briskly to the private aircraft area and two men, both dressed in suits, white shirt and tie, approached them, one of whom Teri recognized from the Agency's Paris office.

"Mister Lachaise," said Teri, "this is Mister James Markham."

"Please to meet you, Mister Markham. This is my associate Mister Claude Poitier." replied Lachaise. "I have been instructed to give you this locked briefcase. The combination is contained in this sealed envelope. If you will sign this receipt Mister Markham, I'll escort you to your waiting aircraft."

Markham signed the receipt, and then accepted the briefcase and brown envelope. "Lead the way Mister Lachaise," said Markham.

The silvery Gulfstream V aircraft was parked on the tarmac not far from the terminal exit. Markham and Flanigan both shook hands with Poiter but Lachaise only offered his hand cupped like a claw to Markham. As they walked towards the aircraft, Markham commented to Flanigan about Lachaise's rude behavior.

"Apparently Lachaise doesn't like you. Tribal rivalry?" asked Markham.

"We met at the agency's Paris office. He doesn't like rejection," she replied.

"Judging from his crab like handshake, I'd say you made a wise decision," said Markham. They made their entry into the aircraft and were immediately met by a male steward who invited them to be seated in the plush seats in the forward area. The steward immediately closed the door to the aircraft and the pilot started the jet engines readying to taxi onto the main runway for takeoff.

"We should be landing in Turino in about one hour and 20minutes," said the young steward. "I have refreshments including tea and coffee and croissants."

"I'll have a cup of coffee and a croissant, please," said Teri Flanigan.

"Please make that tea with cream and sugar and a croissant for me," said Markham.

61

"My pleasure," replied the steward.

Markham opened the sealed letter and read the combination to the lock of the briefcase. He then opened the briefcase and removed all of its contents, giving some of it to Teri to hold. They each pulled up their individual tables and started leafing through the material consisting of letters and reports.

"I've got the polygraph report from the Defense Academy for Credibility Assessment," said Teri.

"Let me see that," replied Markham who quickly read the report then gasped at the signature name.

"What's the matter, Jim?"

"The man who headed the polygraph team and signed the report is an old nemesis of mine named Peter Loefler. The Department of Defense recently changed the name of the Department of Defense Polygraph Institute to the Defense Academy for Credibility Assessment or DACA and Loefler is now apparently the Deputy Director."

"Is that creating a problem in our investigation?" asked Teri.

"According to the report, Loefler and another polygraphist went to Turino at the request of the Turino Police Department and conducted polygraph examinations on fourteen people. In one capacity or another, these people had access to the vault that contained the holy shroud but all tests proved negative. What surprises me is that the deputy director himself would conduct polygraph tests."

"Yes, that does sound unusual, doesn't it," replied Teri.

"I think we're going to pay the Turino Police Department a visit, my dear," said Markham who had several unanswered questions.

Upon landing at Turino International Airport, Markham and Flanigan were met by an awaiting limousine. The uniformed chauffeur opened the first of two rear doors, inviting them to enter wherein they were received by the Cardinal General. Markham immediately recognized the Cardinal General and was introduced to another man of the cloth, Archbishop Bartolini, the Papal Custodian of the Holy Shroud.

"Permit me, Your Eminences, to introduce Teri Flanigan who works for Alex Petrov and has been assigned to assist me in this case," said Markham.

"It is our great pleasure to make your acquaintance, Miss Flanigan," said the Cardinal General. "I hope that your stay in Turino will be a pleasant one."

"Thank you, Your Eminence," replied Teri Flanigan, who felt a bit intimidated, so refrained from further dialogue.

"Have you had a chance to review some of the material that Alex told us he would provide you?" asked the Cardinal.

"Yes, I have, Your Eminence," replied Markham. "My first step is to view the area within the Royal Chapel where the Holy Shroud was stored and stolen. I will need to know all of the security measures that were in place at the time of the larceny."

"That won't be a problem, Jim," said the Cardinal who knew Markham well enough from previous meetings to address him by his first name.

"I will also need a list of all personnel who had even the most remote access to the area where the holy shroud was stored," said Markham.

"Yes. We will provide you with the same list we gave to the Italian Police Department's investigative unit. They had all of the people on the list submit to a polygraph test," said the Archbishop of Turin.

"I noticed that they were polygraphed by two examiners from DACA," replied Markham.

"I see that the report that Alex gave you is quite complete," said the Cardinal.

"I'm not satisfied with DACA's report. I will need to review each and every one of those polygraph tests," said Markham. "In that regard, I will need to discuss this issue with the Italian investigator in charge of the case, as soon as possible."

"That will be arranged," replied the Cardinal. "I told Alex that we needed you on this case, and I see now that I was right. You have the full support of the Vatican, Jim, and the Pope remembers you and sends you his blessings."

Those last words had a profound emotional impact on Teri who now realized the enormous responsibility that had been placed on Markham's shoulders and the importance of her role as his assistant. *My God,* she thought, *in the whole world, we two have been chosen to rescue the Holy Shroud of Jesus, the Holy Grail of Christendom. I cannot fail,* she told herself, and in accepting this awesome responsibility, she sensed a special bond with Markham.

"First we're going to the Hotel Principi di Piemonte where you will both be staying while in Turino. The hotel is only a short distance to the Cathedral," said the Cardinal. "I have taken the liberty of reserving a private room within the dining area of the hotel where we can have a private and informative dinner at 1900 hours this evening. That will give you four hours in which to restore yourselves for the evening."

"That's very thoughtful of you, Your Eminence," replied Markham. "Speaking for both of us, we will be honored to join you for dinner."

"And here we are," said the Cardinal. "We won't come in. Your reservations for two adjoining rooms have been confirmed."

The chauffeur came around and opened the door to the limousine, allowing Markham and Teri Flanigan to exit whereupon Markham turned towards the seated Cardinal. "It is most comforting to see you again, Your Eminence."

The hotel entrance had a unique façade of three stacks of five tall, side-by-side windows fronted with four pine cone plants adorned with the name of the hotel. Upon entering the lobby Markham and Teri were impressed with its luxurious décor and spaciousness and the courtesy afforded them by the reservation desk clerk who expedited their registrations. In spite of their light luggage, a bellhop was quickly summoned to take their luggage and show them to their rooms. In the elevator, Markham remarked to Teri that having their rooms on the fourth floor was most handy for a quick exit, as there was usually a fire escape easily available outside one of the windows. The bellhop opened Teri's room first and after depositing her luggage inside the room and accepting the routine gratuity, he showed Markham his room next door, receiving a second gratuity. It seemed it was a good day for that bellhop. Markham immediately went to Teri's room and after she let him inside, he commented that they were both given super deluxe rooms with a flat screen televisions and a great view of the Mole Antonelliana with the Alps in the background through the two double-pane windows.

"What a spectacular view," said Markham looking at the snow-capped peaks of the Alps.

Teri walked over to the window and stood next to Markham admiring the view. "What is that tall domed building towering over the city?"

"That's the Mole Antonelliana, the tallest brick building in Europe," replied Markham. "The Chapel of the Holy Shroud is supposed to be located nearby."

"Such a beautiful city," said Teri. "Too bad we're here on serious business, James, otherwise this could turn out to be a great vacation."

"Yes, well we'd better get some rest before dinner, 'cause I suspect that the Cardinal and the Archbishop will be using this dinner to gives us a thorough briefing of the case," said Markham. "Bring your small tape recorder with you, Teri, 'cause we won't be able to take notes and I would like to have documentation of all the information."

"They might find the tape recorder objectionable," said Teri.

"Give it to me. I'll stick it in my pocket and no one will be the wiser," replied Markham. "Taking notes slows down the exchange of information, and an audio recording may save us precious time later. By the way, Teri, the Cardinal is addressed as 'Your Eminence' and the Archbishop as 'Your Excellency.'"

"OK, Boss!" replied Teri. "You'd better get your beauty rest."

Markham, dressed in his midnight blue suit, white shirt and tie, accompanied by Teri who wore a dark blue business suit, entered the hotel dining room and after identifying themselves, were immediately escorted to a private room. There the Archbishop was already seated next to the Cardinal at the head of the cloth covered mahogany table. Both ministers stood up to greet their two dinner guests, and after shaking hands, Markham and Teri sat down next to each other facing their hosts.

A formally dressed waiter appeared and after giving them each a leather covered menu, asked for their order of a beverage while they perused the menu. The Cardinal ordered a bottle of Barolo Borgogno '96 for himself and the Archbishop to accompany their meal.

"May I suggest Arneis if you like white wine, or Barolo Borgogno if you prefer red wine, for you and Miss Flanigan?" said the Cardinal.

"Arneis is local to Piedmonte, isn't it?" said Teri in English even though she was fluent in Italian.

"Yes it is, Miss Flanigan," replied the Cardinal. "Apparently you're familiar with our wines."

"I've visited Italy on a number of occasions, Your Eminence," said Teri. "I'll have the Barolo Borgogno, James."

"Very well," said Markham to the waiter. "We'll share a bottle of Barolo Borgogno '96."

"I'm afraid that you have me at a disadvantage, Your Eminence. I don't speak or read Italian and the menu is in Italian only," said Markham.

"That's alright, Jim," said Teri. "I can read Italian so let me translate for you what's on the menu."

"Now I can see why Mister Petrov sent you to assist Jim on this assignment," said the Cardinal.

"Listen, Teri," said Markham. "I'll simplify it. A mixed antipasto, followed by the vegetable soup, then for the main course, either beef or lamb."

"I've got just the thing for you then," said the Cardinal. "The mixed antipasto of the house, the traditional Tuscan vegetable soup, Agnoletti unique to Torino, is a pasta ring filled with ground lamb, pumpkin seeds and chestnuts, drizzled with walnut oil, Grana Padano cheese and black truffle oil."

"Thank you, Your Eminence," said Markham. "I'll try that. "What about you Teri? What would you like to order?"

"I will order the salad and vegetable soup, but I'm going to indulge in their grilled Chianina beef filet," replied Teri.

"Good choice, Miss Flanigan," said the Archbishop. "Have you been to Turino before?"

"Not Turino, Your Excellency," said Teri, without having to volunteer any of her past travels under CIA sponsorship.

The waiter returned with two bottles of wine which he opened and poured a small amount in the Cardinal's empty glass for him to taste before pouring.

The Cardinal lifted the glass to his nose to breathe in the aroma first, then tasted it with approval, thus signaling the waiter to pour the wine into each of the four glasses, and then the waiter opened the second bottle for it to breathe. The Cardinal told the waiter in Italian that he was ready to order for the group.

Markham watched the Cardinal express his culinary wishes with the hands of an orchestra leader. There was a second waiter standing nearby to assist the first waiter which indicated first class service.

"Archbishop Bartolini reserved this room so that our dinner conversation would be private," said the Cardinal General. "He will now present to you the facts of this case in chronological order."

"Three weeks ago, on Good Friday, the 21st of March, at 0700 I retrieved the key and magnetic card from my personal safe located in my office in the rectory, and went down to the basement of the Royal Chapel in the Cathedral of Saint John the Baptist. This is where the vault is located within a room that is secured with a burglarproof steel door," said Bartolini, pausing to take a sip from his glass of water.

"I inserted the magnetic card into the slot in the door to disarm the alarm system within the vault room, then used the key to open the steel door. Once inside the room, which is about 5 meters long, I walked up to the massive vault door and was about to use my combination to unlock the door when I noticed a tiny hole next to the combination dial. I instinctively pulled on the door handle and the door opened. I knew almost immediately that someone had broken into the safe and this was confirmed when I saw the two gas hoses normally connected to the metal sarcophagus that contained the Holy Shroud were unplugged and lying on the floor and the sarcophagus had been moved. I could see that one end of it had been pried open and the Holy Shroud was missing. At that moment, I became very afraid," said Bartolini, a most mild mannered priest.

"If I may ask a question, Your Excellency?" said Markham. "You said that the Holy Shroud was kept inside the vault. How big is that vault?"

"It's actually a bank vault about 5 meters wide by 9 meters deep. It's used to store valuable sacraments and relics, some of which are priceless," replied Bartolini.

"How many people have the combination to the vault's door?" asked Markham.

"Myself and the Cardinal Superior," replied Bartolini who was referring to the Cardinal General's official title.

"And who has access to the key to the steel door to the room that leads to the vault?" asked Markham.

"Only myself, but the Cardinal Superior has the combination to my personal safe," he replied.

"Your Excellency, you mentioned that the magnetic card disarms the security system within the vault room. What does the security system detect?" asked Markham.

"It detects movement, floor pressure above 30 liters, temperature below 65 degrees and above 75 degrees," replied Bartolini.

"When was the safe vault installed?" asked Markham, curious as to its age.

"In 1975," replied Bartolini.

"And the steel door to the vault room?" asked Markham.

"That same year."

"Was there any evidence of forced entry?" asked Markham.

"Not to the room leading to the safe vault, but the massive vault door was penetrated apparently with the use of a powerful drill," replied Bartolini. "As it was explained to me by the chief detective of the Turino Police Department, the thieves drilled a hole into the safe door next to the combination dial and then inserted a gastrovideoscope with a wide angle lens inside the hole to view the tumbler mechanism enabling them to open the vault door."

"But the question remains, how did the perpetrators gain access to the vault room without setting off the alarm system?" asked Markham. "You said that there was no evidence of forced entry into that room and your Excellency is the only person who has both the key and magnetic card to that door."

"That remains a mystery," said the Cardinal, injecting his personal opinion. "There was no record of electrical failure and there is an auxiliary electrical power system in place."

"Is there any chance at all, Your Excellency, that someone obtained the combination to the safe in your office?" asked Markham.

" No, not a chance, sir," replied Bartolini.

"Obviously, once the perpetrators were inside the vault room with the door closed behind them, they were able to take their time to drill their way into the vault," said Markham. Teri listened attentively not wanting to interrupt Markham's train of thought, knowing that he had the criminal investigative experience.

"The interesting thing about this larceny," said Bartolini, "is that nothing else was removed from the vault, including a pure gold chalice imbedded with priceless jewels dating back to the 12th century."

"Mister Petrov's report indicated that 14 people who had access to the area of the vault room and safe were polygraphed by DACA. In what capacity would they have had access to the vault room and safe area?" asked Markham.

"Well, you have the two clerks that work in my office," replied Bartolini. "The cleaning staff who have access to the entire cathedral including the Royal Chapel, a bishop, four priests, sister Lolita and my chief custodian Mister Arturo Musso. He provides me and my staff with the necessary assistance in the conduct of services which often require that he accompany me to the vault to retrieve a valuable chalice or other item necessary for a particular ceremony."

"With due respect, Your Excellency, I must ask you this very important question," said Markham most politely. "Have you ever allowed Mister Musso or any other person to ever hold your key or your magnetic card for even a few seconds?"

"No, I have not. I am certain of that," replied Bartolini defensively.

"I'm sorry, Your Excellency, but I had to cover that angle," said Markham apologetically.

"That's quite alright," said the Cardinal in Markham's defense. "We understand that you must investigate all possibilities."

"When can we be shown the area where the Holy Shroud was maintained and stolen," asked Markham.

"Tomorrow morning," replied Bartolini. "Will 0900 be alright with you?"

"Yes, that will be fine," replied Markham.

"I will have father Albini meet you in the lobby of your hotel at 0900 then," said Bartolini. "He will drive you both to the cathedral where I will be awaiting your arrival."

At that moment, the two formerly dressed waiters appeared with the antipasto which they served, offering choices of dressing and seasoning. The Cardinal General's resumption of the conversation was momentarily interrupted by the taller waiter who started to replenish the wine glasses, then becoming aware that his presence was the reason for their silence, quickly finished his task and left the room with his associate, closing the door behind him.

"You're probably wondering, Jim, as we have, about the real motive behind the theft of the Holy Shroud?" said the Cardinal, and without waiting for a reply continued, "Someone suggested that it could have been perpetrated by a fundamentalist Islamic group who wish to hold it for ransom in negotiations between Israel and Palestine. Others have suggested that a wealthy collector of rare artifacts funded this theft. Then there are those that could have stolen the Holy Shroud for sale to the highest bidder."

"But the Holy Shroud is not a relic that can easily be marketed," added Bartolini.

"I beg your pardon, Your Excellency," said Teri, inserting her comments for the first time. "I haven't had time to research the Holy Shroud, but I seem to recall that there was some question among scientists about the authenticity of the Shroud. Using the carbon 14 method, I believe they dated the Shroud in the 13th century."

"I'm glad you raised that issue, Miss Flanigan, because since then a substantial amount of scientific research has been done on the Holy Shroud by as many as 40 scientists from around the world," said Bartolini.

"I'm truly interested in learning all I can about the results of this latest research, Your Excellency," replied Markham with Teri nodding in agreement.

"A study published in 2005 in a peer-reviewed journal on the radiocarbon sample from the Shroud concluded that the sample used to test the age of the Shroud in 1988 was taken from a rewoven area of the Shroud," said the Cardinal General. "Pyrolysis mass spectrometry results from the sample area coupled with microscopic and microchemical observations proved that the radiocarbon sample was not part of the original cloth of the Shroud of Turin. In fact, Dr. Raymond Rogers, a Fellow at Los Alamos National Laboratory who led the team of scientists assigned to study the shroud reached the conclusion that the shroud images were not painted and in fact none of the scientists could offer an explanation for the images on the shroud. Dr. Rogers had complete respect for the technology and quality of the work conducted by the scientific laboratories, therefore accepted their findings on the carbon dating of the shroud to be in the 13th century. However, two researchers by the name of Benford and Marino wrote a paper that suggested that the sample used in the carbon dating was drastically different and not part of the shroud but was part of a medieval repair using a technique known as invisible reweaving. Dr. Rogers thought that Menford and Marino's idea was preposterous and decided to prove them wrong by conducting tests on sample material saved from the actual cuttings from which the samples used in previous tests were taken. His results were published in 2005 in Thermochimica Acta, a highly respected peer-reviewed scientific journal in which Dr. Rogers stated that the combined evidence from chemical kinetics, analytical chemistry, cotton content, and pyrolysis proves that the material from the radiocarbon area of the shroud is significantly different from that of the main cloth. The radiocarbon sample was thus not part of the original cloth and is invalid for determining the age of the shroud. Dr. Rogers' conclusions were of such importance in refuting the previous results of the carbon dating that questioned the authenticity of the shroud that I made it a point of remembering Rogers' conclusions verbatim so I would not misquote him."

"Your knowledge regarding the scientific research conducted on the shroud is most impressive, Your Eminence," said Markham.

"Could you give us a description of the Shroud, Your Excellency, and what evidence supports its dating to the time of the crucifixion of Jesus Christ?" asked Teri.

"Actually there's quite a bit of evidence," replied Bartolini. "The Shroud is woven in herringbone twill and is composed of flax fibrils entwined with cotton fibrils. Its dimensions are 14 feet 3 inches long by 3 feet 7 inches wide and it bears the image of a naked man with his hands folded across his groin. He has a beard, mustache and shoulder length hair parted in the middle characteristic of Semitic men of that period. What is most interesting about the Shroud is the location of the wounds on the body of the Shroud's figure which coincide exactly with the wounds received by Jesus during his trial and crucifixion as stated in the New Testament, and consistent with Roman weapons and practices of crucifixion. Some of the unique wounds suffered by Jesus were the crowning with thorns that pierced his scalp and forehead. It was also the practice to break the crucified's legs to prevent him from raising himself up to breathe thus accelerating his death, which was not done to Jesus and the image on the Shroud does not show evidence of broken legs, a singular rarity. Instead a soldier pierced Jesus' heart with a lance, and this wound appears on the Shroud's image. Furthermore, examining scientists discovered evidence of two Roman coins imprinted on the eyes of the figure in the Shroud. These coins were identified as leptons minted during the governing of Jerusalem by Pontius Pilate, the Roman judge who condemned Jesus."

"Excuse me, Your Excellency," said Teri. "How was the Shroud folded over the body, and were the scientists able to determine the height and weight of the figure on the Shroud?"

"The man that we believe was Jesus was laid out on his back on the Shroud with his feet at one end and the Shroud was folded over his head then down the length of his body, so that the Shroud covered the front and back of his body," said Bartolini.

"The fact that Jesus was beaten with a flagrum or Roman whip consisting of leather thongs that contained lead pellets was evident from the markings on the Shroud that indicated he had been whipped over his entire back, shoulders and legs," said the Cardinal.

"The nail wounds which were made with seven-inch iron roofing spikes pierced his wrists and a single spike was driven through the left foot covering his right foot, as shown on the Shroud" said Bartolini.

"I don't mean to sound agnostic, Your Excellency," said Teri. "I've never had an opportunity to query persons with such authoritative knowledge of the Holy Shroud and the Holy scriptures. So I hope that you won't take offense to my questions."

"On the contrary, Miss Flanigan," replied Bartolini. "Your questions show an inquisitive mind and a keen interest in the ecclesiastic foundation of the Christian church."

"Well, Your Excellency, I was raised as a Catholic and taught by nuns about the bible, and I seem to remember in the Gospel of John, that Thomas who had been absent when Jesus made a post-resurrection appearance to the Apostles, had stated he wouldn't believe in the resurrection of Jesus unless he put his fingers into his hands, and touched the wound in his side, subsequently being afforded that opportunity. Yet, the Shroud apparently shows a man who was crucified with spikes through his wrists. How is this inconsistency explained, Your Excellency?" said Teri.

"That's a very good question, Miss Flanigan," replied Bartolini. "One plausible explanation is that in Aramaic and Biblical Greek, there is only one word used for both hand and wrist, which may account for the confusion in translation."

"Furthermore, Miss Flanigan," said the Cardinal, "It has been demonstrated that spikes or nails driven at the center of the hands' palm would never hold a man on a cross, especially a man of Jesus' size who had an estimated height between 5 feet 8 inches to 5 feet 11 inches and from 165 to 180 pounds."

In an attempt to rescue Teri Flanigan, Markham redirected the conversation towards the authenticity of the Holy Shroud. "Did the scientific tests ever show how the image of the man became imprinted on the Shroud?" asked Markham.

"There were many tests conducted on the Shroud's cloth in an attempt to determine how the image became imprinted into the cloth," replied Bartolini. "The scientists' conclusion is that the image was not formed by any known substance but by a burst of radiant energy or light of extremely high intensity, such as found in a nuclear blast. We believe that the Shroud was exposed to a brief burst of radiation at the moment of Jesus' resurrection which seared the Shroud with his image. Furthermore, microscopic examination of the Shroud by numerous scientists revealed that some of the pollen obtained from the Shroud originated from Jerusalem at the time of Jesus, and mites from examined samples were peculiar to Egyptian burial linens used at the time of Jesus. Finally, floral images on the Shroud were identified as having originated from a 7 mile area between Jericho and Jerusalem indicating that the Shroud was an ancient Israeli cloth."

"We believe that the Holy Shroud is the silent witness to the Resurrection of Jesus Christ," said the Cardinal General.

"Your Excellency, "said Markham, "the evidence you have presented is most compelling, which raises another question that I feel obliged to ask."

"Please don't be bashful, Jim," replied the Cardinal. "We hold no secrets regarding the Holy Shroud."

"Have there been any miracles attributed to the Holy Shroud?"

The Cardinal looked intensely at the Archbishop, then replied "Several pilgrims exposed to the Holy Shroud during its presentation to the public have claimed to have been cured of their illness, but none have been officially validated by papal investigation."

"So the Holy Shroud may have performed miracles but you just haven't been able to authenticate any of them," replied Markham. "But I can see the difficulty in verifying the miraculous power of the Holy Shroud when, for preservation and security reasons, it must be kept isolated."

"Yes, and apparently we didn't do such a good job of securing it this time" replied Archbishop Bartolini.

"Oh! Was there another time Your Excellency?" asked Markham.

"In 1938, just before the Second World War, Adolph Hitler showed a keen interest in the Holy Shroud and sought it for its *divine power.* In 1939, King Umberto of Savoy whose family had owned and protected the Holy Shroud since the 15th Century and Pope Pius XII worried about the safety of the Holy Shroud, thus decided to hide it with the Benedictines in the town of Avellino, Italy, about 500 miles from Turin under the pretext that transfer of the shroud was to protect it from bombs, when in fact it was to prevent Hitler from acquiring it," said Archbishop Bartolini.

"Apparently your plan succeeded," said Teri.

"Barely," said Bartolini. "In 1943 after a bombing of Avellino, German soldiers entered the Abbey in search for the shroud, and upon seeing a group of monks praying at the altar, the German officer in charge ordered his men not to disturb the monks, who were actually praying for the safety of the Holy Shroud hidden inside the altar."

"Phew! That was a close one," said Teri with Markham agreeing.

"The Lord was with us that day," said the Cardinal General.

The waiters had purposely signaled the cook to take his time cooking the main course dinners in order to accommodate the apparent intense conversation between the two clergymen and the Americans, but now the meals were ready and had to be served which did not seem to impede the conversation, especially with Markham whose impatience needed immediate answers to nagging questions.

"You mentioned earlier, Your Excellency, that when you found the Holy Shroud missing, two gas hoses were dangling from the container," said Markham. "Does this mean that there was a steady stream of gas enveloping the Holy Shroud inside the container?"

"Yes, that is correct," replied Bartolini. "The gas preserves the cloth from deterioration."

"Then the thieves must have had some type of container designed to preserve the Holy Shroud until it reached its destination where I'm sure they would have similar means of preservation for such a valuable prize," said Markham wondering what temporary mobile container was used to transport the shroud.

"I'm thinking offhand," said Markham, "that the thieves could have covered the Holy Shroud with a non-porous sheet and rolled it up, then inserted the rolled up Shroud into a metal cylinder capable of holding a vacuum."

"You are quite correct in your assumption, 'cause that's exactly what the chief investigator for the Turino Police Department theorized," said Bartolini.

"Well, it does make a lot of sense. They had to move quickly and with the least amount of notice," said the Cardinal.

"Did DACA submit a written report of their polygraph findings to the Turino Police?" asked Markham.

"Yes they did and the report failed to develop any useful information," replied Bartolini.

"Do you have a copy of this report, Your Excellency?" asked Markham.

"Yes I do, but it's in my office at the rectory," replied Bartolini.

"After we have examined the vault area tomorrow morning, I would like to visit the Turino Police Department and speak to the investigator in charge of this case and hopefully they will give me access to their investigative file," said Markham.

"You can be sure, Jim, that the Turino Police will give you whatever assistance you need to resolve this most important matter," said Bartolini. "This case has been given top priority by the Turino Police and the Attorney General's office in Rome."

The dinner was concluded with superb Italian pastries endemic of Turino.

The following morning, Markham and Teri were picked up by the Archbishop's assistant who drove them to the Cathedral of Saint John the Baptist where they were lead down circular marble stairs to the basement below the Royal Chapel. They were immediately confronted with a gray stone wall containing a large black steel door at its center.

The Archbishop inserted his magnetic card into the slot next to the key hole. "This disengages the alarm system," said Bartolini who then inserted his key which unlocked the thick steel door. Turning the door handle, Bartolini pulled the door open and the threesome entered the small room that revealed the massive steel door to the vault.

"The door has been repaired and the safe combination has been changed, pending the installation of a new vault door with a more sophisticated locking mechanism," said Bartolini. "If you don't mind, I will ask you to turn around while I use the combination to open the vault door."

"Not at all, Your Excellency," replied Markham who, along with Teri turned and faced the entrance door.

Soon the massive door was opened and Bartolini invited Markham and Teri to step inside. Markham noticed that the door was at least 18 inches thick and a very special drill had to be used to penetrate that very big steel door. "The thieves have had to have knowledge of the safe's locking mechanism to know exactly the depth of drilling that would avoid damaging the locking machinery," said Markham. "Someone who's been inside this outer room must have passed that information to the thieves."

"The repaired container is due to be returned to the safe sometime tomorrow," said Bartolini. "Hopefully it will not go unused."

"I've seen enough, Your Excellency," said Markham, exiting the vault with Teri following him. "My next stop is to the Turino Police Station."

"My driver will take you there," replied Bartolini.

"That won't be necessary, Your Excellency," said Markham. "We may be there for some time. We'll just take a taxi, if you don't mind."

"As you wish, Jim," said Bartolini. "When you get there, ask for Chief of Detectives Roberto Ciminelli. He's in charge of the investigation into the disappearance of the Holy Shroud."

Upon arrival at the Turino Police Station, Markham had the opportunity to witness Teri's use of the Italian language with the desk sergeant, who requested in Italian to see some form of identification.

Teri turned to Markham. "He wants us to show him some form of identification. I think this is the proper time for you to show your Papal credentials."

Markham pulled out the laminated card bearing the Papal seal which he handed to the desk sergeant along with his passport. "You'd better show him your passport too," said Markham.

The desk sergeant looked at the passports and then read the text of the Papal credentials. "I will alert Chief Ciminelli of your presence," he told Teri in Italian, handing her back the credentials.

It didn't take long for Chief Ciminelli, a pepper gray haired man of medium height and weight, to appear with one of his detectives.

"Welcome to Turino, Mister Markham," said Ciminelli in English, "and you must be Miss Teri Flanigan," extending his hand to her and Markham. "The Archbishop told me you'd be visiting me today, so I was expecting you. This is my assistant, Detective Giuseppe Galvani who has been working with me on this high profile case."

Markham shook Galvani's strong hand and sized him up as a former athlete who had not lost his muscular attributes and could prove to be a formidable adversary, luckily on the side of justice.

Markham and Teri were lead to the second floor of the large police station and into a conference room where piles of documents were lying on the long rectangular highly polished wooden table. The room had two windows on one side only, and they were both covered with thick velour drapes.

Markham held a chair for Teri to sit in, then sat next to her. Chief Ciminelli sat at the end of the table with Detective Galvani on the other side, facing Markham and Teri.

"I understand that you are the author of several books on lie detection, Mister Markham," said Ciminelli inquisitively.

"Yes, that's correct," replied Markham.

"We had a couple of your lie detector examiners from the United States government here three weeks ago," said Ciminelli. "They gave lie detector tests to fourteen people who had access to the Royal Chapel where the Holy Shroud was secured."

"Yes, I heard, and that's my primary purpose for being here, Mister Ciminelli," said Markham.

Ciminelli reached for the pile of documents on the table and pulled a brown folder towards him. "I have here a report from the Defense Academy for Credibility Assessment, which revealed no deception in any of the tests conducted on the fourteen suspects. Frankly, Mister Markham, I don't believe those tests are accurate. That's why we don't use them, but the Cardinal General from Rome is convinced that when the tests are properly conducted, they are most accurate, so to satisfy him and the Archbishop, we permitted the United States Department of Defense to send their two top examiners to Turino to help us solve this case. As I predicted, we are no further than when we started."

"The polygraph technique is only as good as the psychological technique that was used and the training of the examiner that applied the technique," said Markham. "Could I see the report, please?"

"Certainly," replied Ciminelli, passing the folder to Markham who quickly read the report and the list of the names of the examinees.

"Mister Ciminelli, I would like to conduct a Quality Control Review of each and every polygraph examination conducted on the fourteen suspects," said Markham. "In order for me to do that, I will need for you to make an official request from your police department to the director of DACA to send you a copy of the computer disks that contain the polygraph charts, test questions, and video recording of each the fourteen examinations for an internal review."

"Will we be able to read those computer disks?" asked Galvani.

"My laptop computer has polygraph software to read those disks," replied Markham.

"What do you hope to find from your review of those disks?" asked Ciminelli.

"The guilty suspect," replied Markham.

"Then I will make my official request most urgent!" said Ciminelli.

"So, at this point in time, you have no viable suspects other than the fourteen persons who had access to the Royal Chapel area," said Markham for confirmation.

"That's correct, Mister Markham. This is a most baffling case. It was done by professionals who left no trace behind them," said Ciminelli.

"I am most anxious to review those computer disks. I would sincerely appreciate it, if you would notify me immediately when you receive them," said Markham. "We're staying at the Hotel Principi di Piemonte."

"You'll be the first to know and I'm looking forward to seeing you again, Mister Markham, and you Miss Flanigan," said Ciminelli with quiet politeness.

Back at the Hotel Principi di Piemonte, Markham sent an e-mail to Alex Petrov informing him of his meeting with Chief Ciminelli. Markham urged Alex to use his influence in having DACA expedite Ciminelli's request for the fourteen computer disks.

A week transpired without any news from Ciminelli or the arrival of the computer disks. Markham sent another e-mail to Petrov and several hours later, he received a reply stating that the disks had been sent to the Turino Police Department by Federal Express that morning and should be arriving in Turino within 48 hours. The wait had been driving Markham crazy with thoughts of various scenarios that might prevent the release of the disks, so the news of its dispatch was a welcome relief to Markham and Teri, who shared his anxiety.

Having been notified of the arrival of the computer disks, Markham, accompanied by Teri Flanigan, immediately went to the Turino Police Headquarters with his laptop computer. They were greeted by Ciminelli and Galvani who placed a small box containing the fourteen disks on the conference table.

"How long will it take for you to review these disks?" asked Ciminelli.

"A minimum of 30 hours, and perhaps longer, depending on whether I find any problems with any of the examinations," replied Markham. "But I plan on working 12 to 14 hour days until the task has been completed."

"Please permit me to offer you and Miss Flanigan any assistance you need including beverages and snacks," said Ciminelli. "The restrooms are located to your left down the hall as you exit the conference room."

"Thank you," replied Markham, immediately removing the disks from the cardboard box as Ciminelli and Galvani left the conference room.

"How will I be able to help you, Jim?" asked Teri.

"Well, you can take notes as I review each disk," said Markham who wished she had been trained as a polygraphist.

Markham separated the disks into two piles. One pile contained seven disks of examinations conducted by Peter Loefler and the second pile contained examinations conducted by his associate George Petrosino who was fluent in Italian. Apparently the seven suspects tested by Loefler understood English. Those who did not, were tested by Petrosino, hence there had been no need for the use of an interpreter/translator. Markham decided to start with those examinations conducted by Loefler and inserted the first disk into his laptop computer with Teri watching over his shoulder.

"That's strange," said Markham. "There doesn't seem to be any video recording of this exam. We have the charts and the test questions, but no audio-video recording."

Markham clicked the Exam file and checked the PF Notes which indicated that the audio-video system was inoperative, but the polygraph functions were all functioning properly in accordance with the Functionality Check filed in the system.

"Make a note, Teri," said Markham. "On your list of suspect names, next to Giovani Netti, indicate no video recording."

Markham removed the disk and inserted the second disk and found it to be without an audio-video recording. Markham then checked the remaining five disks of tests administered by Loefler and found them all to be lacking an audio-video recording.

"Well, he's consistent. I would have found it most suspicious if the video recording had been inoperable to only one test," said Markham. "Let's check the exams conducted by Petrosino."

All seven examinations conducted by Petrosino had been video recorded. "I think that if we're going to find any irregularities in these tests, they're going to be in the ones with no video recording," said Markham, "so let's look at those seven tests conducted by Loefler."

Then Markham had another thought. "No, give me one of Petrosino's disks which has a video recording and let's make a note of the timing of each test question."

Markham watched as the chart progressed from right to left and called out to Teri the time it took for each of the nine questions to be asked. Markham then inserted the first of seven disks of tests conducted by Loefler and called out the time of each question while he analyzed the physiological recording related to each test question. Everything seemed to be normal and the results of 'No Deception Indicated' were supported by the physiological data of the first four tests reviewed. It was the fifth disk that gave Markham some concern when the Preparatory/Sacrifice Relevant question which had taken 10 seconds for all previous tests, only took 5 seconds to be asked in this examination. Markham then decided to closely calculate the timing of the remaining test questions for comparison with the timing of the six previous tests, including the one conducted by Petrosino which all coincided with each other.

"You know, Teri. The timing of the questions on this suspect does not correspond with the timing of the test questions asked of the other suspects including the recorded test done by Petrosino," said Markham. "I think that this particular examinee was not asked the same test questions which would have been revealed by a video recording that conveniently malfunctioned. Circle Mister Arturo Musso as a prime suspect."

"Isn't he the Chief Custodian at the Royal Chapel?" asked Teri.

"Indeed he is, and he assists the Archbishop in the removal of items from the vault," said Markham. "We need to know what Ciminelli and Galvani know about this guy Musso. While I look at this disk again, why don't you get hold of them."

"Sure thing, Jim," replied Teri who exited the room in search of the two Italian detectives.

Teri reentered the conference room with Ciminelli and Galvani in tow.

"What have you found, Mister Markham?" asked Ciminelli.

"The polygraph charts collected from Mister Arturo Musso contain test questions that are significantly different in duration from the polygraph charts of other examinees whose tests were video recorded," said Markham.

"What does that mean?" asked Ciminelli.

"First of all, all seven tests conducted by Peter Loefler, including Arturo Musso's test, were not video recorded, whereas all of the tests conducted by his associate Petrosino were video recorded."

"What was the reason for not recording those seven tests?" asked Ciminelli.

"The computer notes reflect that the audio-video recorder for Loefler was inoperative," replied Markham. "Without a video recording, we're unable to determine the type of questions asked on Musso's test. Even though Loefler programmed the correct test questions on each test which would have been reflected at the bottom of the screen as he administered the test, he didn't have to recite those questions. He could have orally substituted different questions, which could explain the difference in the duration of those test questions on the charts that we have before us."

"He figured that without an audio-video recording of the test, no one would have known the difference," said Galvani.

"That's correct," replied Markham. "Furthermore, he had to stage the test at that particular time and date because the computerized polygraph system is designed to be tamperproof and records the exact time and date the test is administered, plus the written test questions are permanently entered into the computer file."

"I think we can solve your problem, Mister Markham," said Ciminelli, smiling.

"How's that?" asked Markham.

"You see, Mister Markham. Mister Loefler conducted his polygraph examinations in our main interrogation room which is equipped with a hidden video camera that uses 8-hour VHS video tapes," said Ciminelli. "We took the liberty of taping all of the polygraph examinations in case anyone confessed or provided useful information. Since no information was developed and reported from these polygraph examinations, we saw no need to inform Mister Loefler and his associate of the recordings."

"Thank God for that oversight," exclaimed Markham. "Could I view the video tape that contains Musso's test?"

"Giuseppe, would you retrieve that tape of Musso's test for me please," asked Ciminelli.

About five minutes later, Giuseppe Galvani returned with the video tape which he inserted into the video player-recorder on a table beneath a large television set. He then fast forwarded the tape until he reached the beginning of Musso's polygraph examination, which he overshot by a few seconds necessitating that he rewind it to the beginning of the test. They all gathered in front of the television set while the tape reflected Peter Loefler greeting Arturo Musso.

"I hope this test will go well," said Musso to Loefler.

"All the Saints are with you today," replied Loefler, which brought a smile of satisfaction from Musso, and a thought of suspicion from Markham who was watching the video.

"That's an odd remark from Loefler," said Teri to Markham.

"Yes, that's my thought too," replied Markham. "Like a code that the fix is on."

Half an hour passed before Loefler reviewed the test questions with Musso.

"Alright, Arturo. I'm now going to review the test questions with you," said Loefler. "These are the only questions you will be asked on the test and I have to run these questions by you three times. In other words, I'll run three separate charts containing these same test questions."

"I understand," replied Arturo Musso.

"The first question is: Regarding whether or not you stole a five karat diamond from the London Jewelry Company on the 5th of May 2008: Do you intend to answer truthfully each question about that?"

"Yes," replied Musso.

"That's correct. I want you to answer each question as you will answer them on the actual test," said Loefler.

"Next question: Did you steal that five karat diamond from the London Jewelry Company?"

"No," answered Musso.

"The next question is the same as the previous one, but it's worded differently:

"Regarding the five karat diamond stolen from the London Jewelry Company on May 5th 2008, did you steal that diamond?

"No," replied Musso.

"The next three questions are very important, Arturo," said Loefler. "I want you to answer NO to each of these three questions, because I want to elicit a lie from you for comparison with the previous two questions."

"I understand, Mister Loefler. I was explained the procedure before coming here."

"Good," said Loefler. "The first of these comparison questions will be as follows:

Between the ages of 18 and 40, do you remember ever stealing anything?"

"No," replied Musso.

"During the first 18 years of your life, do you remember ever stealing anything from someone who trusted you?"

"No," replied Musso.

"During the first 40 years of your life, do you remember ever cheating anyone out of anything?"

"No," replied Musso.

"Good," said Loefler. "Now during the test, when we come to these three questions, I want you to think of something you did that makes your answer a lie. You understand what I am saying?"

"Yes, I do, Mister Loefler."

"The next two questions are designed to assure me that you are convinced that I will not ask you a surprise question on the test," said Loefler.

"Are you completely convinced that I will not ask you a surprise question on this test?"

"Yes," answered Musso.

"Is there anything else you're afraid I will ask you a question about that I have not already reviewed with you?"

"No," replied Musso.

"This is the last question: Is your last name Musso?"

"Yes," answered Musso.

"Excellent. Now we can proceed with the actual test," said Loefler.

As the four observers watched Loefler place the various components on Musso's person sitting in a large black chair, Ciminelli voiced his astonishment at what he had observed.

"I can't believe that a man in Mister Loefler's position would deliberately fabricate a false polygraph examination," said Ciminelli. "What could have possibly motivated him to commit such a shameful act?"

"Money, Mister Ciminelli," replied Markham. "Lots of it is my guess, from a very wealthy individual or entity."

"The actual test is about to begin," said Markham. "Let's see if those are the same questions he asked on the test."

After completion of the actual test wherein Musso's physiological data was recorded on three separate charts, Loefler was seen scoring the printed charts for several minutes, then turn towards Musso with his final comment.

"You did fine, Arturo. Your polygraph charts will show that you've been truthful to each of the relevant questions. Please do not discuss with anyone the manner in which this test was conducted."

"I understand perfectly, Mister Loefler. Now I can leave the country," replied Musso.

"Mister Musso. Please do not tell me what your plans are," said Loefler with severity. "You must be discreet, Sir."

"Yes, I'm sorry, thank you," replied Musso apologetically, and exited the room.

"You can turn the video and television off, Giuseppe," said Ciminelli.

"This man has probably already left Italy," said Markham.

"We'll immediately check all modes of transportation out of Italy since the date of that video," said Ciminelli.

"We need to know to what country he fled to," said Markham.

"Yes, of course, Mister Markham," replied Ciminelli.

"This man knows too much," said Markham. "I wouldn't be surprised if a hit had not already been placed on him, and what better place for it to happen but in another country."

"While you're locating Mister Musso, I'm going to have a talk with Archbishop Bartolini," said Markham to Inspector Ciminelli.

"I'll have one of our officers drive you to the cathedral," said Galvani. "Finally, we've got a solid lead in the case."

"Inspector...I wouldn't disclose to anyone at this time about the role Mister Loefler of DACA played in the identification of Mister Musso as a suspect. I want him to feel secure until we're ready to spring a trap for him," said Markham.

"Yes, you are quite right, Mister Markham," replied Ciminelli.

As they rode in the back seat of the Italian police car, Teri expressed her excitement at the newly found evidence.

"You think Musso left Italy, Jim?" asked Teri.

"I think so, but the question is, did he go east or west?" replied Markham.

"Why do you want to talk to the Archbishop, Jim?"

"Because now that we know of Musso's criminal involvement in the larceny, the Archbishop may remember some specific incident with Musso that could reveal how the alarm system and locking mechanism of the vault room door was circumvented," said Markham.

Markham and Teri found the Archbishop in his office in the rectory behind the cathedral.

"Your Excellency," said Markham, extending his right hand. "We need to talk to you most privately."

"Yes, of course," replied Bartolini. "My assistant is in the chapel and I don't expect to be disturbed. You have some news regarding the case?"

"Yes we do, Your Excellency," replied Markham. "We discovered from the polygraph examinations and a video tape surreptitiously recorded by the Italian Police that Mister Musso is apparently criminally involved in the theft of the Holy Shroud."

"You mean my chief custodian is the thief?" said the Archbishop in disbelief. "How could that be?"

"Inspector Ciminelli and his detectives are presently attempting to locate him," said Markham. "In the meantime, Your Excellency, I need to ask you a few questions regarding your activities with Mister Musso during the previous 90 days preceding the theft of the Holy Shroud."

"Yes, of course," replied Bartolini seemingly shaken by the revelation.

"At some point in time, before the larceny, Musso had to somehow gain access to your key and magnetic card," said Markham. "He only needed a few seconds to make a wax imprint of the key and slide your card into a magnetic register."

The Archbishop placed his right hand against his forehead in deep thought. "Now that I think of it, Mister Markham, about three weeks before the theft of the Holy Shroud, I suffered a mild heart attack in the hallway outside the door to the vault and temporarily lost consciousness. I had just exited the vault room with Mister Musso after returning the gold chalice to the safe."

"Had you ever suffered a previous heart attack?" asked Markham.

"No. I have no history of heart disease," replied Bartolini. "My doctor only found a couple of red marks on my back which he could not explain."

"Where was Mister Musso when you suffered your heart attack?" asked Markham.

"He was behind me," replied Bartolini.

"Did you feel sort of an electric shock or jolt coming from your back?" asked Markham.

"As a matter of fact, that's exactly what I felt which penetrated through my chest causing me to feel weak and faint," said Bartolini reflecting back on the episode.

"Sounds like he may have used a stun gun, Your Excellency," said Markham.

"A stun gun?" asked Bartolini.

"Yes, Your Excellency. It's a small handheld gadget that transmits 50 thousand volts of electricity to paralyze an individual causing disorientation, even unconsciousness," said Markham.

"My God!" exclaimed Bartolini. "I've known Arturo Musso for many years and trusted him implicitly. Why would he betray me and the church?"

"Money, Your Excellency," replied Markham. "It can only be money."

"So that's how he got access to my key and security card?" asked Bartolini.

"It's the most likely scenario, Your Excellency," said Markham.

The loud ring of the Archbishop's telephone momentarily interrupted their intense conversation.

"It's for you, Mister Markham," said Bartolini.

Markham picked up the receiver and after no more than a minute of mostly listening, hung up the telephone receiver.

"Inspector Ciminelli found out that Mister Arturo Musso took a plane to Rome and then another plane to Islamabad, Pakistan, three days ago," said Markham.

"That's the capital of Pakistan," said Teri. "Why would he go there?"

"My God, my worst fears are being realized," said Bartolini. "The Holy Shroud may have fallen into the hands of an Islamic group."

"I don't think we should jump to conclusion, Your Excellency. This could just be a ruse to throw us off the trail of the real perpetrators," said Markham, attempting to reassure the Archbishop, although he bore the same fears.

"It is most important, Your Excellency, that you not discuss this newly found evidence with anyone other than the Cardinal General," said Markham. "Especially since Teri and I will be leaving immediately for Islamabad in an effort to find Mister Musso."

"I bless you both, as I fear you will be in grave danger. May God protect you," said the Archbishop making the sign of the cross.

CHAPTER IV

Middle East Entrapment

Upon arrival at the Islamabad International Airport, Markham and Teri Flanigan went through Pakistan Customs without incident. Expecting a thorough search of their person and baggage, they brought only those items that would be inconspicuous, and handguns, even composite ones, were left secured in their hotel room in Turino. Teri made sure she brought four pill-size global positioning system transmitters which she concealed in a bottle of vitamins. *At least,* she thought, *if they should get into trouble, the CIA would be aware of their location at all times which could enable a rescue effort.*

As they rode in a taxi from the Airport to the Pearl Continental Hotel in Islamabad, Teri remarked about the modern architecture of the city.

"I read that Islamabad was rebuilt in the 1960's as the capital of Pakistan," said Teri.

"Impressive," replied Markham. "I'm rather surprised at the ease in which we were able to locate the hotel that our man Arturo Musso has checked into."

"Well, he couldn't very well check in under an assumed name. He had to show his passport for identification," said Teri. "Although, his employer's apparent wealth could have provided him with a false passport, I'm sure."

"That is precisely what concerns me, Teri," said Markham. "It's as if they want us to find him."

"Hopefully we won't be too late," replied Teri.

The Pearl Continental had to be at least a four-star hotel, with a marquis and uniformed doorman to greet their arrival. At the reception desk, Markham asked the clerk if a Mister Arturo

Musso had checked in, and he was informed that Mister Musso was indeed a registered guest but his room number could not be revealed. However he could use the hotel telephone and ask the operator to call his room.

"We're friends of Mister Musso," said Markham. "Would it be possible to have a room with twin beds adjoining Mister Musso's room?"

Markham passed a 50 euro bill towards the clerk. "We'd like to surprise him."

The clerk quickly took the 50 euros while looking around to make sure no one had seen him take the bribe. "You are in luck, Mister....?"

"Markham, James Markham."

"Mister Markham, I do have a room next to Mister Musso. Your room number is 412. I will need to see your passports and if you will both register, I will have a bellboy show you to your room."

"I presume that Mister Musso is in room 410?" said Markham.

"Room 414," replied the clerk nervously.

"Thank you," replied Markham who then turned towards Teri. "Let's visit our friend, shall we."

They first entered their assigned room #412 and noticed that there was a door that accessed room 414. The door was locked by a dead bolt controlled by the occupants of each room. Markham unlocked his side of the door but was unable to enter room 414.

Markham stepped out of the room and knocked on the door to room 414 but received no response. Now certain that the room was unoccupied, Markham returned to his room.

"Apparently Musso is not in his room," said Markham. "You speak Urdu, Teri. Chances are that the housemaids in this hotel only speak Urdu. Why don't you step out into the hall and find a housemaid and pretend that you were locked out of your room, then slip her a few euros to let you back in room 414, that is."

"I told you I would come in handy, didn't I," replied Teri with a smile. She walked down the hall until she saw a young maid leaning into a utility room, fetching cleaning items that she placed onto a four-wheel cart.

"Excuse me. I would greatly appreciate it if you would unlock my room door. I locked myself out," said Teri in Urdu, slipping her a 10 Euro bill which the obliging maid readily accepted.

"What is your room number, Madame?" she asked.

"Room 414," replied Teri with a disarming smile.

Upon entry into room 414, Teri immediately closed the door and started to proceed towards the side door when she spotted the body of a man sprawled on his back at the foot of one of the twin beds. Her heart started racing as she approached the bald headed man, dressed in dark suit trousers and a white shirt. A pistol lay near the body but her gaze was fixed on the bullet hole in the middle of his forehead. The man was obviously dead. Quickly, Teri turned the dead bolt to unlock the side door and upon opening it, summoned Markham.

"We've got a dead body in the adjoining room," she said nervously.

Markham entered the room and with the skill of an experienced investigator, examined the body and the surrounding area for clues.

"This isn't a robbery, 'cause his wallet with several hundred euros is intact," said Markham who then pulled a passport from the dead man's jacket hanging over the back of a chair. Markham looked at the photograph on the passport, then at the man lying on the floor and then at the name on the passport. "That dead man on the floor is none other than Mister Arturo Musso."

"Teri, check all the drawers, his luggage, anything that might give us a clue about his contacts," said Markham, who himself started a methodical search of the room.

Markham searched each and every compartment of Musso's wallet and found a business card that contained a handwritten phone number which he placed in his pocket.

Suddenly, there was a knock on the room door and several male voices could be heard.

"Quick, Teri. Take this business card I found on Musso, and get out of this hotel through our room next door," said Markham. "We've been set up to take the rap for this murder."

"Jim, swallow this transmitter pill," said Teri. "We'll track you wherever they take you."

"OK! Now go, go, Teri," said Markham as they heard the door to room 414 being unlocked.

Three suited men entered the room with the hotel manager behind them. One of the men had a handgun pointed directly at Markham who stood still, offering no resistance, while the other two men examined the dead man.

"This man was recently shot," said one of the suited men. "This is not your room," remarked the other man. "What are you doing in Mister Musso's room?"

"I can explain everything if we go down to your office at police headquarters, which is where I'm sure you will be taking me under the circumstances," said Markham.

"Let me see your passport," asked one of the men.

Markham gave him his passport.

While the man examined Markham's passport, the hotel manager whispered something into one of the other men's ear who relayed the information to the man holding the passport.

"Mister James Markham," said the man. "I'm inspector Abdul Kavakian. Where is the woman that you entered the hotel with and registered as a Miss Teri Flanigan?"

"I don't know, sir," replied Markham.

"Search their room and the entire hotel," said Abdul to his two associates. Put an alert at the airports and seaports, also make sure she doesn't seek asylum at the American Embassy."

The two associates immediately used their cell phones to alert police headquarters.

I am placing you under arrest on suspicion of murder, Mister Markham. I assure you that we will find your female accomplice."

Markham was handcuffed and escorted out of the hotel and into a black unmarked police car, fully observed through a plate glass window by Teri who stood inside a clothing store across the street.

For the first time in her life, Teri felt nauseating fear for a man she was beginning to love. Realizing that her only way to save Markham was through the resources of the CIA, she first had to evade Markham's captors and seek safe haven out of Pakistan. She knew that all airports and seaports would be on alert, hence she decided to find the American Embassy. Looking at the clothing in the store, she saw the beautiful Indian Shararas and Saris that the Pakistani women wear and decided that would make a perfect cover. She selected a Sari with a pure silk lavender and yellow flowered wrap. In addition, she bought a bag for her western clothing and left the store as a veiled Pakistani woman. Navigating through the narrow streets of the city, she finally came within view of the American Embassy, but to her chagrin, she found Pakistani policemen stationed outside the main gate. Her fear returned and she reactively swallowed one of three transmitter pills she had left. She then walked to a secluded place where she used her cell phone to call Alex Petrov's private line.

"Petrov," said the voice at the other end.

"It's Flanigan, Sir," said Teri.

"Flanigan. Where the devil are you?"

"In Islamabad, Pakistan, Sir,"

"What's going on?" asked Alex.

"We found Arturo Musso, the Archbishop of Turino's chief custodian, shot to death in the Pearl Continental Hotel in Islamabad, and Mister Markham was taken into custody while I managed to escape, sir,"

"So you don't have any idea where they've taken him?" asked Alex.

"No sir, but he did swallow a transmitter pill, so you'll be able to track him," said Teri.

"I want you to take one of those tracking pills also, so we can keep track of both of you. Did you try the American Embassy?" asked Alex.

"Yes sir, but the Pakistani police are stationed outside the entrance and I'm sure they've alerted all airports and seaports," said Teri. "I've taken the precaution of dressing in Pakistanian attire so as not to draw attention."

"Good move, Teri," replied Alex. "Listen carefully. I want you to work your way into Quetta which is about 900 kilometers. You should go by bus. Once there, I want you to contact Ari Popolzai and explain to him that it is absolutely necessary for him to arrange for you to proceed to Dushanbe in Tajikistan. From there, he will arrange for you to meet with Valery who will provide you with new papers and a passport out of Tajikistan to Sophia, Bulgaria. Once there, contact me for new instructions."

"I've got all of this information memorized, Sir," said Flanigan. "Any backup available?"

"Only in Tajikistan," replied Petrov. "If you have any problem, contact me directly, and only use your cell phone when absolutely necessary, 'cause they may be able to locate your position from the foreign signal transmitted by your phone."

In the meantime, Markham restrained in handcuffs, was quickly escorted to the inside of the main police station in Islamabad. The chief detective leading the escort didn't bother looking at the two policemen guarding the entrance or the complaint desk sergeant who normally registers all visitors including arrestees. Markham was led through a long corridor and then down a flight of stairs into a room with a small metal table and three chairs. The door was slammed shut leaving him alone still handcuffed. A metal shaded light bulb hung over the small table reminiscent of interrogation rooms of police stations in New York City in the 1930's. Markham knew the drill and suspected that Pakistani methods of interrogation could prove quite persuasive, especially when he noted that his captivity had not been recorded. Instead of sitting down, he stood in the far corner of the room, partially hidden by the light's shadow. The room had no windows and his only means of escape was through that solid locked door. But he reasoned that it was too soon to think of escape without first learning of his status with the police. They could release him due to insufficient evidence to arrest him, which he thought quite plausible. He wondered whether Teri had managed to evade the police and make contact with Petrov, but his thoughts were interrupted by the sound of a key unlocking the door. Three men walked into the room. Two of them wore police uniforms but the man obviously in charge was meticulously dressed in a black striped suit, white shirt and black tie. His waxed mustache reminded Markham of Groucho Marx, the comedian, however he was anything but funny as he took control of the interrogation.

"Sit down, Mister Markham" he said in a commanding voice. "We're going to have a long talk you and I."

Markham stepped out of the corner shadow and deliberately moved towards the empty chair which he lifted into sitting position with his handcuffed hands, causing momentary concern to his captors that he was going to use the chair as a weapon, but just as quickly dismissed the idea when Markham sat down facing the small metal table. Markham knew that he could probably take all three out of action if he acted swiftly, but considered it imprudent.

The mustached detective motioned with his left hand to one of the uniformed policeman to remove the handcuffs from Markham. Markham quickly rubbed his wrists, then sat back in his chair waiting for the chief detective's opening statement. There's always an opening statement in an interrogation which is designed to make any resistance futile. Being a master interrogator, Markham was curious about the approach this Pakistani detective would use. Would he start off with an indirect approach in an attempt to establish rapport and trust, or go for the jugular with the introduction of alleged evidence and the threat of punishment if he didn't cooperate?

"Welcome to Pakistan, Mister Markham, or shall I call you Doctor Markham?" said the detective.

"Mister will do just fine," replied Markham.

Looking at the open manila folder laying in front of him, the detective raised his eyes towards Markham and introduced himself.

"I'm Inspector Mohamed Tamani. I'm the chief of the Homicide Bureau and I have taken a direct interest in this case. I noticed from an inspection of your papers that you have a Papal Carte Blanche, no doubt to investigate the disappearance of the Holy Shroud of Turin," he said, then added "Oh, yes, Mister Markham, such news travels fast."

Then you must know that his Eminence the Pope would never sanction murder and as his agent, I had nothing to do with the death of Arturo Musso," said Markham calmly.

"Please do not insult my intelligence, Mister Markham. Many murders have been committed by Christian zealots, and the Roman Crusaders are but one example of mass murder in the name of Christianity."

"I hope that you have more than medieval history to hold me here," replied Markham.

"Indeed, I do, Mister Markham," said Tamani confidently. "We found you at the scene of the crime shortly after Mister Musso was shot with the murder weapon there within your grasp. You also had no reason to be in his room. That, Mister Markham is sufficient evidence in our courts to convict you."

"I realize that my presence at the scene doesn't look good, but my intentions were simply to find Mister Musso, and gain information regarding his access to the missing Holy Shroud. My investigation indicates that he was criminally involved in the theft of the Shroud and his flight to Pakistan raised suspicions that he was meeting an accomplice here in Islamadad. That's the sole reason for my presence at the hotel where he was found, and unfortunately, unable to provide me with any information that would lead me to the Holy Shroud," said Markham. "I had no motive to kill him."

"I think you got the information you wanted from Mister Musso, and then you silenced him to prevent him from warning his accomplices of your investigative progress," said Tamani in a confident tone of voice. "By the way, Mister Markham, where's your female companion, Miss Teri Flanigan?"

Markham remained silent. *The less they knew about her,* he thought, *the better her chances of eluding them.*

"In spite of the evidence against you, Mister Markham, you want us to believe in your innocence, yet you refuse to tell us anything about your female companion. We do need to talk to her to establish her role in this affair and verify your story," said Tamani.

"First of all, Mister Tamani, I don't know where she is, and furthermore she cannot provide you with any information that you don't already know. She is totally innocent, as I am," replied Markham.

"You can at least tell me the reason for her to accompany you on your mission to find Mister Musso," said Tamani, moving closer to Markham.

Markham knew that if he revealed her role and mission, the Pakistani police would significantly increase the scope of their search for Flanigan.

"She was just my administrative assistant, that's all," replied Markham.

"Was she your lover, Mister Markham?" asked Tamani with a sardonic smile.

Markham looked into Tamani's eyes without a reply, hoping that Tamani would accept his silence as proof of guilty embarrassment.

At that moment, a knock on the door caused one of the two uniformed policemen to answer it, and after an exchange of a few words in Pakistani with a plainclothes detective, the policeman walked over to Tamani and whispered a few words into his ear.

"Excuse me, Mister Markham," said Tamani, as he stood up and walked over to the slightly open door.

"You have a message for me," said Tamani to the uniformed officer at the door whom he recognized as the Chief Security Officer.

"Yes, Sir," the officer replied. "I just received a call from the Chief Prosecutor's Office, that Mister James Markham is to be immediately transported to Quicksand Castle under an assumed name, and that no record of his apprehension and detention is to be made."

"Who specifically gave this order?" asked Tamani.

"This order came directly from Chief Prosecutor Abdulah Khan, Sir."

"He must have made powerful enemies to be sent to that ungodly place," said Tamani. "Are there any orders regarding the disposition of his female companion when we find her?"

"No sir," replied the Security Officer.

"Very well, then, he's all yours," said Tamani, who then issued orders for the two policemen to handcuff Markham, this time behind his back.

"Mister Markam," said Tamani looking directly into his eyes. "Even the Holy Shroud can't help you where you are going."

"And where might that be, Mister Tamani?" asked Markham.

"Quicksand Castle, Mister Markham, Pakistan's Devil's Island," replied Tamani with a venomous grin that conveyed the promise of torture and pain.

Two more uniformed policemen entered the room, one manning an assault rifle and the other carrying chains and shackles. They first secured iron rings around Markham's ankles while the armed policemen stood ready to shoot him if he offered any resistance. Then a chain was attached to his waist. His handcuffs were removed and replaced with iron shackles that were fastened to the waist chain facing his groin. Another chain was then attached to the shackled ankles and connected to the waist chain. Through it all, Markham felt as though he was reliving the horrific experience of French Army Captain Alfred Dreyfus, similarly shackled and innocently condemned to Devil's Island in 1894. If he had any chance of escape, it was before they shackled him under the watchful eye of three armed policemen.

The short chain fastened to the shackles around his ankles forced Markham to take quick short steps to keep up with the two policemen, who hustled him out of the interrogation room and down the hall to a paved yard where a black van awaited him.

The two back doors opened at the center and a metal staircase was folded down, permitting Markham to climb up the stairs, with some difficulty from the dragging chains, inviting one of the policemen to strike him at the back of the legs with a long nightstick. Before Markham could turn to see who was hitting him, he was pulled inside the van by another policeman who was to accompany him to the prison.

There were two metal benches fastened to each side of the van. Markham sat at one side near the middle, and his ankle chain was then fastened to a metal ring imbedded into the metal floor of the van. The temperature was nearly ninety degrees Fahrenheit, but luckily, he noticed long and narrow open windows secured with wire mesh on both sides of the van. They were directly above the heads of any seated prisoners providing them with fresh air. Satisfied that Markham was securely imprisoned inside the van, the policeman exited the van, locked the back doors, and then joined the driver of the van for the long trip south.

CHAPTER V

Escape from Quicksand Castle

As Director of Clandestine Operations, Alex Petrov was no stranger to the Central Intelligence Agency's vast Communications Center in Langley, Virginia. He had developed a personal relationship with the Chief of the Com Center whom he referred to simply as Harry.

"Harry, you've met my assistant John Tunney," said Petrov.

"Yes, I remember you," replied Harry shaking John's hand, then turning to Petrov. "Your phone call seemed urgent. Is one of your agents in trouble?"

"That's putting it mildly, Harry," replied Petrov. "I've got two agents in Pakistan. One is on the run and the other has been captured. Both have ingested GPS transmitter capsules, thus can be tracked. Are your satellites in position to pick up their transmission?"

"You're in luck, my friend. Pakistan has been a hot bed of insurgent activity with a significant Al Qaeda terrorist presence. So we've been keeping a close eye from the sky on that area of the world," said Harry. "Let's take a look at our electronic map."

On a massive, elongated wall appeared an electronic map of the entire world. It was controlled by several technicians operating an array of computers keeping track of all deployed vessels and aircraft within and without the United States. It could also use satellite cameras to view and zoom into a specific area of interest that would then be projected onto the electronic map. As often as Petrov had visited the Com Center, he always marveled at the technological advances made in the gathering of intelligence information, and now it could be instrumental in saving the life of his two agents.

"You have the frequency codes for the two transmitters, Alex?" asked Harry.

"Sure do," replied Petrov, handing Harry a slip of paper which was given to one of the technicians.

"It's going to take a few minutes to track and find the location of those two transmitters," said Harry. "It'll show up on the screen as two flashing red dots in that part of Pakistan where your agents are located."

"In terms of accuracy of location, how accurate is this global positioning system, Harry?"

"Our system can accurately pinpoint a subject within three meters or less," replied Harry, "and there's your flashing red dots."

"Zoom into the one on the right moving south," said Harry to the nearby computer technician. "Give us maximum exposure," he added.

A square section of the screen showed a black van traveling south on a paved road.

"Your agent is inside that van," said Harry.

"Looks like a vehicle that's used by the police to transport prisoners," said Petrov.

"Let's look at the other one."

"A bus," exclaimed Petrov. "That has to be Flanigan."

"That bus is heading towards the western border of Pakistan," said Harry.

"That's a good sign. Her first contact is in Quetta," said Petrov. "Let me know, Harry, when she gets there, or if she is detoured for any reason." Then looking at the text message on his cell phone, he added "I've got to get back to my office. Also let me know if and when the signal on my other agent stops moving."

"I'll keep you posted," replied Harry waving goodbye to Petrov who briskly walked away with John Tunney in tow.

The prison van had been traveling due south more than 800 kilometers making one stop, primarily to refuel so the driver and guard could use toilet facilities and get some refreshments. No thought was given to Markham who had to use the bucket in front of him to relieve his bladder. The sweat was pouring off of him and he wondered how long before they reached their destination as he was nearly dying from thirst. Finally, the van turned into a solitary road from which you could see a huge sandstone castle seemingly perched on a large sand dune giving it the illusion of a fairy tale desert kingdom. The van pulled up in front of a large steel reinforced wooden gate which opened from a signal given by one of the turret guards. As the van entered the courtyard, the prison warden Ali Multan, a lean dark haired mustached man, turned to the prison's chief medical doctor Aban Mombasa, a portly, clean-shaven, partly balding man.

"I believe that your patient, Mister Markham has just arrived," said the warden, as he looks out of his second story office window into the courtyard below.

"I hope they fed him some water during that long trip. I don't need a dehydrated patient," replied the doctor.

"They apparently were in hurry to get him out of Islamadad," said the warden. "The prosecutor was especially concerned about keeping his identity secret. Therefore your patient will be listed simply as an 'Infidel'."

"Imaginative but hardly a good identity concealment, wouldn't you say?"

"It doesn't identify the patient to the outside world. That's all that matters," replied the warden.

The warden and the doctor both watched as Markham's shackled feet slowly descended the metal steps of the vehicle, and raising his sweaty eyebrows, he perused his surroundings. The sergeant of the guard immediately issued orders to the two guards that had met the prison van.

"Take the prisoner to an unoccupied cell in the medical building," said the Sergeant.

"But sir, all cells in the medical building are currently occupied," replied one of the guards.

"I have orders that this prisoner is to be incarcerated in the medical building. He is not to be incarcerated with the prison population. Aren't there any vacant cells in either Block 1 or Block 2?" asked the Sergeant.

"No sir. Two of the prisoners that were scheduled to be terminated were held on orders of Doctor Mombasa."

"Very well, then, lock him up temporarily with the Frenchman who I believe is in Block 2. He's due for terminal surgery and soon his tongue will be silent," said the Sergeant.

Markham's chained ankles restricted his gait which gave him an opportunity to survey the prison's layout as he was led by the two guards to the entrance of the south end building. He noticed that the two-story buildings within the interior of the prison were no more than 8 to 10 feet from stone walls which appeared to be of equal height, and the gutters' downspouts looked quite sturdy. He also noticed that the building on the west side had what appeared to be a large air conditioning unit next to a shed like structure. *Probably the offices of the prison warden and his staff, no doubt,* thought Markham. Escape never left Markham's thoughts.

One of the guards used a primitive key to unlock the iron bar door to this seemingly ancient prison and Markham was led up the metal stairs to the second story. There they were met by another guard who, upon recognizing the visiting guards through the small window of the metal door, unlocked it and allowed them inside.

"Which cell is the Frenchman in?" asked one of the escorting guards.

"He's in cell number 9," replied the guard custodian. "Is that where he's supposed to be incarcerated?"

"Yes, with the Frenchman, and after the Frenchman is gone, he's to be secluded in that cell with no other inmates," replied the lead guard.

"So what's this prisoner's name?" asked the custodian.

"He's only to be known as the Infidel," replied the lead guard, looking at Markham with contempt. Markham quickly realized that his incognito imprisonment was that of a condemned man. All of his senses were now in full force like a caged animal seeking any means of escape, but so far no opportunity had materialized.

Markham stood quietly in front of the metal door to cell number 9 as the custodian guard slid the small metal viewing door open to speak to the Frenchman.

"Step back against the far wall where I can see you," shouted the custodian.

Markham had noticed that there was another small metal door at the bottom of the cell door which he figured was used to insert a food tray or bowl. The custodian opened the cell door and Markham was led inside where one of the escorting guards unlocked the padlock that had secured the chain around his ankles. He then removed the remaining iron shackles and gave an order to Markham to remove his shoes which he reluctantly obeyed. The three guards then quickly exited the cell and closed its metal door with a clang that resonated through Markham with the chill of lost hope. Markham stood still with his eyes reconnoitering his new quarters, and marveled at the high 15 foot ceiling and spacious cell that contained a curtained shower, toilet and sink in the immediate right hand corner, two single metal bunks with sheets, blankets and covered pillow cases against the north and south walls, plus a small table in the middle of the room with two folding chairs.

"Bienvenue au Chateau du Sable Mouvent," said the barefooted Frenchman standing against the far wall below an open window with iron bars whose ledge was a good six feet from the floor. "My name is Jean Depardieux," he said in French.

Markham looked at this graying bearded man whose sad eyes and gaunt face betrayed great mental anguish. "Je suis Jim Markham," he replied in French in a reassuringly low voice as he slowly walked towards Depardieux still standing guardedly against the wall. Markham extended his right hand and after a few seconds, Depardieux cautiously offered his hand in a limp handshake.

"I'm an American, Jean, and no doubt you're a Frenchman," said Markham in French.

"Ah Bon! An American who speaks French. Merveilleux," replied Jean in French, "because my English is very poor. I'm originally from Paris, but I've spent several years conducting archeological excavations in Egypt, Libya, and finally Pakistan which landed me in this prison."

"So you're an archeologist," said Markham, continuing the conversation in French. "What did you do to land in this prison… steal an ancient relic?"

"That's very perceptive of you Monsieur Markham," replied Depardieux.

"Just call me Jim, if you don't mind," said Markham.

"I am not a thief, Monsieur Jim," replied Depardieux. "I was framed by the Pakistani archeologist that was assigned to work with me as part of the agreement between me and the Pakistani government."

"Does the French government know of your arrest and confinement?" asked Markham.

"Yes, but they can do nothing because the crime occurred in Pakistan, and I was convicted in a Pakistani court. They sentenced me to 25 years at hard labor," replied a solemn Depardieux.

"Do you have any family members that can help you?" asked Markham.

"My wife Marianne arranged to have my best friend, who was also our trusted attorney, travel to Islamadad ostensibly to assist in my defense but he conveniently arrived after the trial had ended, and only to deliver divorce papers. He was not conversational and his visit was brief. I never suspected he was having an affair with my wife until his visit at the court's holding center," said Jean lowering his head. "I think his betrayal hurt me more than my wife's infidelity." Regaining his composure, Jean continued, "This was the perfect opportunity for my wife to get rid of me and seize all of my assets which, unfortunately, were jointly owned. The trial was held just a few days after my arrest and my conviction was swift. This was a well conceived and executed conspiracy to deprive me of one of the greatest archeological findings ever discovered in Pakistan, and my Pakistani associate's cousin was the chief judge at my trial," said Depardieux. "I know I'll never leave this Chateau du Sable Mouvent."

"Twice you referred to this prison as Chateau du Sable Mouvent, which I translate that to mean Quicksand Castle, why?" asked Markham.

"Your command of the French language is remarkably good," replied Jean whose face had gained some color and animation. "But to answer your question, this prison is surrounded on three sides by quicksand, and the only safe way to enter or exit this prison is by the narrow coble stone road which the guards refer to amusingly as the Chemin de L'Enfer (Road to Hell), because the only way out is by the smoke of your ashes from the fires of cremation."

"Cremation?" murmured Markham.

"We prisoners serve as unwilling organ donors. Why do you think we are given such luxurious accommodations, compared to the rest of the prison population, but to keep us healthy. They have already taken one of my kidneys" said Depardieux, lifting his shirt to show the surgical scar on the right side of his abdomen. "The next operation will be my last. Then they cremate my remains to destroy any evidence."

"My God, Jean, how long have you been here in this prison?" asked Markham incredulously.

"Ten months. I stopped counting the days," replied Jean. "I'm surprised they have kept me around this long, because I've seen and briefly spoken to several prisoners in the exercise yard who've undergone surgery for the removal of organs, and I know of four that have since disappeared."

"This sounds like institutionalized cannibalism for profit... unbelievable," said Markham. "But aren't they afraid that you would tell this to your visitors?"

"What visitors," replied Jean. "When I got convicted, my wife divorced me, and the few people I thought were friends deserted me. This was surely noticed by the prison officials. But I think the time I have left is short, so I am telling you this in the hope that somehow you will be able to tell the world about this devilish organ factory. What have you done to warrant being sent here to this hell hole?"

"They suspect me of having killed someone they found dead in a hotel room in Islamadad," replied Markham.

"You mean they sent you here without having first been tried and convicted?" said a surprised Jean.

"That's correct, and I don't think they intend to try me. In fact, they have listed me in their prison records simply as the 'Infidel'."

"Sounds like you're a political prisoner," replied Jean. "For some unknown reason, I feel strongly that you will attempt to escape from this penitentiary, even though I know that no one has ever escaped."

"Has no one ever tried to escape from this prison?" asked Markham.

"No, not to my knowledge," replied Jean. "Even if you managed to remove those bars in the window and escape, you would fall into quicksand and disappear forever. As I said, there is no way out except by the smoke of your ashes."

"How do you know so much about this area of the desert, Jean?" asked Markham.

"In my archeological search and diggings, I studied the entire southern area of Pakistan which included this desert area," replied Jean now sitting on the edge of his bunk.

"Exactly where are we located?" asked Markham, anxious to get his bearings.

"We're about 50 kilometers southwest of Nawabshah, and about 150 kilometers from the Indus River which travels north and south," said Jean. "But my dear fellow, you are not thinking of escaping, that's shear madness."

"It doesn't hurt to know your whereabouts and options," replied Markham. "Where does the Indus River end going south?"

"Into the Arabian Sea just south of Suyawal," replied Jean. "If you should manage, against all odds, to escape from this prison, they would never expect you to attempt your escape through the desert; therefore they would concentrate their search north into the villages and towns that would eventually lead you to the Pakistan border."

"But you said that it was impossible to traverse this desert because of the quicksand," said Markham inquisitively.

"Impossible for most people, but with your apparent strength and vigor and my knowledge of the desert and luck, you could possibly make it to the Indus River," said Jean.

"You did not include yourself…why?" replied Markham.

"Because I'm too feeble for this long trek of more than 150 kilometers in a treacherous desert full of reptiles, freezing nights and scorching days without water or food. And when they fail to find you in their search north, they may send helicopters over the desert area and the Indus River," said Jean.

"You said that your knowledge of the desert would help me," said Markham. "I'm not worried about the reptiles; I'm concerned mainly with the quicksand. How do I identify those areas to avoid being swallowed by the desert?"

"First of all, three fourths of the perimeter of the prison is surrounded by pits of quicksand but they don't extend closer than about 50 yards to the walls of the prison. However once in quicksand territory, they occupy an area of about 500 yards in every direction including west of the prison wall which is the direction of your escape. What you will have to look for are the peaks of sand dunes that are at least 10 feet wide for you to walk on. You should have a stick of at least 5 or 6 feet to test the stability of your path and the presence of reptiles and scorpions," said Jean who envisioned himself traveling through that veritable minefield.

"If I succeed in escaping this infernal prison, it would be in the nighttime; not much light for navigating that desert," replied Markham.

"You will have to select a night with a full moon giving you ample light for traveling the desert. What you will need most is a sufficient amount of water. You must travel at night and rest during the day by excavating a hole in the sand, deep enough to cover most of your body. The sand is cooler two feet down," said Jean, now excited at the prospect of an escape by Markham who would then tell the world about his ordeal and that of others who suffered the same fate.

"Covering my body with sand during the day will also give me cover from searching helicopters," added Markham.

"Just be careful when digging that you don't disturb a reptile or a nest of scorpions," said Jean. "On a positive note, the Indus River is a fresh water river inhabited by a species of nearly blind dolphins. It also has snakehead fish that can grow to 6 feet in length, but they are not poisonous or a threat to humans."

"If I can just make it to the Indus River, I think I can manage my way to the Arabian Sea," said Markham whose mind was working overtime seeking ways to elude his captors.

"That's a long journey on the Indus River to the Arabian Sea. When the search north fails to find you, they will inevitably turn their search south and west using helicopters. You will be a large floating duck that will surely be noticed from the air," said Jean pessimistically.

"The only solution is to devise a snorkel and swim beneath the surface," replied Markham, already thinking of ways to use a short hose tied to a piece of wood, and possibly place rocks in his pockets to weigh him down.

"Are there any pebbles or rocks along the shore of the Indus River?" asked Markham.

"As a matter of fact there are small stones along the shore. Luckily, you will have fresh water, but you will need food to sustain your strength," said Jean.

"If I can find a knife, I will improvise with a sharp stick to harpoon fish," replied Markham.

"Then there may be another problem. You will only be able to surface at night when it's dark, which will make it almost impossible for you to spear fish," said Jean.

Markham looked at his bunk. "I could take my pillow cover and use it as a net to fish for minnows. That would work in the dark," said Markham.

"That's an excellent idea, Mister Jim, and they would be nourishing and easy to eat."

"You know, Jean, even if I get out of here, I don't know that anyone will believe me when I tell them about this place."

"They'll believe you," said Jean, reaching the far side of his mattress. He inserted his right hand inside a slit along the seam of the mattress and pulled out a gold locket with chain and a ring. "I hid this when they first brought me into this cell." Jean opened the locket and showed it to Markham. "That's the picture of my wife when we were first married, and the inscription inside bearing the name of my wife and me and the date of our marriage. When you are ready to leave this place, please take this with you as proof that you met me in this prison."

"That will only prove that I met you," said Markham.

"Here's my wedding ring inscribed with my name," replied Jean. "That will be sufficient proof that you met me in this prison and I gave those items to you as proof." said Jean who then replaced both items inside his mattress.

"But I don't know anyone in the news media in Paris or in France for that matter," replied Markham.

"One of my childhood friends has been the editor of Le Parisien newspaper for many years, his name is Henri Charlemagne," replied Jean. "I believe he'll be the editor of that paper until he dies. You give him these two items plus a note that I will now write, and this will introduce you to him."

"You mean they gave you a pen and paper to write with?" asked Markham in amazement.

"Yes, they did that to appease me, knowing that they would never mail my letters to anyone, and after a while when I received no response, I just stopped writing but kept the pen and now I have only a couple of sheets of paper from the pad left," said Jean. "I will first introduce you by name to Henri, then briefly describe the horror of this prison and your plan to escape. Henri will recognize my writing and especially my postscript about our excursion with Giselle which will no doubt authenticate my letter," said Jean, smiling at the memory of her.

"I presume that this ménage-a-trois would only be known to the three of you?" said Markham with amusement.

"Yes, and it was a long time ago, before I met my wife," replied Jean.

"I promise you, Jean, that if I get out of this hell hole, I'll do my best to get your letter and jewelry to your friend Henri. Knowing Parisian society, your ex-wife and her collaborating attorney will then have a hard time defending their right of passage in the social register," said Markham with a smile that brought hope to poor Jean who immediately started writing the letter.

Markham slowly paced the floor in deep thought. "All of these preparations are very good," said Markham absentmindedly, "but without a viable plan of escape from this cell and prison, it's all for naught."

At that moment, they heard the opening sound of the metal door at the end of the hallway followed by the footsteps of guards coming towards them. Jean stopped his letter writing and inserted the partially written letter and pen inside the slit in his mattress. The metal sliding window opened, and the guard gave the order for Jean and Markham to stand against the far wall, which they did. The cell door opened and while one guard, a big heavyset man held his handgun at the ready, the other guard, a lean wiry man walked into the cell and threw garments on the lower bunk.

"You will remove your clothes, Infidel, and put on this prison attire," said the lean guard, who stood waiting for Markham to obey his order.

Markham removed his jacket, socks, shirt and pants, retaining his shorts and t-shirt which brought no objections from the guard. Markham then put on the light gray slacks which contained a covered rope around the waist which he fastened with the same type of bow used to tie shoe laces. He then put on the gray shirt which fitted him rather tightly around the shoulders, but he didn't mind that, since he wasn't planning on staying there very long. The guard picked up Markham's clothes then left and secured the cell without further conversation.

"Mon Dieu (My God)," said Jean, "You're now officially known as the prison's Infidel. The word will spread to all of the inmates, most of whom are Muslims. A good thing you're locked up."

"I'm not worried about that. I'm just wondering how much time I've got to get out of here before they decide what organ they want to remove from me," said Markham.

"Watch out for the slim guard, the one that gave you your prison clothes," said Jean. "He's known in the prison yard as the butcher, because he likes to use his curved dagger on inmates that displease him. We're safe as long as we're classified as organ donors."

"I did notice the Arabian-like knife on his belt," replied Markham, "The smaller the man, the bigger the knife." Markham had also noticed that the other guard who was armed with a pistol was about his size and looked more Turkish than Pakistani.

An hour passed, and then the same two guards returned and removed Markham from his cell, escorting him down the long corridor, through the locked metal screen door and to the first of several doors on the left. One of the guards stepped inside the room with Markham, and a male nurse wearing a white coat immediately ordered Markham to remove all of his clothes. When Markham hesitated, he was told that this was only a routine medical examination. The examination included x-rays of his chest, a blood test and even a check of his teeth. The medical equipment left no doubt that this was a full-fledge medical facility. Two doctors surveyed his medical examination and declared him in the best of health. Markham noticed that he was moved from one room to two other rooms through adjoining doors within each room, which formed a large medical complex.

He also noticed the presence of several medical tools that could be of use during his escape, such as knives and hoses. Upon his return to his cell, he told Jean of his observations.

The following morning, the same two guards appeared at their cell and one of the guards placed handcuffs on Markham's wrist and escorted him out of his cell. Markham looked at Jean who simply uttered "Bonne chance, mon ami (Good luck my friend)."

As the two guards escorted Markham down the long corridor, he made note of his surroundings again. One of the guards used an old fashion key to open the metal and wire door leading to another hallway that contained closed doors to four rooms adjacent to each other. He remembered the day before, he had entered the first room for his medical examination. He could hear voices from two of those rooms speaking in what he perceived to be Arabic. Finally, the slim guard with the key ring knocked on the door to the last room in that corridor and after a few seconds the door opened slightly. The guard announced in Arabic that he had the Infidel with him. The door opened wide and a field grade officer in uniform invited them inside the room. Markham immediately noticed a man dressed in a suit sitting in a wheel chair with his back to him, looking out of the window. The officer ordered Markham to sit in the chair facing a large wooden desk then left the room. The armed guard then stepped into the corner of the room next to the entrance door while the second guard stood outside the room in the corridor in case of emergency.

Markham, seated with his handcuffed hands on his lap, waited patiently for the man in the wheel chair to turn around and address him. Then without turning, the man said "You may not remember me, Doctor Markham, but I have good reason never to forget you."

Markham strained his eyesight in an attempt to identify the mystery man, who then slowly turned his wheelchair and began wheeling himself towards Markham. As he got closer, Markham suddenly recognized his former enemy from Tangier, Morocco, even though he had gained weight.

"Mr. Mohamed Bundalai," exclaimed Markham. "I didn't know the Morocco Minister of Justice's jurisdiction extended this far."

Now facing Markham from the other side of the table, only a few feet away from each other, Bundalai openly relished his commanding position.

"The reason for my presence here, Doctor Markham, is a medical one which should be of great interest to you."

"Your health is of no concern to me, but let me guess," said Markham. "You're here to get a knee replacement and surgical repair of related tendons and ligaments as a result of the injuries you suffered during our duel in Tangier a couple of years ago."

"Guess again, Doctor Markham," replied Bundalai, rubbing his right knee as a reminder of his injury during that duel. "This surgical operation will be fatal...to you, I'm pleased to say."

Markham remained silent while his mind wrestled with the various possibilities, none of them encouraging.

"I could wait until the day of the operation to tell you the nature of your donation, but that would deprive me the pleasure of knowing from this day forward until the very second when you lose consciousness on the operating table, you will suffer the agony of realizing your heart will be cut out of your chest and transplanted into my body," said Bundalai with an evil grin, which made Markham regret he had not killed him in the duel. "Sleep well, Doctor Markham...until we meet again, soon."

The two guards then escorted Markham back to his cell where he was immediately questioned by Jean.

"What happened?" asked Jean, "you look troubled...what did they want?"

"My heart, that's all," replied Markham, deeply concerned about his fate and the need to expedite his escape.

"Your heart? Mon Dieu, are they serious?" asked Jean.

"You should know, Jean. They took one of your kidneys. Besides...the man who wants my heart is an old enemy who I crippled in a sword duel in Tangier, Morocco a couple of years ago. He wants revenge, needs a new heart, and I'm the unfortunate donor who happens to be available."

"Do you have any idea how much time you have before they perform the surgery?" asked Jean.

"None, but he wants me to suffer the suspense of waiting for the dreaded event, therefore I expect that he will wait a few days. I must get out of here somehow within the next two days," said Markham, now looking around his cell for any clues helpful to his escape.

"One of the two guards, the slim one, carries a ring of keys that must open almost every door on this floor of the prison," said Jean.

"Yes, I noticed that when they escorted me from this cell a moment ago," said Markham pensively. "Somehow I must get possession of those keys. I'll have to lure him into this cell along with the other guard that is armed. I've got to get both of them inside this cell."

"My time is limited, Mister Jim, so I'm willing to do whatever it takes to help you get out of here."

"Thanks, Jean. I appreciate that," said a grateful Markham. "I noticed a three inch ledge just above the doorway. Now if I can get up there and stand with my heels on that ledge flat against the wall, I could hold that position with my hands pressed to the ceiling. You could cause a commotion that would invite both guards to enter our cell, then I could pounce on the armed guard with both feet breaking his collar bone and possibly his neck. I could then quickly dispose of the other guard and seize his keys and you could come with me."

"Thank you Monsieur Jim, but going with you is out of the question. I'm too sickly. The question is…how are you going to get up there on that ledge, and what kind of a commotion would cause both guards to enter our cell?"

"Good questions, Jean. If you could stand with your back against the wall and two hands clasped together in front of you, I could put one foot into your closed hands, and…no that wouldn't work. There's no way that in your weakened condition you could lift me at 220 pounds."

"Yes, you're right Monsieur Markham, I couldn't lift a person half your weight."

Markham's attention was now drawn to his metal bunk. "That bunk is six feet long," said Markham. "We could place the full length of that bunk vertically against the door and I could climb on top of it which would place me within a few inches from the ledge. Once I'm in place above the doorway, you could put the bunk back. Then you could move the table against the far wall under the window and stand on it so that your head and hands would block the view of the two bars on the window. You could start shouting through the window as if I had made my escape by removing the two bars from the window. That would surely get both of those guards to quickly enter the cell to inspect the window and possible escape. But as soon as the second armed guard enters the cell, I will drop on him like an elephant on a mouse."

"That sounds like a good plan," replied Jean, "but are you sure you can handle those two guards?"

"That won't be a problem, I assure you, Jean," replied Markham. "Hopefully, there will be a full moon tonight, 'cause that's when I will be leaving this place of inequity."

"Tonight?" said Jean with surprise written all over his face.

"Yes, it must be tonight, Jean."

"I suppose you have no time to waste under the circumstances, but the one problem I foresee, Monsieur Markham, is getting the attention of both guards to come to our cell. It's quite a distance from the window of our cell to the gate at the end of the corridor. They might not hear me."

"We'll just have to do it when they deliver our dinner at 1900 hours," said Markham. "Sunset is at about 2030 hours, which will give us a little over an hour to secure the two guards and for me to find the necessary material from those locked rooms that will aid in my escape. The timing is perfect. I will have just enough light as the sun sets to navigate my way from this prison into the desert."

"How are we going to secure the guards?" asked Jean with some concern.

"We'll tie them up and place one in the shower and the other one in my bunk covered with a blanket."

"Frankly, Monsieur Jim, I would like to kill them. They're nothing but murderers. Why bother taking the time to tie them up?"

"I can understand your position, Jean, but we are not murderers. Let providence decide their fate," said a philosophical Markham.

"But after you have escaped and the guards are freed, they will surely torture me to death for my part in your escape," said Jean.

"Whether the guards are dead or alive after my escape will not prevent the prison warden's retribution," replied Markham. "I still say that you should come with me in spite of your physical condition. If you don't make it, isn't it better for you to die in the desert then in this tortuous prison cell?"

"My feeble condition would slow you down and hamper your escape which I am counting on for you to publish to the world my fate and that of the other condemned men in this hellish prison," replied Jean. "I intend to end my life after you leave, Monsieur Markham. There is nothing left for me to live for and I wish to choose the time and method of my death."

"I wish you would reconsider," said Markham.

"I have made my decision and it's final," replied Jean. "Now let's prepare for your escape."

Markham knew that further argument with Jean about his final decision was futile, therefore began preparations for his escape. He realized that he would have to use the guards' own clothing and equipment to tie their hands and feet which would necessitate his having to render them unconscious if not already in that state after the brawl. Markham was no stranger to brawls even though he detested unnecessary violence. In this case, he realized only too well that much depended on his escape, including his own life.

Jean did not have a watch and Markham's wrist watch had been taken from him along with his wallet and other personal effects, hence his ability to tell time was reduced, with help from Jean, to their observation of the sun and its position in relation to the horizon from the cell window.

"I estimate that our dinner will be delivered in about half hour," said Jean.

"OK, let's prop my bed frame against the door," replied Markham, who then removed the mattress and bedding from the metal frame and placed the frame vertically against the cell door. Barefooted, Markham used his toes and fingers to climb up the tight bed springs within the bed frame, then carefully grabbed the top cement edge above the steel door and pulled himself up until he could touch the ceiling. With both hands against the ceiling for balance and his feet squarely on the edge of the bed frame, Markham stepped back planting both heels on the three-inch cement edge.

"You did it," exclaimed Jean. "I hope you can hold that position until the guards arrive."

"Don't worry about that, Jean, you can remove the bed frame now and put it back where it was," said Markham.

Jean pulled the frame down and dragged it across the floor into its original place and replaced the bedding so that nothing appeared unusual. He pulled one of the two chairs against the wall directly below the barred window, and then went to the cell door to await the arrival of the guards. Once he heard the sound of a metal tray sliding against the cement floor to the cell two doors down from him he would alert Markham.

"The guards should be here in less than a minute," said Jean nervously. "Get ready Monsieur Markham."

Jean immediately stood on the chair partially facing the glass-less window with his head turned towards the cell door, when he heard the small top viewing door slide open for the guard to ascertain the location of the inmate before inserting the food tray in the bottom door. That was Jean's signal to start his act.

Yelling at the top of his lungs while facing the open window, Jean shouted "Monsieur Markham, watch out for quicksand, watch out for quicksand, good luck and God speed."

The smaller of the two guards immediately unlocked the cell door and ran up to Jean pulling him off the chair. The armed guard followed with his right hand atop his holstered pistol and as he walked through the door, Markham jumped down with both feet hitting the armed guard's shoulders breaking his collar bone and neck. The injured guard's body served as a buffer between Markham and the hard cement floor allowing Markham to recover from the fall only to be facing the other guard with his Khanjar knife, a deadly weapon carried by most local tribesmen. Jean got up from the floor and grabbed the guard by the neck from behind in a feeble attempt to help Markham. The slim but strong, wiry guard quickly freed himself and plunged his knife into Jean's chest. As he turned to face Markham he was hit square on the chin with a devastating punch that would ordinarily render anyone unconscious, but this robust guard merely staggered against the wall still holding the knife. Markham grabbed the guard's knife wielding wrist with his left hand and the guard immediately reinforced his grip on the knife with his other hand, causing Markham to do the same, then both men struggled for possession and control of the knife. Now pointing upwards between their chests, the sharp shiny blade was within a couple inches of each other's neck. With sweat pouring from the guard's brow, his penetrating dark eyes showed fear of Markham's commanding strength. In a sudden move, Markham shoved the guard's knife hand against his chest and with the power of an engine piston drove the blade up under the guard's chin deep into his head causing mass hemorrhaging and instant death. Markham pulled out the knife, wiped it against the guard's clothing for future use then dropped it to the floor to go to Jean's side and saw that he was still breathing. Markham quickly closed the cell door then returned to Jean who was lying in a prone position on his back. Markham lifted Jean's head slightly and called his name. After a few seconds, Jean opened his eyes and gave a strained smile at seeing that Markham had survived the attack.

"I'm not going to make it, Monsieur Markham but you will, and that is our fate my friend," said Jean with a slight cough.

"Take it easy, don't talk, Jean," replied Markham knowing full well that Jean's wound was fatal.

"You will keep your promise and give my letter and jewelry to Henri Charlemagne, Oui?" said Jean weakly.

"Yes, I promise, Jean,"

"Now I can die in peace," replied Jean whose facial muscles suddenly went limp.

Markham picked up Jean's body and placed him in his bed between sheets and covered him with the blanket. He then pulled off the belt of the slim guard's body containing the sheath for the tribesman's knife and the metal ring containing several keys laying them on the bed. He then checked the armed guard for signs of life by checking his pulse confirming his suspicions that he had died of a broken neck. Markham needed trousers and shirt that contained pockets, and the armed man was about his size and his clothing was not covered with blood. He quickly exchanged clothes, and removed the holster and pistol which he fastened to the other guard's belt containing the sheathed knife and key ring. He then carried the bloodless body to his bunk and covered it with the blanket. Markham dragged the bloody body of the guard who had knifed Jean to the corner shower where the remaining blood would drain under cover of the shower curtain. The big guard's sandals were a nearly perfect fit for Markham who would need them for protection against the desert's hot sand. He also removed the top sheet of his bunk which he planned on bringing with him as a shield from the sun. Markham quickly soaked up the blood on the floor next to the window with the bathroom towels to remove any apparent evidence of the struggle from the cell door's viewing window. He then cut up a section of the bed sheet which he fashioned into an Arabian head turban. Remembering his promise to Jean, he walked over to Jean's bunk and removed the two page letter, locket and ring from inside the mattress which he placed in his pants pocket. Markham took one last long look at the cell's surroundings, then said goodbye to Jean and left the cell, locking it behind him, wondering if in his haste he had forgotten anything. *Alas, he had no time to waste,* he thought, *and must concentrate on the job ahead.*

Markham quietly walked like a panther down the corridor to the locked metal door that led to the perpendicular hallway containing all of the medical offices and exit stairs. After several attempts he finally found the key that unlocked the door and quickly opened and secured it, then unlocked the first medical office door where he had undergone his medical examination. Once inside he refrained from turning on the ceiling lights for fear that someone would notice it from the outside window, but turned on a desk light which was sufficient for his perusal of the room. He noticed a six foot hose still connected to a faucet that serpented to an adjacent basin. Markham found some cord which he cut and tied to one end of the hose, then wrapped the hose around his waist twice tying each end together. Most of all, he thought, he needed something to carry a substantial amount of water, yet it couldn't be too heavy and burdensome to carry. He searched the room in vain, then decided to check the next room and found an open closet that contained first aid equipment with a carry-on back pack. There was a refrigerator in the corner of the room which to his surprise contained several bottles of water stacked neatly on the upper shelf. Markham immediately stuffed as many bottles that would fit into the back pack numbering half a dozen. Returning to the closet he saw a mop and remembered his need for a long stick, so he unscrewed the handle from its base providing him a five foot probing stick. *Perfect*, he thought, *now I'm ready for the long journey across the desert.* But then he noticed several empty plastic cylindrical tubes normally used for blood samples. He grabbed one and removed the cork, then rolled the two-page letter which he inserted into the tube and replaced the cork. Now the letter would be protected from the elements.

Markham placed his ear against the door to the hallway for signs of life and when satisfied that the coast was clear, exited the room locking the door behind him. He proceeded west to the end of the hallway and the exit stairs that Jean had told him led to the roof where the two air conditioners were located. The opening in the roof was protected by a shed like structure with an unsecured wooden door. Carefully, he opened the door, slightly at first, then assured that his presence would not be noticed, moved onto the roof in a crouched position to the western edge of the roof. The view was spectacular with the sun resting on the dark horizon preceded by massive sand dunes whose shadows partially eclipsed their gold slopes. *The beauty of an inviting vixen,* thought Markham, *but forewarned is forearmed.*

The only thing separating Markham from the desert was a thick three-foot stone wall of the same height as the roof but eight feet from the building. Markham, loaded with his backpack and stick, would have to jump at least eight feet to clear the wall, but Markham wanted to land on the wall in order to examine the terrain below. That offered the danger of falling back from the wall into the prison yard below made of cement that would inevitably cause Markham serious injury. With the broomstick in his right hand, Markham ran a distance of twelve feet landing his right foot on the edge of the roof and catapulting himself high into the air landed with both feet squarely on the wall but nearly loosing his balance towards the desert below. Regaining his balance, he immediately squatted so as not to offer a target for the guards on duty in the corner turrets. The wall extended downward into a long sand slope that ended some thirty feet away from the wall which would serve Markham as a sort of safety slide into the sand dunes. He had to select a spot on the wall that would prevent him from sliding into a valley of the dunes where sand pits and quicksand existed.

As it turned out, the spot where he was currently located offered him a slide into the top of a relatively flat sand dune. Without further ado, Markham leaped away from the wall with the broomstick in both hands in front of him in a lateral position that would hopefully impede any burial in the sand. His heels protected by the leather sandals touched the sand slope first, followed by his buttocks as he bent his body forward until his body came to rest at the bottom of the slope with his feet and ankles buried in the mound of sand that felt surprisingly cool as the night air. Markham immediately stood up and freed his feet from the sand then surveyed his surroundings. He knew he had to distance himself from the prison as fast as possible but he also realized that the next 500 yards would be the most dangerous part of his escape route therefore he had to implement Jean's advice to the letter. Using his broomstick, he poked the sand surface in front of him as he carefully walked along the peak of the sand dunes that formed a trail in a westerly direction. He had reached a point where he could see an arid part of the desert some sixty yards ahead that Jean had identified as the end of the quicksand area and thought of quickening his pace when suddenly he heard the unmistakable hiss of a desert snake that was attempting to climb up his broomstick. Markham's first impulse was to drop the stick. Instead, he swung the stick hard into the air sending the snake into the flight of his life. He then continued to poke the tip of his stick into the sand before him, expecting companion snakes to appear, but several scorpions emerged instead which Markham dispersed with several strikes of his broomstick. With mere open sandals on his feet, Markham felt most vulnerable to the deadly bites of these reptiles and insects, but he kept his cool and concentrated on the task before him, proceeding slowly but surely until he finally reached the parched area of the desert signaling the end of quicksand valley.

Markham looked back in the direction of Quicksand Castle which now offered only a distant light that shadowed the monstrous castle of death. He turned his gaze west and observed a sea of sand swells lit only by the full moon that reminded him of his long sea voyages aboard his sailboat, the Caul, presently berthed at the Port of Saint Nazaire, France, and now a wistful memory. As he walked briskly along the relatively firm sand flats he noticed the huge sand dunes he had previously observed as being near were much farther away than he had imagined, and as his journey progressed, those dunes appeared as mountains of sand stretching far and wide in every direction. Guided only by the stars which he had so often used in his celestial navigation aboard his cutter-rigged sailboat, Markham walked through the night until he saw the rising of the sun on the eastern horizon confirming the correctness of his course. He decided that it was safe to walk another hour before stopping to rest and camouflage his body with sand, but as the sun slowly rose, the light and heat formed a blinding glaze against the sand and for a moment created the illusion of a rider in the distance advancing towards him. Markham lifted his right hand to his brow to shade his eyes, focussed on a small dark form riding either a camel or horse that slowly grew larger, materializing into a tribesman in dark clothing with a rifle slung over his shoulder and riding a camel at moderate speed towards him. He unsnapped the cover to his pistol holster and waited for the stranger's arrival and intentions which were made quite clear within a hundred yards of Markham. The tribesman suddenly ran his camel at a full gallop with his rifle aimed at Markham who immediately drew his pistol turning sideways to offer a limited target. The tribesman fired first, missing Markham, who calmly aimed his pistol, shooting the intruder in the head, knocking him off the camel causing the camel to stop a few feet in front of Markham as if to greet his new master. Markham plunged his broomstick deep into the sand and tied the reigns of the camel around the stick. He then walked over to the fallen tribesman now lying on his back with a neat hole in the middle of his forehead. The bullet had penetrated, leaving a sizeable exit wound at the back of his head that bloodied the sand cradling it. Markham decided to remove the tribesman's outer clothing to wear as a disguise to fool any pursuers. An inspection of the camel's gear and pouches revealed dried meat and fruit, and two Bota one liter skins that hold liquids. These thankfully contained water. Markham buried the undressed body in a shallow sand grave, loaded his backpack and broomstick onto the camel, slung the rifle over his shoulder and rode west towards the Indus River. As he was dressed in tribesman apparel, he rode in Arabian fashion with his right knee hooked over the horn on the front of the saddle for stability and comfort. He felt he could reach the Indus River in two to three days now that he was onboard a 'ship of the desert' as camels were poetically referred to by tribesmen. A camel's gait requires both legs on the same side to rise and fall together producing a swaying, rocking motion that can produce seasickness in some riders.

Upon receiving news from his friend Harry, Chief of the Communications Center at the Central Intelligence Agency that the GPS transmitter ingested by Markham had moved out of the prison and was on the march in the desert in a westerly direction, Alex Petrov raced over to the Communications Center to view the electronic map for the latest position of his friend Markham and obtain possible satellite photographs.

"When did you first notice Markham's movement from the prison?" asked Alex.

"At 20:45 hours, Pakistan time," replied Harry. "At first he moved very slowly, then after about an hour, he moved in what we calculated as a fast walk, but now in the last two hours, he's been moving at a gallop pace."

"Have you been able to obtain satellite photos?" asked Alex.

"He seems to travel only at night so photos don't help," replied Harry.

"How do you account for the sudden increase in his rate of travel?"

"Who knows, Alex. Maybe he found a camel?" replied Harry with good humor.

"Well, how far from the prison has he traveled?" asked Alex impatiently.

"As of right now, about 80 kilometers and he's heading due west towards the Indus River," said Harry with confidence.

"That's the best news I've had in a very long time, Harry. Thanks for the quick alert."

"Don't mention it, Alex," replied Harry. "If your guy keeps up this pace, he should reach the Indus River in about two days."

"That's if the Pakistan authorities don't find him first," replied Alex. "They'll use helicopters no doubt."

"The fact that he was able to break out of that prison says a lot about his ingenuity and resourcefulness which I'm sure he'll put to good use in evading his pursuers," said Harry, attempting to boost Alex's morale.

"If anybody can do it, he can," said Alex with finality. "Keep me posted, Harry. I've got to get back to my office."

In his office at police headquarters in Islamabad, Inspector Mohamed Tamani, had just heard the news from the prison warden, Ali Multan, of Markham's escape, the death of two guards and the French inmate. He immediately telephoned the Chief Prosecutor Abdulah Khan who had shown a special interest in the incarceration of Markham at Quicksand Castle.

"Mister Khan…I have some disturbing news, sir," said Tamani with hesitation.

"Yes, Inspector, what is it?" he asked impatiently.

"The infidel James Markham has escaped from Quicksand Castle and he has not yet been found. He killed two guards and the inmate that shared Markham's cell Jean Depardieux was also killed during the escape," said Tamani.

"That name sounds familiar…isn't he the French archeologist that was convicted about a year ago of stealing ancient Pakistan relics?" asked Khan.

"Yes, sir, that him," replied Tamani.

"When did the escape occur?" asked Khan.

"Two nights ago, sir," replied Tamani.

"Why was I not notified of this before now?" asked Khan.

"I was not told of Markham's escape until a few minutes ago, sir. I presume that they thought they would have recaptured him by now and didn't want to cause any undue alarm," replied Tamani.

"I can understand Multan's position, but it shouldn't be that hard to find the infidel. After all, the prison is surrounded by quicksand and the desert is vast and most unforgiving which leaves the infidel with only a northerly escape into the villages and cities where he could be quickly identified as a westerner," said Khan.

"When I spoke with the prison warden Ali Multan, he told me that it was virtually impossible for Markham to survive the desert even if he had managed to avoid the quicksand which is most unlikely, therefore he concentrated all of his efforts north of the prison and so far he has had no success, not even a trace of him, sir," said Tamani.

"I suggest that you have some police or army helicopters fly over the desert in all three directions, east, south and west of the prison and cover an area of at least 100 kilometers," said Khan. "I'm sure he couldn't have walked that far in the desert."

"I'll get some police helicopters to cover the area immediately, sir," replied Tamani.

"Please keep me posted of your progress, Abdulah. Markham is a dangerous man and a threat to national security. He must be found, dead or alive," said Khan with finality.

As the sun was setting on the western horizon, Markham rolled out of the pup tent made from the prison bed sheet held up by the broomstick. The camel lying flat on the sand next to Markham had provided him cover from the wind blown sand. This 'ship of the desert' was indeed a Godsend. He marveled at the camel's capacity to endure the heat of the desert without the need to replenish its water or food supply for a week or more. He had heard that a camel could survive a 40 percent body weight loss and then drink as much as 150 liters of water. Markham surveyed his surroundings which reminded him of his complete isolation from the world which in this case was somewhat comforting. He quickly ate some dried meat accompanied by several swallows of water, then after folding and storing the bed sheet and broomstick, mounted the camel that made a rumbling growl as it stood up on all four legs. Markham resumed his course towards the sun's last position before it sank beneath the horizon. The full moon and shining bright stars against the vivid blue sky made Markham feel that he was inside the greatest of all planetariums. He felt a sensation of cleanliness from the desert's fine but abrasive sand that stripped nature of all unnatural properties. The only sound he heard was the camel's hoofs making a soft contact with the sandy surface and the occasional hum of the desert wind which had been pleasantly mild. As the night wore on, riding with his right leg hooked around the horn of the saddle, Markham wondered if his teammate Teri Flanigan had been successful in eluding capture. It was comforting to know her knowledge of the Arabian language and culture and her training as an intelligence agent of the CIA would be most beneficial in evading her pursuers. He worried nevertheless about her safety in a way that betrayed a deep fondness for a woman and colleague he had shown only respectful friendliness. So far he had not encountered any aerial reconnaissance, and as he distanced himself from the prison, he believed that the likelihood of aerial discovery was now minimal; hence he felt it prudent to conserve the camel's energy by maintaining its normal steady pace. By mid afternoon, signs of a sand storm were apparent coming from the west with a significant increase in the wind's velocity and large brown clouds of sand growing in size as the storm moved closer. A worried Markham knew only too well the destructive power of such storms. He also knew that camels are well equipped by nature to weather such sand storms having a thin membrane covering the eyes that function as clear inner eyelids. This permits enough light to see through double rows of unusually long eyelashes that keep sand out of the camel's eyes with thick eyebrows to shield them from the sun. Unfortunately nature did not provide Markham with such protection; hence he had to find some kind of shelter fast. Atop his camel, Markham quickly assessed the vast desert for some form of natural shelter and spotted what appeared to be a rocky formation about four hundred yards south. He immediately commanded his camel into a gallop in a race against the arrival of the sand storm, and found an abandoned waterless well protected on its west side by the stone wall remains of a demolished one room dwelling. Markham quickly dismounted and brought the camel to rest against the inside west wall that was only five feet in height. The camel seemed to know of the impending storm because it instinctively bent its front legs and dropped to its knees, then folded its hind legs and sunk to the ground. Markham wrapped himself with the bed sheet over his tribesman's attire covering his head then sat with his back against the wall next to the camel just in time to feel the fury of the storm rage over them with the force of a tropical hurricane, only instead of water it was sand, lots of sand.

About fifteen miles west of Quicksand Castle, a police helicopter flying over the desert in search of Markham landed near the partially sand covered body of a man clad only in shorts.

"This man could not be the Infidel Markham," said the policeman in Urdu. "He's obviously a tribesman, judging from the color of his skin, black hair and beard."

"What is he doing out here in the desert without clothing and transportation?" commented the pilot.

"Evidently, someone shot him in the head with a small caliber pistol judging from the small entry wound in his forehead, stole his clothing and transportation, most probably a camel and fled west," said the policeman, "The pistol from one of the guards killed by the Infidel was found missing, and I'll wager that the Infidel used it on this desert tribesman. So we don't have time to waste. Let's fly west before he reaches the Indus River."

"I don't think so," replied the pilot looking west at the oncoming sand storm. "We'd better get out of here fast or we'll never get off the ground."

"Isn't there any way of flying over it?" asked the policeman.

"Not on your life. We're flying back to the base," replied the pilot. "Tomorrow is another day."

The pilot hurriedly wound up the helicopter's engine and the large overhead propeller started kicking up sand as it lifted the aircraft into the air minutes before the sandstorm could saturate the helicopter's engine and bury them in sand. As the helicopter flew east towards the prison, the policeman could not contain his amazement at the size and force of the sandstorm.

"I've lived in this region most of my life and I've never seen a sand storm of this magnitude," said the policeman. "Just look at the height of this storm."

"You're quite right. Now you understand the reason for my insistence on leaving the body and getting out of there quickly," replied the pilot. "A few minutes delay and we'd never have gotten off the ground."

Upon arrival at the police station about four miles north of Quicksand Castle, the policeman called the Warden at Quicksand Castle and reported his findings.

"When do you expect this sandstorm to pass, Lieutenant Abbasi?" asked Warden Multan impatiently.

"The pilot said it wouldn't be until about noon tomorrow, sir," replied Abbasi.

"You get the other helicopters to join you tomorrow in search of the Infidel, you understand Lieutenant," said the Warden.

"Yes, sir, " replied Abassi. "We think the Infidel is heading towards the Indus River, sir."

"I agree, and if you don't find him by the time you reach the Indus River, you will then explore the River both North and South," said the Warden.

"Well, sir, he doesn't have a boat and I don't think he's going to swim some 200 kilometers to the Arabian Sea," replied Abbasi. "I believe that if he does reach the Indus River, he will cross it, and travel west to the Afghanistan border into Balushi country."

"I want you to get one of those helicopters to fly you to the Afghanistan border as soon as the weather permits and contact the Afghanistan Border Patrol and tell them that I am offering a reward of one million rupees to anyone who captures the Infidel Markham and turns him over to us," said Warden Multan. "We need to make that offer to them before the Infidel reaches the Afghanistan border."

"I understand, sir. As soon as the weather clears, I will fly there and make contact with the Afghanistan authorities," said Abbasi.

"And don't forget to get other available helicopters to canvas the desert west to the Indus River and beyond," said Warden Multan sternly.

In the meantime, Alex Petrov learned from Harry at the CIA Communications Center that Flanigan's transmitter had shown her to be in Quetta. An hour later he received the long awaited telephone call from Flanigan.

"Well, I'm glad you made it safely to your first station," said Alex, not wanting to reveal her geographical position on an unsecured cell phone. "You now must immediately proceed to your next station and notify me upon arrival."

Flanigan wanted desperately to ask Alex about Markham, but did not dare pose the question or mention his name on the unsecured cell phone. She was ready to say goodbye when suddenly she heard Alex' voice utter the coded message she was waiting for.

"Our prayers have been answered," said Alex and he hung up.

Flanigan's heart started palpitating with joy at the news that somehow Markham has managed to escape and was on the march to freedom.

As the sun slowly arose above the horizon, its powerfully brilliant light awoke Markham from his sand covered niche that was fortunately protected by the five-foot stone wall that had absorbed most of the force of the sandstorm. Markham stood up, removed the bed sheet that had insulated him and shook off any remaining sand from his clothes. The camel opened its eyes, turned its head towards Markham then rested its head again seemingly undisturbed by the passing sandstorm. Markham looked up at the sky to assess the weather condition but found the sun too brilliant, and for a moment thought he had seen two large seagulls hovering high above him. He was forced to look down then not believing what he had just seen; he looked up again but saw no evidence of flying seagulls. *Perhaps he had just seen an apparition or a mirage,* he thought, *and what would seagulls be doing over this large desert. But maybe, just maybe it was his spiritual friends sending him a warning as they had done in the past when sailing the Caul.*

Remembering his mission to recover the Holy Shroud made Markham realize that this apparition was most likely a spiritual reality, and that the sandstorm may not have been an accidental event. It could possibly have occurred to delay pursuers in which case he must lose no time reaching the Indus River to escape the searching eyes of his hunters. As Markham approached the camel, it raised itself on its hind legs followed by his front legs then shook the sand off itself. Markham removed some of the dried food from one of the pouches and one of the water bottles he had taken from the prison hospital. He took a few swallows of water then poured the rest of the water into the camel's mouth. He knew that camels could go without water for an extended period of time but he felt that the long journey ahead warranted it. After folding the bed sheet and storing it in one of the saddle pouches, Markham used the command "Koosh" to have the camel lie down so that he could climb aboard his 'ship of the desert.' He had decided that because time was of the essence to reach the Indus River, he would travel day and night for as long as he and the camel could withstand the punishment of the journey.

As the day's journey progressed, Markham wished he had a pair of sunglasses. His eyes had become slits from which he saw the head of the camel and not much else. As day became night, Markham felt a need to improve the circulation of his limbs by walking with the camel in tow. He marveled at the ripples in the sand which reminded him of the ridges in the sandy bottom of lake Richelieu where he swam as a boy. After an hour, he mounted the camel and resumed the steady pace until the sun arose again revealing two palm trees in a small patch of land about 200 yards in front of him. Markham decided to make camp and sleep for a few hours between the two trees. When he awakened, Markham realized that about 4 hours had elapsed, judging from his shadow clock, and he needed to make up for lost time by increasing the speed of the camel's stride. After sharing water with the camel, Markham continued his journey with the hope that this would be the final leg of his passage in the desert.

The C.I.A. Communications Center was buzzing with excitement as Harry was presenting Alex Petrov with satellite photographs of Markham dressed as a desert tribesman riding a camel in the Pakistani desert.

"Are you sure, Harry, that's Markham riding that camel?" asked Alex.

"Whoever is riding that camel has your transmitter inside him," replied Harry. "Right now, he's only fifteen miles from the Indus River, but a very peculiar thing happened. A violent sand-storm traveling very fast in an easterly direction across the desert which must have passed over Markham, suddenly slowed down as it came within a few miles of where that prison is located and it's still there preventing any flight departures. Now, whether it's just plain luck or divine intervention, those flight delays are going to give our guy time to reach the Indus River, but what can he do from there to prevent his apprehension?"

"I wish I knew, Harry," replied Petrov, "but as far as I'm concerned, that sandstorm was divine intervention."

"Well, I hope somebody up there is looking out for him because he's not out of the woods yet," replied Harry.

"I know what you mean, Harry," said Alex who then was interrupted by the ring of his cell phone. He looked at the caller's telephone identification number and recognized the caller as Teri Flanigan.

"Petrov," answered Alex.

"Mr. Petrov," said Flanigan, "this is Teri. I'm in Sophia (Bulgaria). Everything went as planned, sir. I presume that I can talk now."

"Now that you're safely out of danger, you can talk freely with the usual cautionary measures," replied Alex.

"Any news about Jim, sir?" she asked with trepidation in her voice.

"Yes, he managed to escape from that prison and we have located his whereabouts which I won't reveal on this phone. However we are very hopeful that he'll make it home safe and sound," said Alex in a reassuring voice.

"I don't mind telling you, Mister Petrov, that I have never prayed so hard in my life," said Flanigan.

"Don't be embarrassed, Teri, I have too," replied Alex. "I now want you to make your way to Turin, Italy and remain there until you hear from me."

"Yes, sir. I will leave on the first available flight," replied Flanigan.

"Have a safe flight and God speed," replied Alex.

Markham was riding the camel half asleep in his saddle when he heard the familiar sound of a marine engine instantly awakening him to the realization that he had finally reached the Indus River. He galloped his camel forward until he reached the embankment of the river to see an old brown hull boat slowly motoring down river with only its pilot and another sailor. *Most likely carrying limited cargo,* he thought. He descended the camel and led it to the river's edge where the camel replenished its supply of water to the delight of Markham who had come to revere that gentle and loyal animal. There were still a couple of hours of daylight left and he needed to use that precious time to prepare for his long underwater journey to the Arabian Sea. Markham noticed that there was a deserted wooden shack nearby which might provide needed materials. First, he removed the tribesman clothing that thankfully had protected him during his desert trip. He then put on the trousers and shirt he had acquired from one of the prison guards. He needed the pockets of those trousers and shirt to store items of importance such as the vial containing Jean Depardieux's letter, plus his ring and locket. During his desert trip he had elected not to re-ingest the GPS transmitter but to secure it in the vial, reasoning that once in the Indus River, he would have no means of retrieving it, especially in the darkness of the river. There was little or no likelihood of his being apprehended once in the river. He removed the five-foot hose stored in one of the camel's pouches and armed with the prison guard's dagger resting in a sheath fastened to his belt; he walked over to the shack to investigate its material possibilities. There were several wooden planks lying about and one of them, about four feet in length and an inch thick contained a knot in the middle of the plank. He also found a short rusty metal pipe about an inch in diameter which he placed on the knot and with the use of a rock pushed the knot straight through the plank leaving a round hole of approximately the same diameter as the metal pipe. He then searched for nails from some of the planks reminding him of his youth in Montreal, Canada, when he built an airplane using a rock for a hammer and rusty nails from wooden planks left in the fields adjacent to a factory. The airplane would never see flight but provided an amusing time for the youth. Using his knife, he removed two nails of sufficient length from the debris. He then positioned a nail one inch from the end of the hose, and drove the nail through both sides of the hose. He then positioned the second nail diagonally from the first nail and drove it through the hose thus forming a cross when looking directly into the tubing. Markham then inserted the other end of the hose through the hole in the wooden plank until its passage was stopped by the four outer ends of the nails protruding from the hose. He now had successfully built his snorkel equipment and needed only find enough stones to fasten to his body in order to remain under water. His two shirt pockets had flaps that held closed with a button thus were the best place to secure his vial, ring and locket. Therefore, his front and back pants pockets could be used to store stones, and the only other item he needed was the pillow case to catch minnows and other small fish. Using his knife, Markham cut the length of his trousers above the knees effectively making them shorts. He also cut off the shirt sleeves at the shoulders to free his arms for swimming and provide less resistance in his displacement of water which was cooler than the air's 100 degree temperature but warm enough to avoid hypothermia. He knew that sooner or later his pursuers would discover the camel and search it for evidence of its use by Markham, thus he had to remove any items that might betray him. Markham went further by removing the saddle and harness which he threw into the river leaving the camel free to roam the desert. With a gentle push, he signaled the camel to leave but he refused. Markham then slapped him hard on the rear end and the camel took off into a gallop that convinced him he would never return.

Stones of all sizes were in abundance at the river's edge and Markham stuffed all four pockets of his trousers, but some of the stones would not remain inside the pockets as he moved. He wasn't certain that there were enough stones to keep him submerged, so he decided to use the two trouser bottoms to store stones by tying each end with rope he'd found in the abandoned shack. He then tied the two stone filled trouser bottoms together to form a weight belt normally used by scuba divers. After securing the belt of stones to his waist, Markham descended into the shallow embankment and submerged himself for a trial swim and discovered that the weight belt did in fact keep him from surfacing yet did not force him to the bottom which was the plan. Now he had to try his homemade snorkel. Markham had cut two incisions into the end of the hose that was to be held by his teeth to give it a grip. With the wood plank and attached hose, Markham entered the river water with his snorkel in place and found that the hose needed to be permanently bent upward towards the surface where it left his mouth. Returning to shore, he used his knife to cut several lateral surface incisions into the hose that would allow it to be bent without allowing water to enter the tube. His second swim trial proved most successful and after one last look at the desert from where he came, he submerged into the Indus River heading for the long swim south.

CHAPTER VI

Rescue from the Indus River

Alex Petrov did not wait for an invitation as he entered the Communications Center of the Central Intelligence Agency to visit his friend Harry who had been chief of the Center for more than a decade.

"What's the status on Jim Markham, Chief?" asked Alex.

"I was just about to call you, Alex," replied the Chief with a knowing smile.

"You look like you swallowed the canary," said Alex. "Alright, let's have it, Harry."

Harry walked over to one of the desks containing a computer operated by one of Harry's technicians. "Pull up Markham's position, Steve," said Harry.

They all stared at the large digitized electronic wall map that showed southern Pakistan and in particular the Indus River.

"You see that red dot, Alex," said Harry. "That's your guy. Give us a close-up, Steve"

"That's your man where the red dot is," said Harry.

"Well, where the hell is he, Harry? All I see is a piece of floating wood," replied Alex impatiently.

"That's where he is, Alex, under that piece of wood," said Harry facetiously.

"C'mon Harry, zoom in and give me a close-up of that piece of wood," said Alex.

"You see that piece of tubing sticking out of the center of that floating plank?" said Harry, and without waiting for an answer, "That has to be a home made snorkel that allows him to breathe while swimming under water and the wood plank shields his shadow from the air. Pretty clever I'd say."

"How can we be sure of that?" asked Alex.

"Because the electronic signal comes exactly from under that floating plank and the plank has been traveling at nearly one mile per hour with the signal constantly emanating from that wood plank," replied Harry confidently.

"Amazing, just amazing," replied Alex with astonishment.

"I'll tell you one thing, Alex. If that guy Markham ever comes to Washington, I want to meet him and shake his hand, 'cause he makes me proud to be an American," said Harry with an unusual display of emotion.

"OK! Now that we know where he is and where he's heading… the Arabian Sea I presume, can he make it on his own with this homemade snorkel?" asked Petrov.

"He's already traveled two miles so he has another 105 nautical miles to go before he reaches the Arabian Sea near the Port of Karachi," said Harry. "He's traveling with the current so he's not exhausting himself."

"If he can maintain that pace of one mile per hour, it will take him about 105 hours and I estimate that he won't be swimming more than 12 hours per day which means that it'll take him at least 9 days," said Alex, "and he has to eat something during that time."

"How important is Markham to you?" asked Harry, "I mean how important is he to your mission?"

"Highly important, Harry," replied Alex with certainty in his voice.

"Then don't take a chance on his surviving 9 or 10 days under those extreme conditions," said Harry. "Go after him; send the Navy Seals to meet him."

"I was thinking of that, Harry," replied Alex. "By going under water the Navy Seals would never be detected by the Pakistan Government. I've got work to do, Harry. See you later my friend, and if any new developments occur, call me on my cell phone if you can't reach me at my office."

On the phone in his office at C.I.A. Headquarters, Alex Petrov had his secretary put a call through to the admiral in charge of Tora Naval Station in Spain. He wasn't sure if Vice Admiral Robert Perkins was still the commanding Admiral there, but hoped he was because it would facilitate and expedite his plan of action.

"Admiral Perkins is on line one, Sir," said Petrov's secretary on the intercom.

Petrov picked up the phone and answered, "Bob...this is Alex Petrov in Langley."

"Well, you old son-of-gun, how've you been keeping yourself?" asked Admiral Perkins.

"Busy as usual and not getting any younger," replied Alex. "I see that you're still at Tora Naval Station. I thought you'd be retired by now."

"Hey! Watch it...you're older than me and you're still leading the charge," replied Perkins kidding, "I assume that is the reason for your call."

"I've got an urgent situation, Bob, that needs immediate action and it's in your neck of the woods," said Alex.

"Don't tell me, Alex, let me guess...one of your agents is in dire trouble and needs to be extricated from an unfriendly country. The last time it was from Tangier, Morocco. Is this Déjà vu?" asked Perkins.

"No, Bob, this is different," replied Alex, "the last time it was merely a military escort service. This time it's a military rescue mission."

"You're splitting hairs, Alex," replied Perkins. "You should have been a politician."

"You can call me anything but that, Bob, seriously, this is a Top Secret mission with international implications and the agent to be rescued happens to be someone you know personally," said Alex, knowing that would get his undivided attention.

"The only man I know that worked for you and could get into this kind of trouble would be Jim Markham. Is it Jim Markham?" asked Perkins.

"Yes it is, Bob, and he is on a vital mission for our agency and the Vatican," said Alex.

"The Vatican?" exclaimed Perkins.

"Yes, Bob, and I'll tell you more about that later. Right now we need to have a team of Navy Seals rendez-vous underwater with Markham in the Indus River. He is currently swimming, using a homemade snorkel, and heading south towards the Arabian Sea," said Alex.

"Good Grief, Alex," said Perkins, "how far upriver is he?"

"About 100 nautical miles," replied Alex.

"No wonder you want the Navy Seals to meet him," said Perkins. "He'll never make it under his own steam."

"That's right, Bob," said Alex. "What ships have you got in that vicinity if any?"

"As a matter of fact, we have two battle groups including two aircraft carriers, the USS Theodore Roosevelt and the USS Enterprise in the Northern Arabian Sea. The Roosevelt has been flying night attacks against the Taliban and Al Queda targets in Afghanistan using Navy F-14 Tomcat fighters. The EA-6B Prowler surveillance aircraft and Marine Corps FA-18C Hornet attack jets are being used in their bombing raids. They're well within range of the mouth to the Indus River," said Perkins.

"What about the availability of a team of Navy Seals, Bob?" asked Alex.

"We do have a nuclear submarine in the Arabian Sea in support of the two battle groups. It's equipped with a DDS, a Dry Deck Shelter that's attached to the subs' rear escape trunk. The DDS houses a 22 foot MK8 Seal Delivery Vehicle that in addition to its pilot and co-pilot can carry a team of Navy Seals and deliver and retrieve them from any underwater objective," said Perkins.

"That is exactly what we need, Bob," replied Alex. "I presume that they would be able to provide Markham with oxygen for the trip back to the sub."

"The SDV has compressed air to extend the range of the seals own air tanks and in this case I'm sure they would bring additional air tanks," said Perkins. "In addition, the SDV has navigation, communication and life-support equipment."

"I need to be there when Markham is rescued by the Seals," said Alex. "If I fly to Tora Naval Station, can you get me aboard one of those aircraft carriers?"

"No problem, that would be a most logical plan of action, Alex," replied Perkins. "Once you arrive in Tora, we'll fly from Tora to the USS Enterprise, and the nuclear sub with its Seal Delivery Vehicle can meet us there."

"I'll be on a plane within the next two hours, Bob," said Alex. "See you soon."

"I'm looking forward to seeing you, and then you can fill me in on the mission," replied Perkins.

Eight hours later, a silver twin jet engine aircraft landed at the Tora Naval Station airfield and the tall figure of Alex Petrov descended the metal stairway onto the tarmac to be met by Admiral Perkins. The men shook hands vigorously, then departed for the officer's club where Alex briefed Perkins on Markham's mission to find and retrieve the Holy Shroud that was stolen from the Royal Chapel of the Cathedral of Saint John the Baptist in Turin, Italy. What intrigued Perkins even more was Markham's escape from Quicksand Castle and his long perilous trek through the desert that brought him to the Indus River. Perkins had sailed with Markham aboard The Caul cutter along the coast of Spain, and they had quickly become close friends. So Perkins now shared Petrov's enthusiasm and commitment to rescue their friend Markham. Perkins arranged for their flight to the aircraft carrier *USS Enterprise* that same evening.

It was daybreak with clear blue skies and a brilliant sun that promised another hot and sizzling day for the sailors on the deck of the USS Enterprise at rest 20 nautical miles off the coast of Pakistan and the port city of Karachi. Inside the war room control center stood Admiral Perkins and several of his staff members perusing a large flat television screen that depicted a map of the region including the Indus River and its exit into the Arabian Sea. Alex Petrov stood next to Admiral Perkins sipping a mug of coffee that had been given to him by the Admiral's Aide.

"We acquired the frequency code of Markham's GPS transmitter from your CIA Comm Center an hour ago, Alex," said Perkins. "This allows us to track him on our own screen."

"Does that red dot on the screen reflect Markham's current position?" asked Alex.

"Yes it does and it shows that he's traveled about 15 nautical miles so far," replied Perkins. "The USS Springfield nuclear submarine is presently on our starboard side, out of sight of the Pakistan mainland, and the Navy Seals team leader is onboard for a briefing."

Alex followed Perkins and his executive officer to a conference room where two Navy Seals, dressed in black wetsuits were waiting. They immediately stood at attention when Admiral Perkins entered the room.

"At ease," said the Admiral.

"Lieutenant William Cordell and Chief Warrant Officer Philip Marshall reporting for duty, Sir," said Cordell speaking for both of them.

"Welcome aboard, gentlemen," replied Perkins. "I would like you to meet Mister Alex Petrov, and my executive officer Captain Jerome Tucci."

The men shook hands, and then Admiral Perkins asked them all to be seated around the conference table.

"The information I am about to give you and indeed this entire mission is classified Top Secret," said Perkins. "In fact, this will be one of the most important missions your team will ever undertake."

"We understand its importance, sir," replied Cordell.

"Good," replied Perkins. "The man you are about to rescue works for the Central Intelligence Agency. He has escaped from a Pakistan prison in the middle of the desert and has traveled some 90 miles through the desert in order to reach the Indus River. There he fabricated a homemade snorkel and is using it to swim underwater towards the Arabian Sea in the hope that the US Navy would be there to meet him."

"The Indus River, sir, flows south into the Arabian Sea," said Cordell. "I hope he's smart enough to ride with the current saving his energy and strength. We will have to go against the current but, fortunately, we will be in the submersible which can easily handle it."

"Markham is an excellent swimmer and I'm sure he's figured that out, Lieutenant," replied Alex.

"Why would Mister Markham presume that the US Navy would be there to meet him, Sir?" asked Cordell.

"Because he ingested a capsule containing a GPS transmitter permitting the CIA and the US Navy to track his position, which is currently about 92 nautical miles from the mouth of the Indus River that spills into the Arabian Sea," replied Perkins.

"I presume, sir, that our mission is to rendez-vous with Mister Markham and bring him back here," said Cordell.

"That is precisely your mission," replied Perkins, "and all precautions must be taken to bring him back alive."

"Yes, sir," replied Cordell, "is that all sir?"

"Not quite, Lieutenant Cordell," replied Perkins. "Is there any way you can identify yourselves or your SDV as friendly so that Markham doesn't go into an attack mode."

"I wouldn't think that would be necessary, sir, in view of his exhaustive physical condition and our superior numbers," replied Cordell.

"Lieutenant...any man that can survive the physical demands that Mister Markham has endured is not to be underestimated," replied Perkins. "Many men have died as a result of it."

"I apologize, sir, for my remark," said Cordell. "We could stick an emblem of the American Flag on the nose of our SDV, sir."

"That's an excellent idea, Lieutenant," said Perkins.

"Will that be all, sir?" asked Cordell.

"Yes, that is all and good luck on your mission," replied Perkins.

As Alex, Perkins and some of his staff rode the large platform elevator down to a lower deck, Alex commented on the extensive possibilities of the ship.

"This carrier is the size of a small city, Alex," said Perkins. The Enterprise has eight nuclear reactors and four shafts. It carries

85 aircraft and a squadron of AH-64D Apache Longbow attack helicopters. This ship has nearly six thousand sailors and everything from soup to nuts."

"I'm impressed," replied Alex. "Glad to see that our tax dollars are being used for a good cause."

Upon arrival at the lower deck, Alex followed Perkins and his staff to a large deck opening. There they witnessed the emergence of the Seal Delivery Vehicle from the dry deck shelter attached to the USS Springfield, whose size was minimized by the enormous shadow of the USS Enterprise. The 22 foot Seal Delivery Vehicle slowly submerged into the Arabian Sea on its way to the mouth of the Indus River and the rendez-vous with Markham.

"Let's go into the control room and watch their progress, Alex," said Perkins as they stepped onto the platform elevator.

"What's your back-up plan in case they run interference with the Pakistan Navy?" asked Alex.

"I don't know that we can do anything while our boys are in Pakistan waters," replied Perkins. "The SDV will be completely submerged during the entire mission, therefore unlikely to be discovered by the Pakistan Navy."

"But isn't the Indus River shallow which would make the SDV visible from the air," asked Alex.

"The water in the Indus River is mostly murky, and once they exit into the Arabian Sea they will be able to descend to a depth that will make them completely invisible," said Perkins.

"Well, there's that stretch of shallows in the Indus River that worries me, Bob," replied Alex.

"Every mission has its risks, Alex, but I have a squadron of Apache Longbow attack helicopters at my disposal in the event that the Seals need support," replied a confident Perkins.

After his first night of sleeping on the northern bank of the Indus River, Markham trolled through the water with his pillow case, as he did the night before, and scooped up several minnows, eating them without regard to their slimy feel or taste as he needed this food for his survival. Swimming during the daylight hours gave Markham the necessary light to navigate the sometimes murky water, but he found that breathing through the hose required a lot of extra effort and energy and a limited diet of minnows hardly satisfied his hunger. He realized he would have to find more sustainable food soon. That's when he heard the familiar sound of the rotor blades of a helicopter, and quickly submerged with the air hose in his mouth, hopeful that he had not been sighted.

The helicopter pilot made a sweeping turn over the river then returned to the desert, and flew along the shoreline for a few minutes before veering east towards his home base. "There is not a sign of him. I believe the Infidel fell into quicksand and we'll never see him again. We are wasting time, I tell you," said the Pilot to the policeman sitting next to him.

"What about that near naked body with a bullet hole in his forehead?" replied the policeman. "Who do you think did that?"

"That could be the work of another tribesman," replied the pilot. "We would have found him by now, don't you think?"

"I guess you're right...let's go home."

Markham swam towards the center of the river and noticed a large six foot dolphin swimming next to him as if he wanted company. Markham felt comfortable with his presence, knowing that he was harmless and nearly blind while having magnificent sonar capability and sense of smell. That's when he spotted a foot long fish riding piggy back on the dolphin seemingly undisturbed by the stowaway. Markham removed his knife from its sheathing and moved closer to the friendly dolphin and with a quick sweep of his hand harpooned the small fish which he took to the bank of the river. He carefully raised his eyes above the water, and satisfied that no one was within his view, examined the fish which resembled a pomfret having a blunt and irretractible muzzle that was most unappetizing, hence he severed the head and cut the fish along the spine pulling off the meat which he devoured with great zest. His hunger temporarily satisfied, he submerged and continued his swim south.

At Admiral Perkins' request, sandwiches and coffee were brought into the control room where Alex Petrov and Perkins were seated, occasionally referring to the video map for an update on the Navy Seals' progress into the Indus River.

"How far up the Indus River would you say they've progressed, Bob?" asked Alex.

"I'd estimate a good 70 nautical miles up river," replied Perkins, "but they had to surface last night to get some rest, which is what Markham was doing anyway, according to the satellite photo we downloaded."

"At that rate they should reach Markham in another 7 or 8 hours," said Alex.

"That depends on Markham's progress too," responded Perkins. "They're moving towards each other, and I wouldn't be surprised if they rendez-vous in another 5 hours."

"I think the Pakistan authorities have probably given up their search for Markham," said Alex, "at least over the desert."

"I think you're right," replied Perkins. "There's no way they would expect him to be this far south and especially submerged."

"I have to tell you, Bob, that his escape is nothing less than a miracle, and it could be because his mission is to recover the Holy Shroud," said Alex. "I'm convinced of it."

"You may be right, Alex," replied Perkins, "and at this point, I'm sure he's grateful for whatever help he can get."

Markham had been submerged and swimming in a relaxed breast stroke with the current for about 4 hours when he noticed a vague black form coming towards him in the distance and as it got closer he was able to discern a torpedo shaped underwater vessel approaching him with three black suited swimmers being pulled by its outside railing. Markham immediately withdrew his knife from its sheath and stopped swimming in wait for the intruders. As the current moved him closer he sighed with relief at the sight of the American Flag emblem on the front of the submersible. He sheathed his knife and approached the SDV and one of the Navy Seals greeted him by handing him a mouthpiece and oxygen tank. Markham raised his hand for the Seal to wait, then quickly surfaced to remove the hose from the wooden plank releasing the hose to fill with water and rest at the bottom of the river, thus eliminating any trace of his method of escape. He then swam over to the submersible and the Seal directed him inside the Seal Delivery Vehicle where he was given a mouthpiece connected to the SDV's supply of compressed air. While the pilot of the SDV turned his submersible around to head south towards the Arabian Sea, Lieutenant Cordell sent a text message from the SDV computer to the USS Springfield and the USS Enterprise Control Room informing them of their successful contact with the target.

Exuberant emotions were freely expressed by Admiral Perkins, his staff and Alex Petrov when the news of Markham's rescue by the Navy Seals was received in the Control Room.

"All we have to do now is wait," said Perkins to Alex.

"He made it this far, so there's no reason he can't make it the rest of the way," said Alex with confidence.

"They've still got a long way to travel in Pakistani waters, and anything can happen," replied Perkins, sounding somewhat less confident. "But there's no need to worry, Alex." He added in an effort to reassure him. "If we see any activity on the part of the Pakistanis that threatens our boys, we'll neutralize them," said Perkins, hopeful that his boast would not be put to the test.

Admiral Perkins' reassuring words were a great comfort to Alex who loved Markham like a brother with memories that spanned nearly half a century.

Several hours passed and the Control Room map placed the submersible exiting the mouth of the Indus River when a message was relayed to the Admiral that a helicopter of Pakistan origin was hovering over the sea area where the Navy Seals were located.

"If that chopper starts firing at our guys, Bob, and one of those bullets hits one of the oxygen tanks, the explosion will kill them," said Alex in a concerned voice.

"I know that, Alex, but they're not in international waters yet," replied Perkins. "We can't take aggressive action until they're past the 12 nautical mile Territorial Sea Limits of Pakistan."

"Can't you at least get some Apache Longbows into the air ready for action," said Alex, always the hawk.

Admiral Perkins got on the red phone and ordered three Apache attack helicopters to scramble and hover at the international water line for further instructions.

"Thanks, Bob," said Alex.

A few minutes later, the voice of the lead helicopter pilot came over the speaker in the control room. "This is Apache One. The hostile aircraft is now firing its machine gun into the water in the vicinity of the submersible. Request permission to engage."

Admiral Perkins turned to the radio controller "Are we on secure?"

"Yes, sir, we are," replied the controller.

Admiral Perkins remained silent, deliberating his options, knowing that if he gave Apache One permission to attack, he would be in violation of the United Nations Convention on the Law of The Sea.

"Bob, you must attack before it's too late," said Alex imploringly.

The voice of the pilot in Apache One was now intense, "the hostile is circling for another attack on our submersible. Request permission to engage."

"Negative, do not engage hostile," replied Admiral Perkins who had seized the microphone.

Commander Studebaker, in charge of the Wolverines Helicopter Combat Support squadron, approached Admiral Perkins. "Sir, our Apaches are equipped with lasers that could temporarily blind the hostile pilot into abandoning his attack."

"The mere entry into Pakistan territory is considered an act of aggression and by default an act of war," replied Perkins. "We might as well shoot him down."

"For God sakes, Bob," exclaimed a frustrated Alex, "at least let's try to scare the hostile with superior forces and if that doesn't work then shoot the bastard down."

While the deliberations in the Control Room were taking place, the Navy Seals with Markham lying prone in the submersible descended to deeper waters in an attempt to avoid the

152

projectiles that were piercing the water disturbingly close to them.

Admiral Perkins looked at Alex, his executive officer, and members of the control room all staring at him in a moment of deafening silence that secretly begged for action. Perkins remembered the importance of Markham's Papal mission, and with the microphone still in hand uttered words that could cost him his career.

"Apache One, you are clear to engage hostile aircraft by placing him in a defensive mode that will cause him to abort his mission. If unsuccessful and hostile continues his aggression, you are clear to destroy hostile."

"Roger," replied the Commander in Apache One who then charged forward at full speed towards the hostile helicopter whose pilot watched with grave concern as the two Navy helicopters that flanked Apache One suddenly fanned out gaining altitude while Apache One slowed to a crawl facing the hostile. Apache One released a laser beam directly at the hostile, momentarily blinding him, allowing his two team mates to fly behind the hostile and remain in that attack mode placing the hostile aircraft in a complete defensive position. The hostile pilot realized that at best he could release one missile at the helicopter in front of him but the two helicopters behind him would easily destroy him. The hostile knew he had to yield or else die, thus decided to live, and disengaged by slowly turning his aircraft in a northeast direction signaling defeat. Once assured that the hostile was not returning, the three Navy helicopters hovered over the Arabian Sea in a protective mode until the submersible and its occupants arrived safely aboard the USS Springfield.

There was jubilation in the Control Room but Admiral Perkins knew that his troubles with the State Department and the Secretary of the Navy had just begun. For the moment he set those thoughts aside and left the Control Room with his Executive Officer and Alex for the lower deck, where they could observe the submersible dock in the USS Springfield's dry deck shelter.

The metal ladder was lowered from the rear deck edge lift along the starboard side of the carrier in wait for the transfer of Markham from the submarine to the USS Enterprise. The wait for the SDV arrival seemed like an eternity for Alex even though the wait was only about ten minutes. Finally, the wave action of the submarine's surfacing exposed the docked SDV and brought a sigh of relief from Alex and Perkins, as they watched Lieutenant Cordell exit the SDV followed by Markham and two Navy Seals who lowered an inflatable dingy that brought them alongside the Enterprise. Out of respect for Markham's accomplishments and long endeavor, Cordell allowed Markham to be the first to set foot on the ladder, and he followed closely behind him in case he fell from the exertion. Without the buoyancy of the water and the return of gravity, Markham's legs felt like heavy lead. He grabbed the ladder's side railings and used what power he had left in his arms to assist his weakened legs in climbing up each step of the ladder with unwavering determination. Admiral Perkins told one of the sailors to go down the stairs and help Markham, but Alex gently put his hand on Perkins' arm and told him, "No, don't Bob. He will be determined to make it on his own. Let's give him that chance."

With great effort and to the surprise of everyone in attendance, Markham made it to the deck in a disheveled state of complete exhaustion. His long gray hair and beard gave Markham the appearance of someone who had just escaped from Devil's Island, a thought that occurred to Alex who walked towards Markham to embrace him and as the two men met, Markham collapsed into his arms and had to be helped by Perkins and his Executive Officer in lowering him onto the deck.

"Get the medical officer over here right away," barked the Executive Officer, "and bring a stretcher."

Markham slowly opened his eyes and upon recognizing Alex and the Admiral, gave a faint smile. "Alex...did Teri make it?" asked Markham.

"Yes, she did, Jim, and she's waiting for you in Turin, Italy," replied Alex.

"Excellent. Now I can sleep in peace," replied Markham who then closed his eyes.

"Is he OK?" asked Perkins.

"He's sound asleep. Look at his deep breathing," said Alex. "If I know him, he'll sleep for the next eleven hours."

The medical doctor arrived and after checking Markham's pulse and other vital signs, declared that the patient was in satisfactory condition and should be moved to the ship infirmary for observation while he regained his strength.

"The debt that Markham and I owe you, Bob, is beyond measure," said Alex.

Perkins remained silent, obviously thinking of the ramifications of his actions in the invasion of Pakistan territory.

"You stuck your neck out for us, and now it's my turn to call in some IOU's from some heavy hitters on the Hill that will squash any repercussions," said Alex. "In fact, Bob, you should get a commendation for your brave actions today."

"That's very kind of you, Alex," replied Perkins. "All I did was save American lives; that's my duty."

Markham didn't awaken from his long slumber until noon the next day. He felt well rested and wanted to get back into action but needed to shower, shave and get a haircut from the ships' barber. He summoned the nurse on the duty to obtain his release, but she needed a doctor's authorization. He then remembered that he had placed the vial containing the Frenchman's letter along with his ring and locket in his shirt pockets. He looked around for his shirt then noticed a metal locker against the wall. He jumped out of bed and opened the door to the locker to find his shirt hanging on a hook. To his relief the vial and jewelry were intact. Markham used the infirmary telephone and was able to reach the Admiral's executive officer who agreed to have him transferred to a cabin in the officer's quarters where he would be given clean clothing. With his hair cut and beard neatly trimmed, wearing white trousers and shirt with blue Navy blazer and black low quarter shoes, Markham entered the ship's dining hall, and was quickly spotted by Alex who was having a late lunch with

Admiral Perkins and his executive officer. Alex waved him over and after being seated, a waiter came and asked Markham what he would like to order.

"Is it too late to order breakfast?" asked Markham hesitantly.

"This dinning room is open 24/7, Jim," said Perkins. "Order what you want."

"In that case, I'd like to order 5 eggs over easy with bacon, hash browns, rye toast and hot tea with cream and sugar," said Markham. "Oh, yes, and I'd like to start with a glass of orange juice, and with the meal would you also bring a large glass of milk, and a banana? Thank you."

"Are you planning on making this your last meal, Jim?" asked Alex kidding.

"I haven't had a decent meal in weeks," replied Markham, "and breakfast is my favorite meal."

"We've already eaten, and just sitting here sipping our coffee, but while we're waiting for your food, Jim, do you mind if I ask you a few questions before you go into the classified debriefing?" asked Alex. This was a signal for the executive officer to leave so that Alex, Perkins and Markham could freely talk about the events that led to his rescue.

"No, go right ahead, Alex," replied Markham.

"What papers did the Pakistan authorities seize from you, Jim?" asked Alex.

"Everything I had, which included my passport, military I.D. card, and my Papal credentials card, and two credit cards," replied Markham.

"I presume they never returned them to you?" asked Alex.

"No they didn't," replied Markham. "In fact, after a short benign interrogation, they whisked me away from the Police station in Islamadad to a prison known as Quicksand Castle a few miles south of Nawabshah. They incarcerated me in a cell with a French archeologist by the name of Jean Depardieux who was convicted of stealing an ancient relic from an archeological excavation in Pakistan."

"So you were not charged or tried, then?" asked Alex.

"No, I was not charged or tried," replied Markham. "In fact, they didn't even record my name in the police blotter and imprisoned me in the name of 'Infidel' so there would be no record of my detention. But that's the least of it."

"What do you mean?" asked Alex while Perkins listened with intense curiosity.

"I was in that prison only for a couple of days when they pulled me from my cell and brought me to a room where I was confronted by the man I had wounded in a sword duel in Tangier, Morocco about two years ago. His name is Mohamed Bundalai, Tangier's Minister of Justice, who apparently needs a heart replacement and he informed me with great satisfaction that I was going to be his heart donor,"

"He wasn't serious, was he?" asked Perkins.

"Oh! He was dead serious, and Jean Depardieux was proof of that. He showed me the scar from their removal of one of his kidneys and he knew of several other inmates who were involuntary donors, most of whom have since been cremated," said Markham. "It's a veritable organ replacement factory."

"Unbelievable," exclaimed Perkins.

"I guess you needed no further incentive to escape from that place," said Alex. "How did you manage to escape?"

"It's a long story, but I had to kill two guards, and in the process of helping me, Depardieux lost his life," said Markham.

"You mentioned the Quicksand Castle," said Perkins. "Why did they give the prison that name?"

"The prison is surrounded on three sides with quicksand and the only way in or out of that prison is through a narrow stone road at the north entrance," said Markham. "It was only with Jean's assistance as an archeologist, who knew the area, that I was able to navigate my way out of the quicksand pits. After a day or so of travel in the desert, I was confronted by a tribesman on camelback who took a shot at me with his rifle. Fortunately he missed, but I didn't, and his camel became my ship of the desert until I reached the Indus River, and the rest is history."

"Fascinating," said Perkins with Alex looking on unperturbed, because he knew of Markham's previous exploits.

"That was quite a trick with your homemade snorkel, Jim, I must say," said Alex smiling.

"Necessity is the mother of invention, you know," replied Markham.

"Is this going to be material for your next novel, Jim?" asked Perkins.

"I don't know…maybe," replied Markham, "the plot is thickening and the story has not yet ended."

"Looks like you're ready to go back to work, Jim," said Alex. "We can fly out of here to Tora Naval Station and from there to Turin any time you're ready."

"Is right after I finish breakfast soon enough, Alex?" said Markham.

"Well, now, you don't have to push yourself so hard, Jim," replied Alex.

"I feel fine and I'll feel a lot better after I've eaten breakfast. I've got a lot of unfinished business to attend to, Alex," said Markham.

"Yes, I know, and Flanigan is waiting in Turin to help you in your investigation," replied Alex. "Here's your new credit-ATM card and agency ID plus two thousand dollars for your immediate expenses. Use your ATM card as needed. The American Embassy in Turin is expecting you to pick up your new passport."

"Are you accompanying me to Turin?" asked Markham inquisitively.

"No, Jim. I'm returning to Langley," replied Alex. "I've got some unfinished business too."

CHAPTER VII

Hunt for the French Connection

Markham entered the Hotel Principi di Piemonte carrying his one piece of luggage and asked the desk clerk for the key to his room, explaining that during his absence, he had lost his room key. As Markham unlocked and opened the door to his room, he heard the door in the next room open and there stood Teri Flanigan in her doorway dressed attractively in a black business suit. Markham dropped his suitcase, walked up to her and embraced her warmly but without the kiss that she would have liked. She held him close and uttered "I'm so glad you're safe, Jim...I really missed you," she said softly in his ear.

"The feeling is mutual, Teri," replied Markham as he stepped back to look at her.

His gaze and smile revealed sincere approval, but in spite of his attraction to her, he knew he had to keep their relationship businesslike in faithfulness to his love for his dead wife Claire and long unrequited love for Michelle. "We've got a lot of catching up to do. Let's have dinner in the hotel restaurant. Is that OK with you?"

"Yes, that's a good choice," replied Teri. "I'm anxious to hear all about your travel, Jim."

After ordering from the menu, Markham was most curious about Teri's escape out of Pakistan.

"How did you manage to evade the Pakistan authorities?" he asked Teri.

"I was across the street in a clothing shop when I saw the police escort you handcuffed out of the hotel and place you in the back of a black police car," said Teri. "I knew then that the only way I could help you was to avoid apprehension and make my way out of Pakistan, so I purchased and wore a Sari with a flowered wrap and navigated through the streets riding buses dressed as a veiled Pakistani woman. I called Alex from my cell phone and he gave me directions and contacts that were most helpful in finding my way to Sophia, Bulgaria, and from there to Turin."

"You were definitely blessed, 'cause so many things could have gone wrong on such a long journey," said Markham. "Thank God you're safe."

"What about you, James?" she asked.

Markham recited in much detail the circumstances surrounding his arrest, imprisonment, escape and rescue by the Navy Seals.

"Talk about being blessed, Jim; that was no less than a miracle that you made it back alive," said Teri.

"I believe that, Teri, and now we must fulfill our mission, the purpose for our miraculous escape," replied Markham, conveying a sense of duty. "In fact, I must at some point contact Henri Charlemagne, the Editor of Le Parisien, in Paris, and give him the letter and two pieces of jewelry from my deceased cell mate Jean Depardieux."

"You think he can do something about the conditions in that awful prison, Jim?" asked Teri.

"He can publish an expose and Jean's letter," replied Markham, "but I don't want to visit him yet; not until we've recovered the Holy Shroud."

"Why is that, Jim?" asked Teri.

"Because, as far as our opponents are concerned, I died in the desert, and I am no longer a threat to them."

"That makes sense," replied Teri. "Here's the business card you took off Mister Musso's body in Islamabad. I thought you might want to look at it."

Markham inspected both sides of the business card. Markham read out loud the side that contained the printing, "Bucceli Security, Inc., 1057 West 56th Street, New York, New York. President Maurice Bucceli. Telephone Number: 212-759-1212." Markham then turned the card over. "A handwritten telephone number: 418-225-7780."

"Well, that's something to start with," said Markham.

"Does that mean we're going to New York City?" asked Teri.

"Yes it does. I'll need to check out that handwritten telephone number. The area code should give us a clue about our second destination," said Markham. "I'd better call Alex and let him know what our next move is."

"Archbishop Bartolini wants to meet with you as soon as you arrive in Turin," said Teri.

"I'll bet, and so does the Turin Police Department," replied Markham. "I do want to meet with them, if only to impress upon them the necessity to keep all information on the case secret, especially the fact they we know that Arturo Musso and Peter Loefler are criminally involved in the theft of the Holy Shroud."

"The moment you walk into that police station, everyone will know that you're still alive and in Turin," said Teri.

"You're absolutely right, and I don't intend to meet Inspector Ciminelli at the police station. In fact, I will kill two birds with one stone by inviting the Inspector to join us at the Royal Chapel where we'll meet with the Archbishop," said Markham.

"Sounds like a good plan to me," replied Teri.

Markham wasted no time in telephoning Alex at C.I.A. Headquarters, primarily because he wanted no interference with any of the Federal law Enforcement agencies.

"I presume, Jim, you're going to New York to check out this Maurice Bucceli," said Alex.

"That's correct. I will have Flanigan pay a visit to the Bucceli Security Corporation in order to prevent them from knowing my status," said Markham.

"Are you sure that's a good idea, Jim?" asked Alex. "She doesn't have your field experience, you know."

"I'll be close-by in case of any trouble, and I'll coach her on the target issues," replied Markham. "She's a very capable agent, Alex."

"I know. I'm sometimes too protective of my female agents," said Alex.

"I don't want the FBI, the New York City Police Department or the Department of Defense for that matter to know anything about this investigation until it's completed.

If word gets out to Peter Loefler at DACA, he'll warn his accomplices and run for cover," said Markham.

"Alright, Jim, not a word," replied Alex reluctantly, "but you must promise me that if you get into trouble, you'll contact me right away."

"I promise, Alex, stop worrying," replied Markham. "By the way, could you check out this phone number, 418-225-7780. That's the telephone number written on the back of Bucceli's business card. It just may mean something because it was found in Musso's possession at the time of his death."

"Have a safe trip," replied Alex.

Markham and Teri were seated in First Class on United Airlines to JFK airport, New York, so that they could talk with some privacy. Markham briefed Teri on the issues that needed to be explored and the various methods she could use depending on the circumstances. He also gave her methods of signaling him for help should the need arise.

She would be armed with her Agency issued pistol and a pen size can of mace.

Inside the lobby at 1057 West 56th Street, Markham noted to Teri that Bucceli Security Corporation was on the 3rd floor. He told her he would remain in the lobby while she paid a visit to the Bucceli Corporation.

Upon entering the security office, Teri was immediately confronted by the secretary, a woman in her early thirties, as to whether she had an appointment.

"No, I just arrived in town, and I was informed that if I needed the services of a private investigator to contact Mister Maurice Bucceli," said Teri.

"I'm sorry Ma'am, but Mister Bucceli is no longer with us. Mister Bucceli sold his security business about one month ago. Mister Percival Feist is now the President of the company," said the secretary.

"Oh! Well, did he leave a forwarding address?" asked Teri.

"No, but we'll be glad to offer you our services," replied the secretary.

"I really would like to get in touch with Mister Bucceli; he was highly recommended and this is a most private matter," said Teri.

"I'm afraid that he's no longer in the security business, Ma'am. He retired somewhere in Paris," replied the secretary.

"You mean Paris, France?" asked Teri.

"Yes, that's correct," said the secretary. "His wife died of cancer a year ago, and he always wanted to live in Paris."

"I hope he can speak French," said Teri.

"He ought to, he was born and raised in Montreal," replied the secretary, then realizing that she had perhaps volunteered too much information, abruptly informed Teri that Mister Feist was not in at the present time but if she wished to make an appointment, she would be glad to take down her name and telephone number.

"That won't be necessary, Miss. If you will give me your business card, I'll call you when I have decided my next course of action. Thank you for your kind assistance," said Teri, and without waiting for a reply, she turned and exited the office and quickly got into the elevator anxious to meet Markham with the newly developed information.

Upon learning the news from Teri, Markham commented, "Paris...at this rate I should just establish permanent residence there. Book us a flight for two to Paris, I'll call Alex and brief him on this new development."

Alex was surprised to hear from Markham so soon after their last conversation. After providing Alex with the latest developments in the case, Markham requested that a check of Maurice Bucceli's financial status be made with any recent monetary deposits into his bank accounts in the United States, France and certain other foreign banks whose purported secrecy the C.I.A. had long ago penetrated. Markham also requested that Alex check the American and French Embassies plus his friends at the Renseignment Generaux for Bucceli's current address in France.

Markham told him that they would be using the same suite at the InterContinental Paris-le-Grand Hotel in Paris.

Alex assured Markham that within three days of his arrival in Paris, he would have most if not all of the requested information.

Upon arrival at the InterContinental Paris-le-Grand Hotel located near the Opera House in the center of Paris, the desk clerk reminded Flanigan that while she was away, the large hotel bill that had accumulated had been charged to her credit card. When she told the clerk that she had expected no less, the clerk gave her the key to her suite with an avariciously approving smile. *Like in any big city*, she thought, *money talks and poverty walks.*

Markham was not a patient man. He was in action mode and the wait for information from Alex was tempting him to visit Henri Charlemagne, the Editor of Le Parisien but being a pragmatist, he abandoned the idea as being premature. Finally, the call from Alex came.

"I got most of the information you requested, Jim," said Alex.

"Great, I'm all ears," replied Markham with Teri waiting anxiously next to him.

"First the money," said Alex. "Three months ago, ten million dollars was deposited into Maurice Bucceli's bank account with Bank of America in New York City. The money came from an account with the Bank of Zurich under the name of LaGrange Enterprises, Incorporated, which turned out to be a shell corporation. The money was transferred from the Bank of America to the Banque National in Paris two months ago.

In fact, he had opened that account with the Banque National several months prior to that and when he sold his security business, he deposited three hundred and fifty thousand dollars into that French account. His only known address in France is 58 Rue des Montiboeufs in Paris. His unlisted telephone number is 011-33-569732789. He's a widower with no children."

"So we don't know the source of his ten million dollars," said Markham.

"That's correct," replied Alex.

"What about the telephone number on the back of Bucceli's business card?" asked Markham.

"That number is from the law office of Marceaux, Gilbert et Brussin in Quebec City, Canada," said Alex. "I don't think we're going to get anything from them...they simply can plead ignorance."

"Perhaps, but Musso must have had a good reason to have Bucceli's business card in his possession and either Bucceli or Musso wrote that telephone number on the card, therefore that number must have had some meaning to one or both of them and I suspect the latter," said Markham.

"Which brings us to Quebec City," replied Alex.

"Let's see what comes out of our investigation of Mister Bucceli," said Markham.

"Keep me posted, Jim."

Markham rented a black four-door Peugeot and drove with Teri to the street address of Bucceli's residence in the west end of Paris.

"What's your plan, Jim?" asked Teri.

"First we must determine the type of residence that Bucceli lives in, and see what kind of security system he has," replied Markham. "If he's readily accessible, we'll just go right up to him and I will confront him with the fact that we have sufficient evidence to have him tried and convicted, mentioning the fact that France is largely Catholic and its populace will not be happy with the man who caused the loss of the most sacred relic in the Christian world."

"Yes, but he's got ten million three hundred thousand dollars in his bank account," said Teri. "Why would he want to cooperate with us and give up that money?"

"Because that money won't do him any good in prison, and I'm going to make him an offer that will be difficult to refuse," replied Markham.

"Isn't that a line from the Godfather, Jim?" said Teri, chuckling.

"Perhaps, but my methods are different," replied Markham. "I'm going to offer him the possibility of serving little or no prison time if he turns the ten million dollars over to the authorities or to the Vatican, as would be appropriate, and he provides us with the name of the person that is the source of the money and has custody of the Holy Shroud. If we do recover the Shroud intact as a result of his assistance, there is no reason why he shouldn't be given immunity from prosecution. Of course I don't have the authority to guarantee his immunity from prosecution, but I can certainly obtain it if he decides to cooperate with us."

"What if he is involved in the assassination of Arturo Musso?" asked Teri.

"That's something we'll have to clear up at the outset," replied Markham.

"I certainly hope he goes for it," said Teri as they turned into Rue des Montiboeufs.

"We're looking for number 58," said Markham as they rode along the iron fenced grounds of an estate bringing them to a swing iron gate that was closed and apparently locked. The number 58 was etched into the right hand cement column that formed the arch over the gate.

Markham got out of the car and pushed the black button under the house number with no response. He pushed the button several more times and received no answer.

Markham got back into the car and drove away disappointed but not deterred.

"What now, Jim?" asked Teri.

"First, let's go to the American Embassy and get a photograph of Mister Bucceli," said Markham. "If they don't have one of his passport photos, then Washington, can e-mail one to the Embassy."

"Good idea, James," replied Teri.

At the Embassy, Markham identified himself with his CIA credentials and made his request for the passport information. They were able to provide him with a passport size photo of Bucceli after receiving it as an attachment to an e-mail from the American Embassy in Washington.

"What's next, James?" asked Teri.

"I'm going to telephone Bucceli and give him certain information that will worry him enough to agree to a meeting in a public place," said Markham. "Apparently no one was in when we called at his residence, so we'll wait until later then I'll phone him. Why don't we go have dinner at the Cheval Noir which is not far from the hotel?"

"I've never eaten there," said Teri. "What's their specialty?"

"Steak mainly," replied Markham, "but you can also order fish or surf and turf."

"You're making me hungry, Jim, but can we first go back to the hotel so that I can freshen up?" said Teri.

"I'm totally at your service, Ma'am," replied Markham.

"I wish you were, my dear," she replied with a huge smile.

Having dined a la Francaise with great enjoyment, and while still seated in the restaurant, Markham called Maurice Bucceli's home number. A woman answered the phone.

"May I speak with Monsieur Maurice Bucceli?" asked Markham in French.

"One moment please," replied the woman in French.

"This is Maurice Bucceli."

"Monsieur Bucceli, my name is James Markham and we have a mutual friend who left me your calling card," continued Markham in French.

"And who may that be?" asked Bucceli whose French accent was definitely Canadian.

"Arturo Musso, who is now deceased," said Markham for emphasis.

"I don't know any Arturo Musso, and I think you have been misled, Monsieur Markham," replied Bucceli in a terse voice.

"Monsieur Bucceli, I suggest that you contact the man who paid you ten million dollars to arrange for the theft of the Holy Shroud and mention my name to him. I think you owe it to yourself Monsieur Bucceli to meet me in a public place for a discussion as to what I can do for you that will prevent your assured imprisonment. All I want Monsieur Bucceli is to recover the Holy Shroud. I will be waiting for you in the Petit Gourmant restaurant on the left bank at 1900 hours tomorrow evening. Just give your name to the Maitre D and he will escort you to my table. A toute a l'heure," said Markham hanging up the phone.

"You sure put him in a tough spot," said Teri. "I'd like to know who he's calling right now."

"That's the $64.00 question, my dear," replied Markham. "We both had better be armed tomorrow just in case of an ambush."

Bucceli made a long distance call to Quebec City with great hesitation, as he had been instructed upon being paid for his services that he was to sever all relations and communications with his benefactor.

"May I speak with Monsieur Henri Marceaux, Please," said Bucceli in French.

"Who may I say is calling, sir?" replied the receptionist.

"Monsieur Bucceli."

"One moment please. I'll see if Monsieur Marceaux is available," replied the receptionist.

"Please call Monsieur Marceaux on this number, 418-225-1243."

Bucceli immediately dialed the new phone number and received a brusque response. "I thought I had made it very clear that you were not to contact us, ever," said Marceaux.

"But sir, something very important and unexpected has come up that I am sure will be of great interest to you," replied Bucceli in French.

"And what might that be, Monsieur Bucceli," asked an angry Marceaux.

"I received a telephone call a few minutes ago from a man named James Markham who said that Arturo Musso had left him my business card," said Buccelli.

"Are you sure he identified himself as James Markham?" asked Marceaux.

"Yes sir, I wrote his name down as soon as he hung up the phone," replied Bucceli. "Oh! Yes, he also said that Arturo Musso was now deceased," said Bucceli.

"What else did he say?" asked Marceaux.

"He knew that I had received ten million dollars to arrange for the theft of the Holy Shroud. He seemed to know everything, Monsieur Marceaux, and that's why I'm calling you," said Bucceli.

"Did he give you a reason for calling you?" asked Marceaux.

"Yes, he did," replied Bucceli. "He wants me to meet him at the Petit Gourmand restaurant on the West Bank in Paris at 1900 hours tomorrow evening to discuss a proposition for the recovery of the Holy Shroud."

"Monsieur James Markham is a very dangerous man who cannot be trusted," said Marceaux. "He must be eliminated, but first we must learn what he knows and for that reason, Monsieur Bucceli, you must keep that rendez-vous with Monsieur Markham tomorrow evening."

"Are you sure that is a good idea, Monsieur Marceaux?" said a fearful Bucceli.

"You do not have to worry. I will have professionals there to protect you. He would not dare do anything inside the restaurant," replied Marceaux. "During your meeting with Monsieur Markham, just listen to what he has to say but don't volunteer any information. If he asks you for your cooperation, just tell him you will have to think about it and have him call you back the following evening for your answer. Make sure you leave the restaurant with him so that my people will identify Markham, then walk away from him and my people will do the rest."

"I'm sorry to have troubled you, Monsieur Marceaux, but you can see that this is a most urgent matter," said Bucceli.

"Yes, Monsieur Bucceli, you did the right thing," replied Marceaux, "now don't forget what I told you. Just listen to what Monsieur Markham has to say and do as I have instructed you and everything will be fine, I promise you."

"Thank you sir and have a nice evening," replied Bucceli receiving no response except a click and a dead phone line.

Markham had made a reservation at the Petit Gourmand restaurant for 1830 hours, and upon arrival with Teri, requested a table that gave him a view of the front entrance.

"Can I see that photo of Bucceli, again," asked Teri. "This photograph must be recent because his new passport was issued last year according to the Embassy."

"He could have grown a beard or a goatee since then, but that won't matter," replied Markham. "We won't order any food until Bucceli arrives, and then we'll invite him to have dinner with us which will give us plenty of time to persuade him to join our side."

"Are you going to conduct this interview in French or English?"

"English," replied Markham. "He's an American citizen who spent most of his adult life in New York City. Our credentials will carry more weight as Americans."

"Always thinking, James," said Teri with a smile of approval.

At exactly 1900 hours, Markham noticed a portly middle-aged balding man dressed in a dark pin-striped suit approach the Maitre D and then both men looked in Markham's direction.

"Mister Bucceli has arrived," said Markham to Teri.

As Bucceli came up to the table, Markham stood up while Teri remained seated.

"Mister Bucceli, I presume...nice of you to come. I'm Jim Markham and this is my colleague Teri Flanigan."

"I've come against my better judgment but I'm curious about your proposition Mister Markham," replied Bucceli who seated himself facing Markham with Teri to his left.

"I would first like to reassure you Maurice, that we are not working for your employer to test your loyalty and discretion, and in that regard here are my credentials as an Agent of the Central Intelligence Agency, and Teri also is an Agent of the Agency," said Markham, showing his CIA identification card. "As a formality, Maurice, I need to see some photo identification; I'm sure you understand."

Bucceli pulled out his wallet and produced a New York State driver's license.

"I guess you just haven't had time to get a French one, huh!" said Markham smiling. "We're having dinner but we haven't ordered yet. Why don't you join us for dinner, the tab's on me?"

Bucceli realized that if he didn't accept the invitation, he would be walking out of the restaurant alone, contrary to Marceaux's instructions, hence graciously accepted.

"Wonderful," said Markham. "They've got a great menu and the service is impeccable."

They each ordered their food with a bottle of red wine, and Markham continued the conversation in English about the wonderful city of lights compared to New York, avoiding the topic of interest until the meal was well in progress, then he laid the bait.

"I'm sure you're wondering how I knew that you were given ten million dollars for arranging the theft of the Holy Shroud of Turin," said Markham looking straight into Bucceli's eyes for signs of stress and wanting to establish dominance.

Bucceli remained silent, wondering how to respond to such a direct question.

"Arturo Musso was assassinated in a hotel in Islamabad, Pakistan and he left your calling card," said Markham which did not elicit a response from Bucceli.

"We also know how the Shroud was stolen and all the players involved, except that we need confirmation on the identity of the person who ordered and paid such large sums of money for the theft of the Holy Shroud of Turin," said Markham who now observed sweat beads forming on Bucceli's forehead and upper lip.

"You know Maurice that what happened to Mister Musso can easily happen to you," said Markham. "Now that your employer knows that your identity and criminal involvement is known to me and the authorities, you've become a security risk and a liability to your employer."

"What's your proposition, Mister Markham?" said Bucceli, finally breaking his silence.

"If you agree to give us the name and address of the person who ordered and paid for the theft of the Holy Shroud and its current location, I will present this to the authorities who have prosecutorial jurisdiction and request that they give you immunity from prosecution but you will have to return the ten million dollars or what's left of it to the proper authorities," said Markham.

"Can you give me that guarantee in writing?" asked Bucceli.

"Yes, if the prosecutor agrees to these terms and you promise to deliver the goods, then it will be in writing," answered Markham. "You do understand, Maurice, that until such an agreement is made, your life is in jeopardy, but if you provide us with the evidence we need, there won't be anyone to carry out such a threat."

Bucceli waited for the waiter to place the padded check holder on the table next to Markham, and after the waiter left, Bucceli leaned over and asked Markham one final question.

"How much time do I have to give you my answer?" asked Bucceli.

"Until tomorrow evening, do you have a cell number?" asked Markham.

"Yes," replied Bucceli who pulled out a business card and wrote the number on the back of it which he handed to Markham.

"Just remember, Maurice," said Markham, "time is not on your side."

Bucceli made sure that Markham and Teri had finished their meal, then offered to pay the check, assuring himself they would all leave the restaurant together.

"That's a very generous offer, Maurice, but the agency is picking up the tab." Markham inserted his credit card in the leather check holder and while he waited for the return of his credit card, he made one last appeal to his potential source.

"If I were you, Maurice, I would lay low until tomorrow evening," said Markham as a warning of possible danger.

With his credit card back in his wallet, Markham engaged in small talk with Maurice as they walked from their table; Teri following close behind them. Upon exiting the front entrance, a black four-door sedan raced up to the curb with the back window open and the muzzle of a gun pointed in their direction. Markham quickly dove at Teri, flinging her to the ground, when he heard rapid fire and the screeching of tires as the sedan sped away from the scene of the shooting. Markham turned to see Bucceli lying on the ground on his back moaning. Assured that

Teri was safe, Markham ran over to Bucceli and could see his white shirt had a round patch of blood at the center of his chest where a bullet had penetrated, and another bullet wound was spurting blood from his stomach. Markham knew this man was dying.

"Maurice," said Markham only inches from his face, "who has the Holy Shroud?"

Bucceli coughed: "He doubled crossed me, that son-of-bitch."

"Who double crossed you?" asked Markham.

"Henri Marceaux," said Bucceli struggling with the words.

Bucceli closed his eyes and Markham thought for a moment that he had given up the ghost.

"Maurice, open your eyes, Maurice, does Henri Marceaux have the Holy Shroud?" asked Markham desperate for an answer.

Bucceli slowly opened his eyes: "No, he's the lawyer…masterminded the whole thing."

"Who then has the Shroud?" asked Markham.

"His older brother Philippe," said Bucceli who was having difficulty breathing and kept closing his eyes.

"Maurice, where is the Shroud?" asked a pleading Markham.

Bucceli opened his eyes wide and replied "the home of Philippe Marceaux… Quebec City," then closed his eyes, forever.

Markham checked his pulse and convinced that he had in fact expired, grabbed Teri by the hand and swiftly left the scene as the police and ambulance sirens could be heard approaching, no doubt summoned by the restaurant management. Markham needed to put some distance between them and the scene of the homicide, especially since he and Teri were carrying firearms in violation of French laws that pertain to Intelligence agents of foreign countries. They boarded their rented sedan parked a block from the restaurant and drove directly to their hotel.

"Pack your bags, Teri. We're leaving Paris," said Markham.

"Where are we going?" asked Teri.

"To Montreal," said Markham succinctly.

"Break your plastic gun down into pieces and put it into your check-in baggage,"

"I know the drill, James," replied Teri. "When making intercontinental flights, don't carry anything onto the plane."

"The sooner we check out of this hotel, the better," said Markham. "We'll return the rented car at the airport, then I'll call Alex and brief him on what we've discovered and our preliminary destination."

"Preliminary?" asked Teri.

"Are you packed yet?" asked Markham.

"Yes, just about," she replied.

"What do you mean preliminary?" asked Teri.

"I'll explain on the way...let's get out of here," said Markham.

At the Charles de Gaulle Airport, Markham obtained two first class tickets from Air France directly to Montreal, Canada with a departure time of 2330 hours which meant they had less than a half an hour wait before boarding their flight. "Perfect timing," said Markham to Teri.

"Phew! Maybe now I can catch my breath," said Teri. "You know, Jim, when I was sent over to France to find you, I was told this would be a routine search and rescue operation, but it's turning out to be the biggest roller coaster ride of my life."

Markham laughed at her remark which showed that she still had a sense of humor under stressful conditions.

Markham dialed Alex's home telephone number and after several rings, his wife Anne answered the phone in a sleepy voice.

"Anne, this is Jim Markham. I'm sorry to call you at this time of night, but this is an emergency. I must speak with Alex."

"Jim, he's asleep and he hasn't been feeling well," said Anne. "Where are you anyway?"

"The airport in Paris," said Markham impatiently.

"Paris? Well how much of an emergency is it, Jim?"

"I know where the Holy Shroud is?" said Markham.

"I'll wake him. He'll be with you in just a moment, Jim," said Anne who was privy to her husband's search for the shroud.

Markham could hear Anne trying to awaken her husband and after several attempts managed to get him to the telephone.

"Jim, do you know what time it is?" asked Alex, and before Markham could answer, he added "This better be important."

"I'm at the DeGaulle Airport in Paris with Teri Flanigan," answered Markham. "Maurice Bucceli whose business card was found on Arturo Musso's body in Islamabad was shot to death as we exited a restaurant in Paris and before he died he told me that Philippe Marceaux has custody of the Holy Shroud and his brother Henri is a lawyer and the mastermind of the operation,"

"Did Bucceli tell you where the shroud was located?" asked Alex now fully awake.

"Yes, Quebec City," replied Markham.

"Any witnesses to Bucceli's dying declaration?" asked Alex.

"Yes, Teri," replied Markham.

"I presume you're heading for Quebec City," said Alex.

"Not directly, Alex," replied Markham. "First of all, I rejected the idea of getting the Canadian authorities to issue a search warrant of Philippe Marceaux's residence, because he obviously has significant resources and by the time the search warrant is served, the shroud would have been moved to another location."

"I agree with you, Jim," said Alex, "and I doubt that the Canadian authorities would issue a search warrant on the sole testimony of two American witnesses to an unrecorded dying declaration."

"I thought of that too, Alex," replied Markham, "so we're going to Montreal where I will make contact with Jean Galian, a former Provincial Police investigator and polygraphist whom I trust like a brother. I'm going to seek his assistance in acquiring information about the Marceaux brothers and in acquiring the necessary equipment to conduct a covert entry into the premises where the shroud is purportedly located."

"Jim, be very careful. Canadian authorities don't take kindly to home invasions," said Alex.

"Don't worry, Alex," replied Markham, "I'm going to conduct a surveillance of the target premises and its surroundings before I go in."

"Good idea. Let me know if you need personnel assistance, Jim," said Alex.

"More personnel might bring attention," said Markham. "I'll let you know if I need anything."

"OK! Be careful, Jim, and call me before you make your final move," said Alex.

"Will do. Now you can go back to sleep, Alex," said Markham with a chuckle.

"Are you kidding?" said Alex. "Now I'll be awake thinking of all the things that can go wrong with this operation."

"Good night, Alex," said Markham concluding his conversation.

Teri Flanigan had been standing near Markham during his conversation with Alex and the name of Jean Galian prompted her curiosity.

"I heard you mention Jean Galian," said Teri. "Does that mean that I will be meeting Michelle?"

"Probably, why?" asked Markham.

"Oh, nothing, just curious," replied Teri who saw an opportunity to redirect Markham's misguided romanticism.

Upon arrival at the Montreal Dorval International Airport, Markham found an ATM machine and using the Agency's card withdrew three thousand dollars.

"Why so much money, Jim?" asked Teri.

"I'm going to give Jean three thousand dollars for the needed equipment and other expenses," replied Markham.

"That should make him happy," said Teri.

"Actually as soon as we get to the hotel, I'm going to send an e-mail to Alex and ask him to send Jean a check for ten thousand dollars made payable to Galian Polygraph Service right away. I know he would do the job for nothing," replied Markham, "but he shouldn't have to and I won't let him."

"You do take care of your friends, don't you," said Teri.

"Why not, they take care of me when I need them," said Markham.

"I'm your friend. Will you take care of me when I need you, Jim?" she asked with a mischievous look on her face.

"If you behave, young lady," he replied with a disarming smile.

Markham rented a black sedan and drove with Teri to the Comfort Inn in Dorval, after a quick phone call that insured they had two vacant rooms. From there, they were only a short drive to Jean Galian's residence. They unpacked their personal belongings then reassembled their handguns with silencers and loaded the clips with ammunition. Markham then called Jean Galian.

"Hello," said Jean, whose caller ID showed a restricted number.

"Jean, my friend," said Markham recognizing his voice, "I just landed in Montreal."

"You're kidding, Jim…and you didn't give me any warning," he said jokingly.

"Believe it or not, Jean, I just arrived from Paris and unfortunately, this is not a pleasure trip, my friend," said Markham.

"Did you come to Montreal to do a polygraph test?" asked Jean.

"No, Jean. This is the most important case I have ever worked on and I'm going to need your help," said Markham.

"Hey! Jim. Whatever you need, my friend," replied Jean with sincerity. "Where are you now?"

"I'm at the Comfort Inn where I stayed before, remember?" said Markham, "and I have an associate with me; her name is Teri Flanigan."

"Hey! You son-of-gun…is she pretty?" he asked in his usual joking manner.

"As a matter of fact she is, but this is strictly business, Jean," said Markham, concerned that Michelle might get the idea that he was romantically involved with Teri.

"I'll take your word for it, Jim," replied Jean, "so what's this case you're working on?"

"I'll tell you all about it over dinner," said Markham. "It's now 1620. How about dinner at 1800? You pick the restaurant and the tab is on me, no arguments."

Markham heard Jean talking to Michelle, then return to the telephone.

"How about the Rib & Reef restaurant in the city? We'll pick you up at 5:30, is that OK?" asked Jean.

"Perfect, Jean. Looking forward to seeing you and Michelle," said Markham genuinely happy to reunite with his old friends.

"I'm anxious to meet mademoiselle Michelle," said Teri. "This promises to be a most interesting evening."

Markham shuddered at the thought of these two women meeting.

"How old is Michelle?" asked Teri.

"I don't know… in her mid-fifties but she could pass for forty," replied Markham. "Look Teri, stop comparing yourself with her, this is strictly business. We've been friends for many years."

"I'm not making any comparisons, Jim, really. I'm just curious, that's all," she said unconvincingly.

Jean and Michelle arrived at the Comfort Inn ten minutes late and no apologies were made because it is fashionable for ladies to be late. Jean, wearing a sports jacket over an open collar shirt gave Markham a vigorous handshake, then Michelle with her blond hair flowing loosely over her shoulders, wearing an elegant, light blue dress, walked up to him and hugged him tightly.

"You haven't changed a bit, Jacques," said Michelle, sizing Markham up and down. She loved to call him Jacques, knowing that was his name during his adolescent years in Montreal's French Canadian schools.

"Like good wine, you got better with age, Michelle," replied Markham whose flattery stirred Teri's suspicion that their chemistry was still synapsing.

Michelle turned her attention to Teri who was not to be outdone in a smart black dress that accentuated her athletic yet shapely figure. Her coal black hair emphasized her pale porcelain facial skin contouring two exotic green eyes that greeted her with a calculating look and a warm handshake.

"I hear that you and Jim were in Paris together," said Michelle inquisitively, "that must have been quite exciting."

"Yes, it was, but not what you would expect," replied Teri who had been told by Markham that she worked closely with Jean and shared all of his secrets, hence would be made privy to their current investigation.

"What do you mean?" asked Michelle who was then interrupted by Markham.

"Before we go to the restaurant, I think it's timely that we both show you our credentials and a brief description of our mission, then we can go to dinner and discuss the details," said Markham who pulled out his C.I.A. identification card and motioned for Teri to do the same which they presented to Jean and Michelle.

"When did you start working for the C.I.A., Jim?" asked Jean visibly surprised.

"Just recently because of this case, Jean," replied Markham.

"I never would have taken you for a special agent of the C.I.A." said Michelle addressing Teri. "Just shows you can never tell a book by its cover."

"So what's the gist of your mission, Jim," asked Jean.

"The Holy Shroud of Turin was recently stolen from the Royal Chapel in Turin, Italy and our investigation has taken us to Pakistan, New York City, and Paris where we finally found an accomplice that identified the man who is in possession of the Shroud, and it is located in Quebec City. I have been commissioned by the Vatican to recover the Holy Shroud," said Markham now showing the card with the Papal Seal giving Markham full authorization to investigate the disappearance of the Holy Shroud.

The faces of Jean and Michelle were momentarily frozen with surprise.

"Mon Dieu," exclaimed Michelle, "this is incredible," she said in French.

"Do you know his name?" asked Jean still amazed at the declaration.

"Yes, Jean, and before I tell you his name, you and Michelle must promise me that you will never divulge his identity to anyone unless I release you from your promise," said Markham.

Jean looked at Michelle, then they both simultaneously shook their heads while giving their affirmative answer, anxious to learn the identity of the sacrilegious thief.

"His name is Philippe Marceaux and his brother Henri is a lawyer who masterminded the whole operation," said Markham.

Jean and Michelle looked at each other, then Jean responded "Do you know who Philippe Marceaux is?" and not waiting for an answer "He's the owner and CEO of Marceaux Industries with headquarters in Quebec City. Philippe Marceaux is probably the wealthiest man in Canada...he's a billionaire."

"That figures," replied Markham. "Only a man with his wealth could have financed this project."

"Whew! Jim. You've got a big tiger by the tail, my friend," remarked Jean.

"There's someone else criminally involved that you know real well, Jean, and because of your polygraph association with him, it's imperative that you know his identity," said Markham.

"Who's that?" asked Jean with a worried face.

"Peter Loefler," replied Markham.

"Peter Loefler...are you kidding me?" asked Jean.

"No, I am not kidding, Jean. We have hard, conclusive evidence, but we don't want to alert him of our investigative progress as it might jeopardize the outcome," said Markham.

"I understand. We won't breathe a word," said Jean turning his head towards Michelle who agreed with Jean.

"Great," said Markham who then pulled out a brown envelope which he gave to Jean.

"What's this?" asked Jean.

"Three thousand dollars in cash for you to purchase equipment that I have listed on the sheet of paper also in the envelope. We need this equipment for the recovery of the Holy Shroud," said Markham. "I know what you're thinking, Jean, but I insist that you take this money...it's from the Agency and this equipment is an absolute necessity."

Jean opened the envelope and when he saw all of those bundles of twenty-dollar bills wrapped with rubber bands, he asked the expected question.

"But why in twenty-dollar bills, Jim?" asked Jean.

"Because the ATM only issues money in that denomination," replied Markham. "That money is for the equipment, Jean. A check in the amount of ten thousand dollars made payable to Galian Polygraph Service is being mailed to you by the Agency for your services," said Markham.

"Jim, that's too generous. I would do this job for nothing, especially when it's about the theft of the Holy Shroud," said Jean with Michelle agreeing.

"You have expenses, Jean, and your time is as valuable as mine, so take the money and enjoy it with Michelle," said Markham. "Now, let's go to dinner where I can fill you in on the details and our plan of action."

"I don't know. You already gave us a lot to digest," said Michelle humorously.

The four of them exited Markham's room through the back French doors directly into the parking lot and found Jean's dark blue Mercedes Benz SUV.

"We girls will sit in the back while you two guys sit up front and talk business," said Michelle now standing in front of the rear door waiting for Jean to open it for her.

On route to the restaurant located on Decarie Boulevard in the city of Montreal, the two women exchanged histories while Markham and Jean discussed the recovery of the shroud.

"Tell me, Jim...how did Loefler get involved in this case?" asked Jean.

"He administered a polygraph examination on the person who stole the shroud from the Royal Chapel and rigged the test and its results so the thief would pass the test," said Markham.

"Holy cow! He must have been paid a lot of money to risk his position at DACA," replied an astonished Galian.

"Yeah! And he doesn't know that we have the evidence to prove it," said Markham.

"So what's your plan now, Jim?" asked Jean.

"First, I want you to know that I don't want you involved in the actual recovery of the shroud, Jean," said Markham. "I don't want you to take any unnecessary risks."

"Hey! Mon ami," responded Jean, "you're like a brother to me, Jim. You just let me know what you need and I'm at your service."

"That's very kind of you, Jean," replied a grateful Markham. "All I will need from you is information and equipment."

"What kind of information?" asked Jean.

"I need to find out where Philippe Marceaux resides. I assume that he's living in a secure mansion somewhere in the City of Quebec, so if you can possibly get the architectural plans of the building and its security system, that would be most helpful," said Markham.

"That's no problem, Jim," replied Jean. "I know lots of people with many contacts, and I'll be discreet, don't worry."

"Once I have the address with the plans of the building and the security system, Teri and I will take a trip there and conduct a surveillance, which may take more than a few days, to learn Marceaux's daily habits and all that," said Markham. "You know the drill on stake-outs."

"Yeah! I could tell you some crazy stories," replied Jean. "I'll go to work on that tomorrow, Jim, 'cause I know that time is critical."

"Very critical now that the Marceaux brothers know that I was last seen with Bucceli just before his death," said Markham.

"Yeah! You're a marked man, Jim. It's hard to believe that you're going after the Holy Shroud of Turin…that's the Holy Grail of Christianity," said an astonished Jean. "Even if I could tell someone about it, they wouldn't believe me."

"I'm in the same boat, so don't feel lonesome," replied Markham.

Upon arrival at the Rib & Reef restaurant, the foursome were seated in a semicircular table in the east corner of the room which offered them privacy yet an open view of the restaurant interior. It became apparent that Michelle and Teri's exchange of history in the vehicle had cemented a warm relationship based on an apparently honest divulgence of their mutual relationship with Markham. Michelle sensed that Teri had intense feelings for Markham and Teri sensed that Michelle was very fond of Markham but in love with Jean and perhaps not the threat she had imagined, but she had to make sure.

During dinner, Teri listened to Jean and Michelle relating stories of past visits by Markham in Montreal, which revealed the rich and deep affection they had for their American friend that made her somewhat envious but more understanding of Michelle's relationship with Markham.

After Markham and Jean ordered dessert, Michelle invited Teri to join her to the ladies room and once inside, Michelle revealed the motive for her invitation.

"You know, Teri...now that I've come to know you, I truly believe that you are the one person who could truly make Jim happy, and I don't think you can deny the fact that you are in love with him," said Michelle with a confidence in her voice that discouraged a denial by Teri.

"You're right, I can't deny that, but Jim is in love with you, Michelle," replied Teri nearly in tears.

"Where did you get that idea, Teri?" asked Michelle who had secretly suspected it.

"While in Paris visiting the Louvre Museum, Jim saw the painting of a fair-haired woman extending her hand towards a white swan at the edge of a small pond which literally sent him into a trance," said Teri. "When I asked him who it reminded him of, he answered that the woman in the painting had captured the memory of someone who had left a lasting impression and imprisoned his heart, but left his soul with guilt because she belonged to his best friend, and when I asked him her name, he said Michelle."

"I don't know what to say, Teri," replied Michelle, herself feeling guilt.

"In fact, I inadvertently stumbled upon a poem dedicated to you, Michelle which was in the drawer of the navigation table on his sailboat."

"I'm really astounded by this revelation, Teri," said Michelle. "I never realized the extent of his feelings for me, I assure you."

"His heart has no room for me or anyone else, Michelle, only for you," said Teri now wiping tears from her face.

Michelle attempted to put her arms around Teri to console her, but Teri tenderly resisted her kind gesture in an effort to recompose herself in case someone entered the room.

"I want to reassure you, Teri, that I am not in love with Jim. I'm in love with Jean and intend to remain with him for the rest of his life," said Michelle. "I think I know how to convince Jim of this in a manner that will not be offensive to anyone. You just leave it to me, Teri," said Michelle with a certainty that was most reassuring.

"Now I understand why Jim is so mad about you, Michelle."

"Oh, nonsense, Teri," replied Michelle.

Upon returning to the table, Jean confessed to Michelle that he had slight indigestion and wondered if she had any antacid tablets in her purse.

"You usually don't complain unless you're feeling pain, Jean," said Michelle in a low voice. "Where's the pain?"

"Right over here," he said pointing to the left side of his chest with his right hand.

"But I'm sure it's only gas from the food's acidity."

"I'm a registered nurse, Jean, so don't kid me," she said. "I want you to make an appointment with Doctor Boivin tomorrow and have your heart checked out."

"I'm telling you, Michelle, it's nothing but gas," replied Jean somewhat annoyed at her persistence, even though he knew it was because she cared for him and loved him.

"Listen, Jean, you kick the bucket and I'm going to become a rich recluse," she said, exploiting the nature of the conversation to execute her plan to discourage Markham's romantic aspirations.

"You a recluse...I don't think so. There'll be half a dozen men knocking at your door the day after my funeral," joked Jean.

"At my age, looking for that jewel of a man in a mountain of stones is not for me. I will be contented to spend the rest of my days with my grandchildren, thank you," said Michelle with a brief look at Teri who recognized the message that she had sent to Markham. His disbelieving eyes stared at Michelle, who was now looking down at her uneaten cheese cake unable to face Markham who felt betrayed because of his love for her.

Teri sensed the turmoil taking place in Markham's mind and heart. She slowly moved her right hand placing it tenderly over his left forearm in a gesture of compassion and empathy which became too much for him to endure. He suddenly excused himself to go to the restroom where he washed his face with cold water to wipe the tears that betrayed his true feelings. Markham reminded himself that when one door closes, another one opens; therefore he steeled himself for a new beginning.

Michelle's statement did not go unnoticed by Jean who now felt reassured that Markham had never been a threat to his relationship with Michelle. Jean immediately changed the subject by asking everyone if they desired a digestif and they all ordered their favorite liqueur to complete the evening.

The following day, Jean went to his office and telephoned some of his colleagues in the investigative world, and by noon he had received a fax from a friend in Quebec City showing the building plans of a three-story mansion in Charlesvoix, about 30 miles north of Quebec City where Philippe Marceaux, a widower, resided. He also had received a schematic of the alarm system from a former detective of the Provincial Police who now conducts private investigations. Jean was calling in several I.O.U.'s and they all proved productive. Now armed with this information, he called Markham and they decided to meet at his 36 foot Regal Commodore Yacht named Antidote. Jean told him it was still docked at slip 325 at the Port de Pleasance de Lachine where Markham had stayed a few years past. Markham reminded Jean to bring with him the needed equipment from the list he had left in the cash bag.

"I heard you say Lachine," said Teri to Markham.

"Yes. Lachine is on the west side of the city of Montreal and the Port de Pleasance is a narrow Presque-Isle accessible from Lachine by a short, narrow bridge. The Port overlooks the Channel des Iroquois that leads to Lake Saint Louis and eventually to the Saint Lawrence Seaway," said Markham.

"Is the Port de Pleasance far from here?" asked Teri.

"No, not far, about a 30 minute drive," replied Markham.

The short and narrow bridge that connected the Boulevard St. Joseph in Lachine to the Port de Pleasance Presque-Isle marina ended with a bar gate controlled by a marina guard who required membership identification before lifting the gate. Fortunately for Markham, Jean had left a spare pass card with the guard on duty for Markham. Upon verification of Markham's identification, the guard gave him the pass card which he inserted into a slot in a box situated at the base of the gate opening it. Markham drove about three hundred yards on a dirt road flanked by yachts of all sizes before coming to a one-story utility building where he parked his rented car in the small parking lot adjacent to it.

"This narrow Presque-Isle with all these boats is so quaint. I wonder which one of these boats belongs to Jean?" said Teri as they walked single file down a wooden platform to Dock number 55.

"His boat, the Antidote is in slip 325 right over there on the left," said Markham who then saw Jean sitting in the cockpit facing the dock.

"Hey! Mes amis," exclaimed Jean in a loud greeting voice, "Welcome to Antidote, the pride of Port de Pleasance."

At that point, Michelle climbed up the stairs from the cabin below to greet her guests. Michelle was an accomplished sailor and Jean enjoyed watching her maintain the boat's appearance and pilot the boat when out to sea. Markham remembered those occasions when he went boating with Jean, and Michelle taking over the navigation and piloting when their nautical position was in question. It had occurred to Markham that she would have made a wonderful sailmate on his cutter sailboat, but alas that dream was now gone forever.

"Jim, Teri, what would you like to drink?" said Michelle. "We have soft drinks like Coke and Seven-Up and Molson Canadian."

"I'll have a coke," said Teri.

"I'll have Canadian beer," replied Markham.

Michelle returned with two bottles, "We serve right out of the bottle if you don't mind."

"I prefer my beer from the bottle," said Markham who then sat down next to Jean in front of a deck table where Jean had laid some papers and a folded map.

"Well, Jim, I've got a map that will take you directly to the Marceaux mansion, and here are the architectural plans of the building plus I've got the plans for the electronic alarm system," said Jean while Michelle stood behind him looking over his shoulder.

Teri was seated next to Markham to his left, leaning close to Markham in order to read the directions on the map and the mansion's architecture.

"Does that show the location of the owner's bedroom?" asked Teri.

"Actually the plan does not specifically state the location of the master bedroom, but one can assume from the size of the room and the fact that this particular room on the third floor is the only room that has a steel reinforced door and alarm system. That room is the largest on the third floor or any floor for that matter," said Jean.

"That's most interesting," said Markham. "Of course the alarm system would cover all exterior doors and windows."

"Actually no," replied Jean. "For some reason the windows on the third floor are not covered by the alarm system, probably because no one would attempt to enter the premises through a window on the third floor. Those ceilings are 12 feet high in French Chateau style which makes these stories higher than normal."

"If that room on the third floor is in fact the master bedroom of Philippe Marceaux, then the window to that room will be the perfect entry point," said Markham, "but we'll have to conduct a surveillance of the premises in order to firmly establish that."

"You'll be needing these binoculars," said Jean, handing him the marine binoculars from his boat.

"Thanks Jean," said Markham. "I'll return them upon completion of the surveillance. But I will be needing a second pair of binoculars for Teri and one more thing, probably the most important item, and that's a tubular container four feet wide that can contain a roll of linen fifteen feet in length, so I would say the container would have to have a diameter of at least eight inches but no more than ten inches."

"You're going to store the Shroud in that container, is that it?" asked Jean.

"That's correct," replied Markham.

"I'm thinking of archer's who carry their arrows in a tubular container with an attached strap that fits over their shoulder," said Jean.

"They're usually about 3 feet in length with no cap, which is not big enough for the shroud," said Markham. "But I'm thinking that a tubular map container would do the trick. They come in all sizes and material such as leather and aluminum and some of them have an attached carrying strap."

"Sounds like the perfect solution, Jim," said Jean. "I will add that to the list you gave me. I see from the list that you need a black jumpsuit for yourself and one for Teri and also black low-quarter sneakers and you've indicated the sizes, which is good."

"You'll notice, Jean, that I need a strong braided rope, which I would guess, should be at least 50 feet long and preferably black or a dark color with one end looped. You'll have to put a knot every two feet in the rope and that would shorten the rope, so maybe we should get 60 feet of rope to compensate for it. The best place to purchase this is at the Boat House in Montreal. In fact, Jean, you can also purchase the other items on the list from the Boat House which include a 6-foot tether and 2-foot tether plus 6 carabiners which are boat equipment. In addition, those two suction cups on the list each have a handle and they're used on the hull of a boat to hold a person from sinking while he cleans the hull of his boat. We're gonna need those suction cups when we cut a hole in the window on the third story, so a glass cutter will also be needed. We'll also need a utility belt preferably black for Teri and me that can hold equipment. Did I list a pair of leather gloves for Teri and Me?"

"Yes you did," answered Jean. "You apparently thought this out real well."

"Now you understand why you've been given that money," said Markham kiddingly.

"At this rate, will we have enough?" said Jean, "no, just kidding."

"We'll do the shopping first thing in the morning, Jim," said Michelle.

When will you be leaving for Quebec City, Jim?" asked Jean.

"This afternoon," replied Markham. "We have to find out exactly what we're facing up there and what equipment we'll really need which means that we'll have to return to Montreal tomorrow or at the latest the next day to pick up the equipment from you. We'll check into a modest hotel so as not to attract attention."

"I figured you'd need a place to stay, so I found the Hotel Baudelaire located at the north end of the city within close proximity to the mansion and I told them that you would call them sometime this afternoon to make your reservations," said Jean. "I figured you'd want to use your own credit card."

"You figured right, Jean," replied Markham. "Good thinking."

"You sure you don't want me to accompany you to Quebec?" asked Jean.

"No Jean. This is an agency operation and if anything goes wrong, you wouldn't be covered by the agency."

"Nothing will go wrong, Jim, 'cause rescuing the Holy Shroud is a sacred cause," said Jean.

"Just the same, say a prayer for us. I'll keep in touch with you while in Quebec," said Markham. "We will most likely return by the same route, hopefully with the Holy Shroud, and if possible, pay you a short visit before we deliver the shroud to its rightful place."

"Good luck you two, and God Bless," said Michelle.

CHAPTER VIII

Deadly Recovery of the Holy Shroud

As Markham drove the rental sedan East along highway 20 towards the LaFontaine tunnel, Teri commented on the charming friends he had and the wonderful compatibility between Jean and Michelle whom she found very sympathetic.

"After this mission is complete, what will you do, Jim?" asked Teri.

"I must go to Paris to see the Editor of Le Parisien and give him the letter and jewelry that belonged to Jean Depardieux," replied Markham.

"And after that?" asked Teri.

"I think I'll stay in Paris for a while and become reacquainted with the city of lights," said Markham.

"You know that I'm scheduled for retirement from the agency soon," said Teri hesitantly.

Markham remained silent, sensing that her next statement may be provocative.

"I would love to keep you company in Paris, Jim," said Teri pleadingly. "I wouldn't take much room in your apartment and I would take care of you when you get sick."

Markham continued his silence, not knowing how to respond, then Teri placed her left hand on his shoulder near his neck.

"You know that I love you, Jacques," she said, using his French first name for effect and it worked.

"I know, Teri, and I realize that I was a fool about Michelle, and I'm discovering feelings for you. Let's talk about this after we've recovered the shroud," said Markham in his deepest baritone voice that made her heart tremble with newfound hope.

They were now continuing their drive on highway 20 East towards Quebec City and upon arrival followed 20 East through the city outskirt towards the municipality of Charlesvoix.

"According to the map we should be near the Rue Principal which should then take us to the 999 Montee des Rois…there it is, Rue Principal," said Teri.

"We're now on Montee des Rois," said Markham, "look for 999."

"Good Lord," exclaimed Teri, "this place is like a fortress."

"I expected as much at the front entrance, but the rear of this park-like estate probably will have serious security weaknesses," said Markham, continuing to drive around the full three mile circumference of the estate that was secured by a ten foot fence topped with barbed wire and behind high hedges. At the back of the mansion was a thick wooded area with a dirt road that ran the length of the fence for half a mile.

"What we need are wire cutters," said Markham who stopped the car on the dirt road, and exiting the sedan, approached the fence with Teri following. As he grabbed the fence to test its stability, he heard the growl of a pit bull, and could see him rapidly advancing towards the fence hitting it with such force that Markham believed the dog suffered a nose bleed.

"My God," said Teri, "I wonder how many of those beasts are patrolling the grounds?"

"He doesn't need many," replied Markham. "We're gonna need a tranquilizer gun for this job. I'd better call Jean and ask him to get us one compressed gas gun with tranquilizer darts."

"You think that will work on those wild dogs?" asked Teri.

"Oh, yeah! The police use them on animals that pose a threat and they're also used in zoos to tranquilize large animals," said Markham.

"Listen, Jim, I don't mind telling you that those pit bulls scare the hell out of me. You don't mind if I hang onto your shirt tail, when we go in there, do you?" said Teri half jokingly.

Markham laughed. "Don't worry, Teri. When that dart hits them, they'll sleep like babies."

Markham started walking west along the fence until he found a spot hidden from the dirt road with a tree surrounded by high bushes.

"This is where we can conduct our surveillance without being seen from the road," said Markham.

"What about the car?" asked Teri.

"We'll have to find a place nearby where we can park it without bringing attention to it," said Markham. "Let's drive around and see what we can find."

Driving through the back roads, Markham found an area off one of the dirt roads that could accommodate a car. It ran parallel to the road adjacent to the fence surrounding the mansion and was only a one hundred yard walk through the forest to the fence where they would conduct their surveillance.

"OK! Let's lock up the car and walk over to check our stake-out spot," said Markham.

"We should have brought a couple of those folding seats used for camping," said Teri.

"Tomorrow we're driving back to Montreal to pick up those things Jean got for us, but let's see what else we may need before I call him and ask him to buy two folding seats and wire cutters," said Markham.

"The mansion is situated at a slight angle to us so while we have a good view of its rear, we can also see people entering and leaving the premises as they come into view on the path leading to the main entrance," said Markham. "You can keep your eyes focused on the front entrance and I will focus on the back of the mansion."

"I wish we had that second pair of binoculars," said Teri.

"Tomorrow you'll have them, Teri, in the meantime we'll just have to use this one pair and see what comes up."

As Markham scoped the area around the mansion, he recited out loud to Teri his observations and findings. "I don't see any activity in the back of the mansion, and everything seems to be very quiet," said Markham.

At 7:00 p.m. Markham observed a black four-door sedan drive through the main entrance gate towards the front of the mansion and out of Markham's sight.

"Someone just arrived at the mansion but I couldn't see who it was or how many people there were," said Markham.

At 9:00 p.m. flood lights covering the front and rear of the mansion were turned on, and all of the windows on the main floor reflected light within those rooms, while the second and third floors remained in darkness.

"Did you notice, Teri, that the two flood lights covering the rear of the mansion are situated at both ends of the building and the lighted areas of those flood lights don't overlap or even meet at the center which leaves a dark area for us to travel and hide against the building," said Markham.

"Yes if our target is in that location," replied Teri who was becoming restless from the lack of activity. "It's now 10:30, Jim, how long are we going to stay here?"

"Until the old man retires to his room so that we can confirm the location of the shroud," said Markham.

"But, do we know if Philippe Marceaux is in the mansion?" asked Teri.

"Good question, Teri, and I will find out immediately," he replied. Pulling out his restricted cell phone, he dialed the telephone number of Philippe Marceaux at the mansion.

"May I speak with Mister Philippe Marceaux, please," said Markham in his most officious French tone.

"May I ask who is calling, sir?" asked the butler in French.

"The foreman at his Quebec plant, it's a most urgent matter," replied Markham.

"Very well, sir, I will inform Mister Marceaux," replied the butler.

After more than a minute, a gruff voice answered.

"This is Philippe Marceaux, who is this?" he asked.

Markham hung up the phone.

"Now we know that Mister Philippe Marceaux is inside the mansion," said Markham to Teri.

"According to the architectural plans we saw and Jean's information, the most likely location of the master bedroom is right up there at the first and second window from the left on the third floor," said Markham. "If the lights go on in that room, it will confirm our information."

"So we'll just have to wait until Mister Marceaux goes to bed," replied Teri.

It was 11:00 p.m. when the lights went on in the first and second window on the third floor, which brought sighs of relief and joy from Markham and Teri. Markham was looking through his binoculars at the two lit windows when he saw a man lifting open the second window. The facial features reflected a match to the photographs Jean had brought to the boat as part of the portfolio of Philippe Marceaux whose photograph had been prominently pictured in many newspaper and magazine articles in the past.

"You won't believe this, Teri, but Mister Marceaux opened his window and confirmed his identity in the process," said Markham.

"Let me see," said Teri grabbing the binoculars. "He's no longer at the window."

"That's alright," said Markham. "Now we know that he retires at 11:00 p.m. but does he follow this routine every night, that is the decisive question?"

"We'll just have to monitor him for a few days, that's all," said Teri.

"Now that the target room has been confirmed, let's take a look at how we are going to reach it," said Markham who then focused his binoculars at the two windows and roof. "The roof overhangs the windows and above window number two to our right is a horizontal wooden beam that extends from the building to the overhang stabilizing it. We could throw our rope over the beam and then connect the loop end of the rope to the rope hanging on the other side of the beam with a carabiner."

"But how are we going to get the rope up there over that beam and secure it with a carabiner?" asked Teri.

"See that metal drain pipe going from the roof down to the ground right next to that window," said Markham giving her the binoculars.

"I know what you're thinking, Jim, but it wouldn't hold your weight," said Teri.

"No, but it would hold yours…you're a hundred pounds lighter than me," said Markham, "and besides, you were a mountain climber."

"How did you know that?" asked Teri.

"You told me just before you climbed up the mast of my sailboat to change a light bulb," replied Markham.

"Me and my big mouth," said Teri smiling.

"Well, what do you think, Teri…is it doable?" asked Markham.

"Looking at that drainpipe, I would say that it is strong enough to hold me," said Teri. "I think it would work, Jim."

"Great," replied Markham. "OK! Let's go back to the hotel and get some shut eye. We'll call Jean and Michelle tomorrow morning after breakfast, so remind me to ask him to get us some wire cutters and wire ties and a tranquilizer gun."

"Perhaps you should call him now about getting these items because he may leave early tomorrow morning before our call," said Teri.

"I'll call him right now, although I'll probably be waking him up," said Markham who dialed their phone number and Jean answered the call.

"Sorry to wake you, Jean. We confirmed the location of Marceaux's bedroom just a few minutes ago. As a result of our surveillance, we found we are going to need additional items. I was afraid that if I waited until morning I might miss you," said Markham.

"That's alright, Jim, I was just getting ready to go to bed. What are the additional items you need?" asked Jean.

"Wire cutters strong enough to cut through a heavy gauge wire fence and wire ties to hold the cut fence in place. We'll also need a tranquilizer gun because the grounds are protected by very aggressive pit bulls," said Markham.

"No kidding...pit bulls, hey!" said Jean. "That's going to be a tough item to get, Jim. Any type of gun is hard to get in Canada, especially in Quebec Province."

"It's either that, Jean, or I'll have to kill the dogs," replied Markham.

"I'll see what I can do about the tranquilizer gun, the rest is no problem," said Jean.

"Call me when you have gotten all of the items on the list including the wire cutters and tranquilizer gun, Jean," said Markham.

"Will do, Jim, Good Night and Good Luck," said Jean meaning luck with Teri.

Markham did not receive a call from Jean until 3:00 p.m. the following day, and with great fanfare announced that he had successfully procured all of the items on the list including a tranquilizer gun with a dozen darts which he acquired from a friend who has a relative working in the Montreal zoo. Markham told him they would be in Montreal by 6:00 p.m. and they all could dine at the restaurant of Jean's choosing, courtesy of the Agency.

During dinner at the Beefsteak restaurant, Markham and Teri related their experience in Charlesvoix and all agreed that one more night of surveillance would be required before executing the recovery of the shroud. The sacredness of the mission assured all of them that Markham and Teri would be protected from harm and their safe return was predicted.

The following evening Markham and Teri resumed their stake-out position behind the fence facing the rear of the mansion and it wasn't long before two pit bulls made their appearance at the fence. But this time Markham was ready for them and sprayed them with pepper which they found most unpleasant and after a second spray the dogs left the area. They had not brought the portable chairs, figuring that this would be the only evening that the chairs would be needed, but after two hours of waiting they wished they had brought them. It was not until 11:05 p.m. that the lights came on in the master bedroom on the third floor.

"This is a self-disciplined man and a creature of habit who appears to follow a rigid schedule," said Markham to Teri.

"He's only five minutes later than yesterday," said Teri. "I think you're right, Jim."

"OK, then!" replied Markham. "We go tomorrow night, and I think that the best time to make our move is at 8:00 p.m. which will give us three hours before Marceaux returns to his bedroom."

"Three hours should give us more time than needed, I agree," said Teri.

Markham and Teri left the area and returned to the Beaudelaire hotel for a well deserved rest in preparation for the next day's mission.

It was a cloudless night with a full moon on the 4th of July, a day of celebration for independence in the United States, but fireworks were not expected in Charlesvoix although that would have been a welcomed distraction. Markham and Teri, both dressed in black jumpsuits and black silk head covers walked stealthily through the woods each carrying a black bag. Markham also carried a long brown leather tubular canister slung over his left shoulder. Upon arrival at the secluded area near the fence, they dropped their bags and Markham began using the wire cutter to cut a rectangular hole in the fence when the two pit bulls suddenly appeared at the fence growling. Markham immediately drew his gas operated tranquilizer gun and fired a dart into each one of the dogs with remarkable accuracy which silenced the dogs into a deep sleep.

"Amazing," said Teri, surprised at the quickness in which the tranquilizers took effect.

"Yes. Hopefully they will remain asleep until we get out of here," replied Markham who continued cutting the fence until he had a wide rectangular opening that would allow them to pass through the fence without having to crawl on their bellies. Markham used wire fasteners to fasten the top of the wire cutout so it would function like a swinging door which would hide the hole when not disturbed.

"OK! Teri," said Markham looking at her with renewed respect and admiration. "Are you ready?"

"Yes I am, Jim," she replied.

Markham allowed Teri to move through the opening in the fence first, and then followed insuring that the fence 'door' was down. Markham then stopped her so he could survey the area.

"You follow close behind me, and if I tell you to get down, you immediately lie down flat, OK?" said Markham.

"Yes, I understand," replied Teri.

Markham with the tubular canister slung over his left shoulder and carrying a black bag ran the one hundred and fifty yards towards the rear of the mansion with Teri running closely behind him. Upon arrival at the metal drain pipe, Teri pulled out the black rope from her black bag and hooked the looped end on a carabiner attached to the utility belt fastened around her waist. Without wasting any time, she started climbing the drain pipe while Markham stood with his back against the wall, the tranquilizer gun in his right hand ready for more assault dogs. Teri swung the looped end of the rope over the roof beam and then with a wire coat hanger she had brought for that occasion, reached for the loop and brought the end of the rope towards her and fastened it to the rope with a carabiner. She then let loose of the rope for Markham to test the strength of the beam and when he was satisfied he gave the signal for Teri to climb down the rope which she did with very little effort.

"Those knots in the rope make it easy to climb but are a hindrance for a quick descent," she whispered.

"I know, but while we're up there busy cutting glass, we're gonna need to use our feet on those knots for support," replied Markham. "Alright, let's go up as planned."

Markham climbed up the rope with a shoulder tether attached to his black bag containing glass cutting equipment. In order not to overload the weight on the beam, Teri was to follow him with the empty tubular canister once Markham had made a successful entry into the master bedroom. Markham was now facing the second window from the left as planned. He first tried to raise the window, hoping it had been left unlocked, but that failed. He noticed that the window latch was at the top and middle of the lower window. He then fastened a two-foot tether to the rope at a level with the upper window and then fastened the other end of the tether to a metal loop on his utility belt to free his hands. He pulled out one of the two suction cups and pressed it securely against the bottom part of the window and tested it. Using the glass cutter, Markham cut a round hole the size of a basketball directly underneath the window latch, then fastened the second suction cup against the cut class which he pulled out without a break in the window. Markham looked down at Teri and motioned for her to step aside then dropped the suction cup with round piece of glass to the grassy ground below which made no discernable sound. Markham then unlatched the window and raised it to its full extension. He carefully threw his black bag inside the open window so that it would fall just beneath the window sill and not crash against anything breakable, then he removed the tether from his belt and climbed inside the room. Using a small, focused flashlight, Markham quickly inspected the room and its surroundings then turned to the open window and signaled Teri to join him.

Teri pulled out her pen flash light and joined Markham in inspecting the room when both search lights simultaneously lit up the Holy Shroud of Turin. It was securely displayed in a glass covered container hanging on the wall above the head of the king size bed.

"Pull the curtains over the two windows, Teri," said Markham

With the curtains covering the two windows, Markham turned on one of the bedside lamps that offered just enough light for them to conduct their removal of the shroud. Markham carefully inspected the container made of an aluminum frame with safety glass covering the shroud. He inspected both sides of the container and found that at the foot of the shroud was a panel with hinges signifying that the shroud could be removed from that end of the container, but it was locked at both ends as Markham had expected. Teri who had been a technical agent during the early part of her CIA career always carried a pocket size leather case containing a set of lock picks which now became useful. It took her more than five exhausting minutes to open the first lock but less than a minute to open the second one. Markham then stepped in and very carefully opened the end flap exposing the foot of the Holy Shroud. Unknown to Markham and Teri, this set off a silent alarm to a handheld device that Philippe Marceaux kept on his person at all times.

"This is the third time in two days that this alarm device has sounded and so far they have all been false alarms," said Marceaux to his trusted accountant with whom he was having dinner. "I'm going to fire that security company if they don't do something about this damn thing,"

"There's no sense in having this thing spoil your dinner, Philippe," said his accountant. "Why don't you wait until after we have finished eating dinner before you check on it?"

"You're right, Claude," said Marceaux, "I'll check it out after dinner."

In the master bedroom, Markham and Teri were trying to figure out how to remove the container from the wall without damaging the shroud with the glass covering.

Markham noticed that there was a hose and also an electric wire connected to the container and he surmised that the hose introduced gas into the container while the electrical cord probably lit up the shroud. He disconnected the hose and electrical cord from the container and with Teri's assistance removed the container from the wall mounted hooks that held it in place, and laid the container on the bed. Markham slowly and carefully started to pull the shroud from the container's opening and it surprisingly slid out of the container without apparent damage. Teri meticulously started rolling the shroud like a carpet until it was fully rolled then Markham wrapped three thin Velcro cloths around the middle and at each end of the shroud to hold it in place, then they inserted it into the tubular canister. With the shroud safely inside, Markham was putting the cap on the canister when he heard a noise in the direction of the door.

"Did you find what you're looking for, Mister Markham, I presume?" asked Marceaux pointing a pistol in Markham's direction.

Teri slowly took a few of steps sideways to distance herself from Markham in accordance with her training. This move would make it more difficult for Marceaux to shoot them both without one of them getting a clear shot at him.

"You can stop moving mademoiselle," said Marceaux menacingly.

"I was right, you are indeed Mister Markham," said Marceaux with a slight smile. "Now put that container down on the bed."

Markham slowly and with great deliberation placed the canister on the bed all the while staring into the eyes of Marceaux. Teri took advantage of Marceaux's focus on Markham and drew her pistol, clearing its holster but froze when a bullet from Marceaux's pistol pierced her chest causing her to collapse to the floor. Marceaux simultaneously collapsed with a bullet through his heart from Markham's gun. Markham holstered his pistol and went to Teri who lay on the carpeted floor, her eyes still open with a look of despair. With the wound oozing blood from the center of her chest, Markham knew she only had seconds to live.

"I love you, Teri," he said realizing the lateness of his declaration.

"I know, Jim," she replied weakly. "I guess Paris is out but Heaven is definitely in." Then she took a breath and whispered "Jim, go quickly, you must save the Holy Shroud."

That was her last breath and Markham knew that her soul had gone to heaven. He picked up the canister slipping it over his shoulder and was placing Teri's pistol in the black bag along with her set of lock picks when he heard someone banging on the bedroom door. Apparently the sound of the two pistol shots had alerted security of a disturbance transpiring in Marceaux's bedroom. He heard someone calling to another person to get the passkey. Markham kissed Teri on the forehead and bid her adieu, then climbed out of the window grasping the rope and rapidly descended. One of the security persons unlocked the door, turned on the lights and then saw Marceaux and Teri both lying on the floor and the Holy Shroud missing from its container. He walked over to the open window with two other security persons that had now entered the room.

"There he is running away," said the security man in the window pulling out his pistol and fired several shots in Markham's direction.

Markham was running as fast as he could in the direction of the fence when he suddenly felt a burning pain on the left side of his abdomen which brought him to his knees.

"I got him, I got him," exclaimed the security man in French to his two companions.

"Let's go downstairs and get the son of a bitch" said one of the other security men in French.

Markham took his folded handkerchief from his back pocket and held it against the exit wound and started running again with the same abdominal pain he used to feel when running cross-country in high school, even though he continued running to finish the race. *He must continue and finish this race,* he thought, and finally reached the cut 'fence door' closing it behind him, then continued his run now a slow trot through the woods until he reached his rental car. He placed the canister and bag on the floor of the backseat, and drove away with lights out until he reached the highway. Then sped west until he reached a rest stop where he took off his belt and wrapped it tightly around his abdomen over the handkerchief covering the exit wound attempting to slow down the bleeding. He got back in the car and turned onto route 20 West towards Lachine. He knew that due to his physical condition and the death of Teri and Marceaux, he could not leave Canada by air or auto, and the only way out was by boat through the Saint Lawrence Seaway to Lake Ontario and the Niagara River on the United States coastline.

CHAPTER IX

Miracle on the Saint Lawrence Seaway

Markham knew that his only hope to get himself and the Holy Shroud into the United States where he could safely get medical help and transportation to Turin was from his trusted friends Jean and Michelle. He used his cell phone and called Jean.

"Jean, it's Jim," said Markham haltingly.

"You sound exhausted, is anything wrong Jim?" asked Jean.

"Yes, Jean. I have the Holy Shroud, but Teri is dead and so is Philippe Marceaux."

"Oh my God! I'm so sorry to hear that," said Jean, Michelle now standing next to him.

"Where are you? Are you alright?" asked Jean.

"Actually I've been shot but I don't think the bullet hit any vital organs. It went right through me just below the spleen on the left side of my abdomen," said Markham. "I'm now driving towards the Port de Pleasance on Route 20 West."

Michelle got on the phone, "Jim, you must keep the pressure on the wound to keep from bleeding out."

"I know Michelle," said Markham. "Can you meet me at the boat?"

Jean got back on the phone. "Jim, we are leaving for the boat and will be there before you. Michelle will bring a first aid kit, but you'll probably need a doctor."

"No, no doctor, Jean," said Markham emphatically. "I need you to take me by boat west bound on the South Channel to Lake St Louis, and then onto the St. Laurence Seaway, eventually into Lake Ontario going south until we reach the Niagara River. The Youngstown Yacht Club is my destination and where I will get off. Can you do that for me, Jean?"

"As the bearer of the Holy Shroud how can I refuse you?" said Jean. "Drive cautiously and don't get any tickets. We'll be at the boat waiting for you. You still have the marina entry card?"

"Yes, it's in the glove compartment. Thank you," said Markham.

Michelle reached for Jean and fell into his arms for comfort. "My God, Jean, Teri is dead. How could that happen? They were on a religious mission."

"It was written, it was her destiny and the Holy Shroud was recovered," said Jean.

"She will surely go to heaven," said Michelle. "I wonder if Jim realizes how much she really meant to him as he did to her."

"I don't know, sweetheart," replied Jean. "I just wouldn't want to be in his shoes right now."

The Quebec police were at the mansion within thirty minutes of the call from the chief of security. A search of Teri's belongings revealed only her real name of Theresa Brenner on a Virginia driver's license. No other card or identification was found by the police nor was the weapon used to kill Philippe Marceaux found. The police were told by the mansion security officer that the other intruder, a male, was wounded, but escaped. The Quebec police immediately issued a bulletin for the arrest of a white male, armed, possibly American, suffering from a bullet wound.

Markham was driving at about ten miles over the speed limit when a marked police car coming in the opposite direction made a U-turn across the narrow strip of road, crossed the medium, and stayed about 50 yards behind Markham for half a mile. He moved into the fast lane and drove up to Markham's vehicle, gave him a long look, then sped away, to Markham's relief.

After an hour and a half of driving, Markham pulled into the Port de Pleasance marina and parked next to Jean's Sport Utility Vehicle. He first hung the shroud canister strap over his shoulder, then removed his bag and Teri's bag, containing their regular clothing, from the trunk of the car and started walking down the dock to the boat when Jean and Michelle ran up to him and relieved him of his bags.

"Jim, how are you feeling," asked Michelle.

"Thirsty," replied Markham. "I need to lie down."

"We've fixed the V berth for you and I brought dressing and other first aid stuff," said Michelle.

Markham was familiar with the yacht, having stayed on it a week at a time in the past. He descended the stairs from the cockpit into the galley which led to the V-Berth.

"Is this the Holy Shroud, Jim?" asked Michelle as she and Jean looked at the tubular canister with great curiosity..

"Yes, it is," replied Markham. "It must not be opened unless absolutely necessary to keep air from reaching the shroud."

Markham released the canister from his shoulder and laid it on the window ledge of the V-Berth, out of the way where it would not be damaged. He removed his belt and jumpsuit exposing the bloody handkerchief covering the exit wound.

"Oh! Let me look at that, Jim," said Michelle, showing the concern of a former registered nurse. "You are lucky, Jim, that the bullet went right through you. At least you won't be suffering from lead poisoning."

Jean looked on as Michelle continued her examination of the wound.

"You lost a lot of blood, Jim," said Michelle. "I'm going to cleanse the wound with disinfectant, then I'm going to dress it and tape your abdomen to cover both the entry and exit wounds."

"Thank you nurse," said Markham jokingly. "I want to thank both of you for helping me," said Markham.

"Don't mention it, Jim," said Jean. "What are friends for?"

"Jean," said Markham, "could you take everything that identifies me and Teri out of the rented car when you come back? I'm afraid you'll have to wipe the car clean of blood on the driver's seat, and then you could you just drop it off at the airport where I rented it."

"No problem, Jim, consider it done," replied Jean.

"If you don't mind, I think we'd better get going before the authorities start looking in this area," said Markham.

"You're right Jim," replied Jean. "Thank God I filled up the gas tank a few days ago."

While Markham lay down on his back on the V-Berth with a light blanket covering him, Michelle went up to the cockpit with Jean to discuss the sea route they were going to take to reach Lake Ontario. Michelle was truly a sailor and Jean relied heavily on her navigation skills and seamanship.

"We're gonna have to take the south channel to the Lake Saint Louis opening and travel west about fourteen miles to the Saint Lawrence Seaway. That will take us to the first of two Beauharnois locks separated by a distance of about 900 meters," said Michelle in French, without looking at a map.

"I've never been through those locks, honey," said Jean in French.

"You climb about 30 feet in each lock and 60 feet when finished with the second lock. The locks are about 600 feet long by 70 feet wide," said Michelle.

"Are we going to encounter any bridges?" asked Jean.

"Yes, after we've exited the second lock we're going to be traveling in a channel for about 2 miles then reach the first of two bridges. You'll have to honk the horn three times for the bridge to open; it's an elevator bridge. The second bridge, also an elevator bridge, is about 2 nautical miles from the first bridge. Then we'll be going through a 1000 foot breakwater made of cement and the two-way channel is about 300 feet which will take us into Lake Saint Francois. We'll be heading west for about 15 miles reaching the Cornwall Narrows , then dodging small islands, we will follow the marked Saint Lawrence Seaway," said Michelle.

"Phew! You'd better write this all down, sweetheart," replied Jean.

"I will while you're under way which should be right now, Jean," said Michelle.

"You might as well give me the rest now," said Jean.

"Well, finally we'll arrive at the Snell and Eisenhower locks in American waters, where fortunately, there are no customs or immigration requirements. The Snell and Eisenhauer locks are about 2 miles apart. When we exit the Eisenhauer lock , we'll be in the Saint Lawrence River navigating west for about 15 miles to the Iroquois locks. We'll by pass it by going through the Iroquois control dam then continuing down the Saint Lawrence River into the beginning of the Thousand Islands. We past Kingston into Lake Ontario and from there we'll travel southwest until we reach the U.S. shore and entry into the Niagara River where the Youngstown Yacht Club is located," said Michelle.

"That's a lot more detail than I care to know, frankly?" said Jean. "I'll depend on you, sweetheart, to give me the proper directions."

"I'll write it down anyway," replied Michelle, "but right now you can start the engine while I untie the dock lines."

"Aye, Aye! Skipper," replied Jean in good humor.

With Markham asleep in the berth below deck, the Antidote got under way with all running lights on under a star lit sky and a quarter moon. Whenever they were not confined inside locks Jean put the boat into near full throttle reaching speeds of 30 to 35 knots. He knew that time was critical in getting Markham to a doctor who would be waiting at the Youngstown Yacht Club. Dr. Peter O'Reilly, a medical doctor and long time personal friend of Markham, resided with his wife Cecilia in Lewiston, New York, about 5 miles from the Youngstown Yacht Club. Jean knew Markham planned to use his cell phone to call Peter when they were 5 miles from their destination, which would be about 6 o'clock in the morning and still dark.

They had traveled through two locks and were approaching the first of two elevator bridges when Michelle told Jean that she was going into the cabin below to check on Markham's condition. "Don't forget to honk the horn three times, Jean," said Michelle before going down into the cabin.

"I know, otherwise he won't open the bridge," replied Jean.

Michelle placed her right hand on Markham's forehead which was hot to the touch. She removed the blanket and saw a mass of blood on the mattress on both sides of his abdomen apparently leaking from the entry wound in his back. She took out her thermometer and checked his temperature which showed it to be elevated at 104 degrees.

"Jim, Jim," said Michelle attempting to awaken him.

Markham opened his watery eyes and just stared at Michelle.

"Jim, I need for you to turn over so that I can take a look at the wound in your back," said Michelle, "can you turn over?"

Without saying a word, Markham slowly turned his body on his right side exposing the wound on his left lower back. She realized that she needed to put on new pressure pads and a tighter wrap. She started cutting the old bandage wrap and removed the old pads and using all of her strength, managed to apply enough pressure to slow the bleeding and replace the bandages. But she was truly worried about his worsening condition, especially the high temperature. Now lying on his back again, Markham attempted to talk to Michelle.

"How am I doing?" asked Markham.

"I will be honest with you, Jim, you've lost a lot of blood and you have a high temperature which I must bring down," said Michelle. "I'm going to give you an aspirin and I'm also going to put a wet compress over your forehead. You don't need that blanket; I'm going to replace it with a sheet."

"Listen, Michelle," said Markham realizing the seriousness of his condition. "I told Jean what to do in the event that I don't make it."

"There's no need for you to talk like this, Jim. You're going to be alright, I promise," said Michelle nearly in tears.

Markham looked into her angelic face which started to fade from view as he slowly fell into a coma.

Michelle went up on deck and alerted Jean of Markham's worsening condition.

"I don't think Jim's going to make it in time for the doctor to help him," said Michelle.

"Why do you say that?" asked Jean. "The bullet didn't hit any vital organs."

"No, but he has lost too much blood; it may be because of a severed artery and his temperature is 104. I figured we won't arrive at the Youngstown Yacht Club for another 4 hours. By that time he may be dead," said Michelle. "I think we should head for the nearest port and summon an ambulance…that's the only way we can save his life, Jean."

"We can't pull into any port. The moment we call an ambulance and they see that it's a bullet wound, they'll call the police, and then what happens to the Holy Shroud?" said Jean. "Those are two good reasons why we can't pull into any port and we must stay on course as Jim wants, no matter what. I don't know if he told you, Michelle, but he told me at the very beginning that if he died on this trip, to call Alex Petrov of the CIA who is aware of this whole operation for the recovery of the shroud. Petrov would make sure that Markham's body was removed and the shroud delivered to the Chapel in Turin."

"He didn't give me any details, just that he told you what to do in the event of his death," said Michelle. "Our dear friend is dying down there…isn't there anything we can do to save him?" she asked rhetorically, and then an idea came to her.

Michelle quickly descended into the cabin below and removed the sheet covering Markham who was motionless and appeared to be comatose. A pool of blood had formed beneath his abdomen. She reached up to the elongated window, removed the tubular canister, and opened the end cover exposing the Holy Shroud. She hesitated for a moment, and asked Jesus to forgive her for what she was about to do. She slowly pulled the rolled shroud from the container and unraveled it to its full fourteen feet length which she then folded in half with the face of Jesus at the head of the fold. Carefully, she placed the seven foot Holy Shroud over Markham's entire body with Jesus' face covering Markham's face, and then stepped back, got down on her knees, and prayed to Jesus that he would save Markham's life. She offered her own life in exchange for his and that's when she saw crystal lights emanating from the shroud. The figure of Jesus slowly filled the shroud with a rainbow of lights each emitting a different sound, suddenly exploding into a blinding light that paralyzed Michelle, then traversed through the roof of the cabin into space for what seemed like an eternity but lasted only a few seconds. It was long enough for Jean to hear the sound and see the beam of light thinking he had been struck by lightning. He immediately brought his boat to a slow crawl and turned on the autopilot, then ran down below to see what had happened, discovering Michelle on her knees praying. As he slowly approached her, he noticed the Holy Shroud spread over Markham's body, and at first thought he had died. Michelle kept repeating the Lord's Prayer over and over again, until Jean realized that whatever had happened had put her into a state of shock. He kneeled next to her and gently put his arm around her and called her name. She turned her gaze towards him and then threw herself into his arms crying "I saw Jesus, I saw him, I saw Jesus Christ appear inside the Holy Shroud," she said to Jean with tears streaming down the cheeks of her face. "Oh, my God! Jean."

Michelle raised herself and approached Markham still covered from head to toe with the Holy Shroud. She carefully lifted the head of the shroud uncovering Markham's face and saw that he was breathing steadily. She felt his forehead, "His temperature is gone, Jean," she said. Then she slowly pulled the shroud down uncovering the rest of Markham's body and her mouth dropped open with disbelief.

"It's a miracle, Jean, it's a miracle," said Michelle as Jean approached.

"There's no sign of blood anywhere, not even on the bandages...I don't understand," said Michelle, who then used a pair of scissors cutting the bandages.

"The bullet wound is gone," said Jean. "There is no evidence of his wounds, not even traces of his blood."

"We have just witnessed a true miracle, Jean, and I undeniably saw the spirit of Jesus Christ."

"I heard the sound and saw the beam of light that shot through the roof of the cabin into space like a thunderbolt," said Jean, "but other than our testimony, Michelle, we have no proof of this miracle, no wound and no blood, not even on the bandages."

"He's in a deep sleep. Let's not disturb him. We'll go on deck," said Michelle.

Jean disconnected the autopilot and sat at the controls on the upper deck and Michelle joined him on the adjoining seat, still bewildered by the spiritual event.

"My God, Jean, don't you see the message Jesus has sent us?" said Michelle. "Jesus wants us to believe in him through our *faith* in his love and compassion for humankind, and that's why he didn't leave physical evidence of this miracle."

"And the irony of it all is that we can't tell anyone about this miracle without revealing our participation in the home invasion and recovery of the Holy Shroud which cost the lives of two people, God forgive us," said Jean.

"I can't believe this has happened," said Michelle.

"Yeah! Just wait 'till Jim wakes up and finds his wounds are all gone...he'll think he just came out of a bad dream," said Jean.

"Or a good one," replied Michelle who thought she heard a noise and turned to see Markham standing barefoot wearing blue slacks and an unbuttoned white short-sleeve shirt. His thick curly gray hair and white beard framed his face with eyes that seemed distant yet intense with wisdom as he slowly walked towards them.

"I believe that I have been visited by Jesus Christ," said Markham holding his left hand against the left side of his abdomen. "I thought I had been dreaming until I woke up to find my wound completely healed. I saw the shroud folded on the bunk. The last thing I remember was Michelle taking my temperature."

"Oh! Jim," said Michelle embracing him, then stepping back to allow Jean to also embrace him in a brotherly gesture of friendship.

"I thought you were dying, so I covered you with the Holy Shroud and a veritable miracle happened...I actually saw the spirit of Jesus appear through the Holy Shroud and the proof is in your miraculous recovery," said Michelle.

"I owe the two of you so much ...how can I ever repay you?" said Markham.

"Nonsense, Jim, we did it out of love, and it's Jesus Christ you should be thanking," said Michelle, and with a nod of his head, Jean agreed.

"Don't worry my friends, I have a feeling that God's got other missions for me to complete as repayment for today's miracle," said Markham with a knowing smile of past experiences. "But I am exceedingly grateful to God and you, his now devoted disciples I am sure."

"This experience has forever changed our lives, Jim," said Jean with Michelle nodding her head in agreement. "I'd better replace the shroud in the canister," said Michelle.

"I already did that, Michelle," said Markham. "How close are we to the mouth of the Niagara River?"

"Another forty-five minutes and we should be there," said Jean.

"I'd better call Peter O'Reilly and announce my arrival," said Markham, "he doesn't know I'm coming and hasn't seen me in a couple of years."

"I'm sure he's going to be ecstatic over you calling him at this hour of the morning?" said Jean.

"He's a doctor who is used to early morning hours, and I'm certainly glad I won't have to use his medical services," said Markham.

"Are you going to tell him about the miracle of the Holy Shroud?" asked Michelle.

"No, I'm not, and I never intended to reveal the contents of the canister, because it would invite their curiosity and removal of the shroud, requiring too many answers to questions that I am not at liberty to disclose," said Markham.

"I understand, Jim," said Michelle.

"It makes a lot of sense," said Jean. "You would have to reveal our role in this investigation and I'm sure the CIA would not want their role to be revealed either."

"The less said about this whole affair, the better for all of us," said Markham, but the investigation is not over yet," said Markham.

"Why not?" asked Jean.

"Because Philippe Marceaux's brother Henri is still at large and in control of assassins who killed Musso and Bucceli, and I'm sure that he's figured out that I am responsible for his brother's death," said Markham. "I also have to deal with Loefler, remember?"

"Oh, shit! That's right, I almost forgot about that," said Jean. "Man, there's never a dull moment with you, is there?"

"As I said, there are more missions for me to execute. I just wish I would get a respite like a nice trip to Hawaii," said Markham.

"Watch what you wish for, Jim, you just might get it," said Jean.

"Yes, and it could turn out to be another job," said Michelle.

Markham walked back to the stern and dialed Peter's telephone number and after several rings, Peter answered.

"Peter, it's me Jim Markham."

"Jim…glad to hear from you but do you know what time it is?" asked Peter.

"Of course I do, Peter. I'm sorry to awaken you at this early hour but this is an emergency," said Markham.

"What…are you hurt?" asked Peter genuinely concerned.

"No, but I'm on a classified mission which I can't discuss over the telephone, Peter. I will be landing at the Youngstown Yacht Club on a 36 foot yacht named Antidote in about 30 minutes. I hope you don't mind having me as your guest for a few hours until I can get a flight out," said Markham.

"Are you kidding, Jim, we haven't seen you in at least two years. Cecilia will be glad to see you as well. I'll be at the dock in half an hour," said Peter.

"Thanks, Peter, see you soon," replied Markham.

Michelle navigated the Antidote through the numerous sail-boats in the Niagara River that were tethered to moorings facing the Youngstown Yacht Club, until she finally saw an empty space at the wooden dock running along the shored grounds of the club. Michelle adroitly pulled alongside allowing Markham to jump onto the dock to receive and cleat the bow and then the stern lines thrown to him by Jean. With the engine running in case they needed to make a swift departure, Michelle and Jean descended to the cockpit to join Markham who was now ready to leave with the canister strapped over his left shoulder and one black bag containing his and Teri's stuff. It included Teri's wallet minus her driver's license, plus her CIA credentials and a watch which she had left in the car. It was an awkward moment when they stood there facing each other, lost for words, then Jean extended his hand which Markham shook vigorously.

"Be careful, Jim, and don't be a stranger, come visit us again, only this time for pleasure, Hen!" said Jean smiling.

Michelle stepped forward with tears in her eyes and embraced Markham for several seconds then stepped back trying to control her emotions.

"You've changed our lives immeasurably, Jim, and we'll never forget you," she said looking directly into his eyes moist with sadness at his departure. "God protect you and come back to us soon; you are now family and we love you, Jim."

The words 'love you' resonated deeply in Markham's mind but he knew this was a spiritual love and her corporal love belonged to Jean. He had recognized only too late his love for Teri who evidently was not destined to share her life with him.

"I'm not good at 'goodbyes'. I'm going to miss you both terribly and I'll especially be thinking of you when I'm sailing solo. I love you guys, God Bless You," said Markham in a choked voice that betrayed the deepness of his love and respect for his two friends.

Markham stepped onto the boat's cowling then jumped onto the dock and laid down his bag and the canister so that he could untie the dock lines connected to the boat. As the boat pulled away piloted by Jean, Michelle stood at the stern, with tears rolling down her cheeks, staring at Markham, the man she could have loved in another time.

Markham watched Michelle standing at the stern and wondered whether she was thinking the same thing passing through his mind that her love belonged to Jean and he was merely a medium to a spiritual event that would change her soul.

CHAPTER X

Return of the Holy Shroud

Markham started walking towards the street entrance of the deserted yacht club when he saw headlights descending down the steep road to the flat road surface at the club's entrance. He opened the door and stepped into the narrow street to greet the silver sports utility vehicle, which stopped abreast of Markham, and upon recognizing Peter he entered the vehicle. Markham shook hands with Peter who then drove up the ramp onto the main street towards his house in Lewiston.

"My goodness, Jim, where have you been?" asked Peter.

"Many places, Peter. I'm currently working for the Central Intelligence Agency on a classified mission. The only way I could get here under some very unusual circumstances was by boat and the hour was not my choice," said Markham. He continued to explain before Peter could ask any questions. "I'll be catching a plane out of the Niagara Falls Air Force Base sometime today, and I'm going to ask you to please understand that I may not be able to answer all of your questions for security reasons."

"No problem, Jim," said Peter, "I'll explain it to Cecilia and I'm sure she'll understand too, so tell me if I encroach on an area that's off limits."

"Thanks Peter, I most sincerely appreciate this," replied Markham. "So how have you been these past two years?"

"Well, I've only got two years to go before retirement, then Cecilia and I will be spending the winters at our house on Veli Losinj island in Croatia," said Peter. "You ought to take time off Jim and visit us in Croatia."

"I'd love to, Peter," replied Markham, "but right now I have several things that demand my immediate attention and who knows how long it will take."

"You're not getting any younger, Jim," replied Peter, "you have to take time off before the clock runs out, which reminds me, how's your health my friend?"

"Excellent, Peter, thanks for asking," replied Markham.

Peter pulled his SUV into the wide driveway of his large home surrounded with beautifully manicured bushes and flower beds. Cecilia greeted them at the door and embraced Markham who in traditional Croatian fashion kissed her on both cheeks.

"You got a bit grayer, Jim, but you don't look a day older than when we last saw you two years ago," said Cecilia demonstrably happy to see Markham.

"Your flattery is misplaced. It is you, my dear, who isn't aging," replied Markham.

"So what's this thing you're carrying, Jim?" asked Cecilia.

"It's contains the arrows I use to pierce women's hearts," replied Markham lightheartedly.

"I don't doubt it, knowing you, Jim," she replied mockingly.

"Cecilia, let me talk to you for a minute," said Peter taking Cecilia aside, "Excuse us, Jim."

"Jim is on a classified assignment with the Central Intelligence Agency and can't discuss what he's doing or what he's carrying, so he asked us not to pry too deeply into his activities at the moment. He'll be catching a plane later today," said Peter.

"So he's going to be with us only for a few hours?" asked Cecilia.

"That's right, so why don't we go out to the patio and have breakfast there," said Peter, "It's a nice, sunny day."

"OK! Find out what Jim wants for breakfast," she said, feeling a bit disappointed.

Back in the living room, Peter learned from Markham that he would be content with eggs and bacon or ham, rye or wheat toast and hot tea, and Peter informed him that all of those ingredients were available and would be served on the patio.

While on the boat, Markham had anticipated Cecilia's curiosity and sealed the cover of the canister with duck tape that Jean always carried on his boat. Hence, he confidently placed the canister along with his bag in the corner of the living room while excusing himself to go to the bathroom to wash his face. Upon his return he was invited to the patio where a glass of orange juice had already been poured for Peter and Markham. Sitting leisurely around the patio table, Markham admired the beautiful flower beds surrounding the in-ground swimming pool and the clear view across Lake Ontario of the Canadian National Tower in the city of Toronto. While Peter and Cecilia were busy in the kitchen, Markham took that opportunity to call Alex Petrov at CIA Headquarters but walked off the patio onto the lawn where he wouldn't be overheard.

"Petrov," answered the Chief of Clandestine Operations.

"Alex, it's Jim Markham,"

"Jim, I was worried about you," said Alex, "where are you and what happened?"

"I'm at a friend's house in Lewiston, New York, and I have the Holy Shroud with me. Teri was fatally shot by Philippe Marceaux and in turn I had to fatally shoot him. I wasn't able to take Teri's body with me and I'll explain the details when I see you. But you need to know that while running from the mansion I caught a bullet on the left side of my abdomen. I managed to get to my rental car and called my friend Jean Galian for assistance, and then met him and his wife Michelle at his boat in Lachine. My condition got worse and Jean's wife Michelle, a trained nurse, believed that I was dying from the loss of blood. In desperation she covered me with the Holy Shroud, and a miracle occurred in that there is absolutely no sign or scar that I was ever wounded. Now the Quebec police no doubt are looking for a wounded man and they're not going to find one," said Markham who was interrupted by Alex.

"Jim...you're not kidding me, are you?" asked Alex. "This is not something to joke about."

"This is no joke, Alex, this is the real thing, and I have two witnesses to vouch for it. In addition, I'm sure that the Quebec police all-out bulletin will reflect the suspect as a white male, armed and wounded," said Markham.

"What really counts is that you're alright and you've recovered the Holy Shroud intact," replied Alex, "but do you realize the implication of what you have just told me, Jim?"

"Yes, I do. It's changed my life completely, Alex, as it will yours when you hear the details," said Markham. "I need a plane to take me directly to Turin to deliver the Holy Shroud to Archbishop Bartolini so they can secure it in a temperature controlled container. Lewiston is located about 8 miles from Niagara Falls Air Force Base, which is an active reserve installation. Can you have an agency aircraft, capable of flying me directly to Turin, pick me up at the Niagara Falls Air Force Base today?" said Markham.

"I can arrange an aircraft to pick you up at Niagara Falls, Jim," replied Alex, "but tell me, what identification was on Teri Flanigan's person when she was shot?"

"Only her Virginia driver's license bearing her real name, nothing else, Alex," replied Markham.

"Good. I'll arrange for her body to be delivered to a funeral home in Riverhead, Suffolk County, New York where her sister resides," said Alex. "I'll have to make some calls to my national security counterparts in Ottawa to smooth things over. I'm going to assign John Tunney to follow through on that, because I will be on that plane with Scott Spencer, whom you have met, to escort you and the Shroud to Turin, Italy. This is an incredible event. I will call you when I have confirmed our arrival time at Niagara Falls Air Force Base."

"Thanks Alex. See you soon," replied Markham who terminated the call just in time to see Peter arrive on the patio carrying a plate of fried eggs and ham and another plate with rye toast. He placed it on the table just as Markham entered the patio.

"Here you are sir," said Peter, "I hope this meets with your satisfaction."

"Indeed, it's better than the Ritz," replied Markham who felt much better knowing that he would be flying to Turin before the day's end, although he loved and appreciated Peter and Cecilia's gracious company.

An hour later, Markham received a telephone call from Alex informing him that a company Gulfstream jet aircraft with him and Scott on board would be arriving at Niagara Falls Air Force Base at 1430 hours and for him to be there with the Holy Shroud.

That gave Markham a few hours to talk with Peter and Cecilia about old times and the current status of their children whom Markham knew quite well. The time came for Peter to drive Markham to the Air Base, where Markham showed his military identification to enter the Air Base with Peter as his guest visitor.

"This is a busy Air Base for a reservist station," said Peter.

"Yes, it is, and I wouldn't be surprised if it became an active duty station soon, considering the situation in the Middle East," replied Markham. Peter had never served in the military and was most curious about military installations. "OK! Peter, you can park in that spot over there; it's not reserved."

Inside the terminal, Markham, followed by Peter, walked nearly the full length of the terminal before they reached the flight control room. As Markham looked at his watch it was exactly 1430 hours.

"Has a private Gulfstream jet aircraft landed yet?" Markham asked one of the Air Force Sergeants manning the control room.

"As a matter of fact, it has landed and is taxiing to terminal 7, sir," said the Sergeant.

"Thank you, Sergeant," replied Markham who then walked with Peter to terminal 7 located less than 50 yards away. They both stood behind the large, elongated Plexiglas window over-looking the runway watching the silver Gulfstream jet aircraft maneuvering through the ground signs and lighted hand signals of the ground crewman, as he directed the pilot to his final parking place. The side door to the aircraft was lowered into a stairway and the tall figure of Alex Petrov descended onto the tarmac followed by Scott Spencer. The two men walked confidently towards the entrance to terminal 7, and at the sight of Markham, Alex broke into a large smile. He quickened his pace to greet his long time friend and colleague with a huge bear hug. Markham shook hands with Scott, of whom he had the greatest respect for his professionalism and integrity. Markham introduced Peter to his two colleagues, then Peter excused himself and said farewell to Markham. Peter admired Markham but did not envy his lifestyle.

As the three men walked back to the aircraft, Alex asked the obvious question.

"Is the Holy Shroud inside that canister you're carrying?" asked Alex.

"Yes, it is, Alex, and it must not be removed from the canister until it is turned over to Archbishop Bartolini for transfer into a climate-controlled container," said Markham.

"I understand, Jim," replied Alex, "I was only asking."

"And I'm only informing," said Markham with a smile meaning no disrespect.

After being seated in the aircraft with no other passengers onboard and the plane was in the air, Alex asked Markham to recount all of the events that had transpired leading to the shooting, the recovery of the Holy Shroud, the boat ride and the miracle.

Alex and Scott listened to Markham's accounting of the events in complete silence and could not contain their astonishment at the description Michelle had given of the appearance of Jesus with the crystal bright lights and sound that had literally paralyzed her into a mesmerized state and her discovery of the miraculous healing of Markham's wounds that left no scars and no evidence of spent blood. Markham also related his own experience of seeing the image of Jesus Christ while comatose in what he thought was a dream but now realizes it was an actual apparition. Markham related that during this apparition, Jesus gave him what appeared to be a message.

"What was the message?" asked Alex with Scott listening anxiously beside him.

"He said *Love and Peace are the Keys to my Kingdom*" replied Markham.

"Is that all he said?" asked an incredulous Alex.

"Yes, that's all I heard him say," replied Markham. "I was in a comatose state; I'm surprised I even remember that."

"It was meant for you to remember, Jim," said Alex. "You were chosen to deliver that message."

"All I know, Alex is that Jesus cured me, he healed my wound and I'm alive today because of him," said Markham.

"Looking back at the past, it's not the first time he saved your life, my friend," said Alex. "Remember those two large winged seagulls that have always appeared when you were in danger at sea."

"Yes, I remember only too well. Oh, God! Alex, I'm getting too old for these adventures," said Markham desperate for a respite. "It's about time I hung up my running shoes don't you think. I need a long vacation; in fact I should be retired."

"Not yet my friend," said Alex. "We've still got some unfinished business. Do you think that Jesus saved your life so that you could retire, Jim?"

Markham remained silent as he thought about Alex's last statement.

"You're just exhausted from all that action, your trek through the Pakistan desert, your swim down the Indus River, your travel across two continents and your being wounded in the recovery of the Holy Shroud; that would put any man into his grave, Jim. What you need is a nice rest to rejuvenate your body and spirit, so why don't you just lie back while Scott and I move to another section of the plane giving you some quiet time," said Alex.

"Sounds like a good idea, Alex," replied Markham reclining his seat and closing his eyes.

Seven hours later the Gulfstream jet aircraft landed at Turino Airport and Markham was awakened from a sound sleep that had totally refreshed him even though it was now 3:00 a.m. Turino time. The three men descended the aircraft with the canister containing the shroud strapped to Markham's left shoulder while he carried his black bag with his right hand. Alex and Scott each pulled a small wheeled carrying case. They all entered the airport terminal and stopped at a rental car agency. Scott pulled out a credit card and within fifteen minutes they were driving out of the airport to the hotel where Alex and Markham had stayed before, the Hotel Principi di Piemonte, located a short distance from the Cathedral. After checking in, they all agreed that a good time to meet in the morning was 10:00 a.m.

Alex was a man who could function on very little sleep, while Markham was the opposite. Alex awakened at 8:00 a.m. and called Archbishop Bartolini at the Cathedral to inform him that the Holy Shroud had been recovered and was in Markham's possession in his hotel room at the Principi di Piemonte. The Archbishop expressed his undying gratitude and told Alex that he would receive them at 11:00 a.m. Afterwards the Archbishop called the Cardinal General at the Vatican to give him the good news.

While having breakfast at the hotel, Alex informed Markham that he had called the FBI providing them with all of the particulars of the case including the evidence acquired from the Turino Police Department as to the video tape of the falsified polygraph test conducted by Peter Loefler, the Deputy Director of the Defense Academy for Credibility Assessment.

"Are you sure we're not jumping the gun, Alex?" asked Markham.

"We've got the Holy Shroud, so we don't have to worry about Loefler interfering with its recovery," replied Alex.

"You're right about that, but I'm hoping that the FBI get to his banking records and other evidence before they reveal he's a suspect," said Markham.

"They've been at this for a long time, Jim," said Alex, "I'm sure they won't arrest him until they have all of the necessary evidence to convict."

"I hope so, Alex," replied Markham, "just remember that there are still at least two assassins on the loose in Paris at the beck and call of Henri Marceaux, attorney at Law, and the brother of deceased Philippe Marceaux."

"Do we have any evidence against his brother Henri?" asked Scott.

"Not that I know of," replied Markham, "and he's a crafty lawyer."

"That means that you, James, could still be a target," said Alex.

"That's if he and his thugs can find me," replied Markham.

"Just the same, I'll be glad that in an hour's time you'll be relinquishing the Holy Shroud to the Archbishop to be secured in their new vault in the Royal Chapel," said Alex.

"I think that as a precaution, I should call Robert Ciminelli, the Chief of Detectives of the Turino Police Department and ask him to make at least one copy of the video tape containing Loefler's polygraph test of Arturo Musso," said Markham.

"A very good idea, Jim," replied Alex, "in fact I think they should copy the tape on a compact disk and make a couple of copies, one of which I could keep in my folder, just in case the original becomes missing."

"I like the way you think, Alex," commented Markham.

"Do you think you're going to have much trouble getting Teri's body transferred from Quebec City to a funeral home in Suffolk County, New York?" asked Markham.

"They'll be holding the body as part of crime scene evidence so there will be some delay, but I'm sure they'll release it soon, Jim," said an empathetic Alex.

"I must attend her funeral, Alex," replied Markham, "so please let me know when she is transferred to the funeral home in New York."

"Don't worry, Jim, I'll let you know," replied Alex who remembered Markham's equally intense reaction when he lost his wife.

The three men with Scott driving, arrived at the Cathedral of Saint John the Baptist and Markham who had been there before, led Alex and Scott to the office of the Archbishop in the rectory behind the Cathedral. Archbishop Bartolini and two other priests were there to greet them and upon seeing the leather canister hanging from Markham's shoulder made the sign of the cross. Markham presented the canister to the Archbishop.

"It is my privilege Your Excellency to return the Holy Shroud to you for safekeeping," said Markham.

"And it is with immense gratitude that I humbly accept the return of the Holy Shroud, Mister Markham," replied his Excellency.

"Your Excellency, would it be possible for Mister Petrov and Mister Spencer to witness the removal of the Holy Shroud from the canister and insertion into the climate-controlled container in the Vault Room? They have been of great assistance in the recovery of the Holy Shroud, Your Excellency," said Markham.

"We owe you so much, Mister Markham, that I can hardly refuse your reasonable request," replied his Excellency. "Let me introduce you to Father Lombardo and Father Picollo, my newly appointed assistants."

"Father Lombardo is from the Vatican in Rome and Father Picollo comes to us from Naples," said the Archbishop, "If you will follow me to the Royal Chapel we will go down into the Vault Room and secure the Holy Shroud."

After Archbishop Bartolini used a magnetic card to disarm the exterior alarm system, he inserted a key into the lock of the steel door which opened with surprising ease in view of its thickness. They then entered the vault room and the Archbishop asked all present to turn around and face the entrance door while he worked the combination to the door of the safe and upon unlocking it allowed his five guests to view the interior of the safe whose door had to be two feet thick. Inside the large safe was a large climate-controlled container with a bullet-proof glass front ready with gas tubing and electrical security device to receive the Holy Shroud. The Archbishop with the assistance of Father Lombardo carefully removed the Holy Shroud from the canister and unrolled it to its full fourteen foot length which they examined for damage, while Alex and Scott with Markham behind them watched the two priests handling the Holy Shroud with a venerability that only the Holy Shroud deserved.

"Your Excellency," asked Alex with great hesitation, "Would it be possible for Scott and I to gently touch the Holy Shroud?"

Archbishop Bartolini looked at Alex then at Scott, and turned to Markham who nodded in agreement.

"You may only touch the corner of the Holy Shroud," said the Archbishop.

Alex allowed Scott to step forward and upon approaching the Holy Shroud which had been folded in half exposing the front of Jesus' body, Scott got down on his knees and touched the corner of the Holy Shroud then made the sign of the cross after which he stepped backwards to make room for Alex who also genuflected before touching the Holy Shroud, then made the sign of the cross and said a silent prayer. They then stepped back and thanked the Archbishop.

"Mister Markham, do you wish to touch the Holy Shroud?" asked the Archbishop.

"I already have, Your Excellency, thank you," replied Markham.

After installing the Holy Shroud into the climate-controlled container and its end secured with a locking device and the alarm activated, they all exited the vault room and retired back to the Archbishop's office at the rectory for a briefing.

Markham briefed the Archbishop in the presence of Alex and Scott but without the presence of the Fathers Lombardo and Picollo whom the Archbishop had politely excused. At no point during Markham's lengthy briefing did Archbishop Bartolini interrupt him, but when finished with his briefing, the Archbishop asked him only one question.

"Would you mind terribly if I could see where you were wounded, Mister Markham?" asked the Archbishop.

"No, I don't mind at all," replied Markham who removed his jacket and then his shirt exposing his chest and abdomen so as to leave no doubt.

"Amazing, simply amazing," said the Archbishop, "I have no doubt that a miracle has happened and the Cardinal General and the Pope must be apprised of this immediately. When will you be leaving Turino?"

Markham looked at Alex for an answer. "What have you in mind, Your Excellency?" asked Alex.

"The Cardinal General and the Pope will most certainly want to see and hear Mister Markham's detailed description of the miracle of the Holy Shroud," said the Archbishop.

"I can truly understand your need for my briefing the Cardinal General and the Pope, Your Excellency," said Markham, "but I have a very urgent matter that must be attended to immediately. Can this briefing wait until I return?"

"Jim, what urgent matter do you have that can't wait until the Pope has been briefed?" asked Alex.

"Briefing the Cardinal and the Pope will require that I go to Rome, and I need to go to Paris to keep a promise with an Editor, and then I must fly directly to New York to attend Teri's funeral," said Markham with a look of determination that Alex knew only too well to challenge.

"I'm afraid that I have to agree with Jim, Your Excellency," said Alex. "Teri lost her life during the recovery of the Holy Shroud, and Jim made a promise to the man who made it possible for him to escape from the Pakistan prison. I'm sure the Cardinal and the Pope will understand this unavoidable delay which will be rectified as soon as possible."

"I understand and I completely agree with you that you must keep your promises Mister Markham," said the Archbishop. "I will brief the Cardinal and he will brief the Pope and we will await your return Mister Markham with God Speed."

CHAPTER XI

Death and Resurrection of Love

At the Principi di Piemonti Hotel, Alex made several telephone calls to the United States, including the FBI, the State Department, as well as his office while Scott and Markham relaxed in comfortable sofa chairs.

"The State Department has cleared the way for Teri's body to be sent to a funeral home in Suffolk County," said Alex to Markham. "I'm going to have to go to Riverhead in Suffolk County and explain the circumstances surrounding Teri's death to her sister; I believe her name is Jennifer."

"That's your old stomping grounds, isn't it?" said Markham.

"Yeah! That's where I served as a New York State Trooper," replied Alex. "As you know, Jim, I grew up in Nassau County, next door to Suffolk County."

"That should bring back memories," said Markham. "Can you fly me to Paris on your way to the states?"

"Sure, we can do that, but how long will you be in Paris? If you want to make the funeral, Jim, you're going to have to make your Paris trip a very short one," said Alex.

"I know that," replied Markham. "I'm only going to visit Henri Charlemagne, the Editor of Le Parisien newspaper and give him the note and jewelry that Jean Depardieux gave me in prison, and then I'll catch a plane to New York and rent a car to Riverhead."

"Are you familiar with Riverhead or Suffolk County?" asked Alex.

"No, not really," replied Markham.

"Then I recommend you stay at the Hilton Garden Inn, Jim. I'll be there before you, so call me on my cell if I'm not in the Hilton; I may be on the way or at the Saint Isidore Cemetery. You have my cell number," said Alex. "Scott, you'll have to remain at the Agency to assist John Tunney who has his hands full with his wife due to have a baby any day.

"That sounds like a good plan, Alex. When are we leaving Turino?" asked Markham.

"We'll get a bite to eat downstairs then I'll call the airport to notify our pilot that we're coming and to adjust his flight plan to take us to Paris," said Alex.

Markham arrived at DeGaulle International airport aboard the Gulfstream jet aircraft at 1530 hours, with enough time left to visit Le Parisien newspaper before closing time. Le Parisien was located near the center of Paris and the taxi driver who thought Markham was French Canadian, due to his accent, praised the Canadians at the expense of Americans to increase his gratuity only to learn from the meager tip that it's best to say nothing if you can't say something good.

Upon entering Le Parisien newspaper building, Markham learned that the Editor-in-Chief's office was on the second floor, and proceeded to mount the stairs when two well dressed men descended the same staircase in conversation and as they passed each other, he heard one man addressing the other as Henri. Markham realized that if this was indeed Henri Charlemagne he would possibly be missing him until the next day or perhaps even longer. Not wanting to take that chance, Markham caught up with the two gentlemen at the bottom of the stairs and introduced himself.

"Excuse me," said Markham in French. "Are you Monsieur Henri Charlemagne?"

"Yes, I am," said the taller gentlemen in French.

"My name is James Markham, sir. I have a very important message from Jean Depardieux whom I met inside a prison in Pakistan and who is now deceased."

"Do you mean Jean Depardieux the archeologist?" asked Charlemagne.

"Yes, sir, I do," replied Markham. "I have come a long way to talk to you, sir and I have a letter and some personal jewelry that I promised Jean I would give to you."

"Mon Dieu, this is incredible," replied Charlemagne, "let's go back up into my office, shall we?"

Inside Charlemagne's office, Markham gave Jean's handwritten letter, the locket and his inscribed ring to Charlemagne who after reading the letter and examining the ring and locket took a deep breath.

"Tell me, Monsieur Markham, about the prison and how Jean died," said Charlemagne.

"I will be glad to," replied Markham who then related all of the events that led to his escape without divulging his mission regarding the Holy Shroud.

"I will not only publish Jean's letter and the circumstances surrounding his death, but I will have my best reporter investigate this matter and motivate the French Government to take action," said Charlemagne.

"I am deeply indebted to you sir, as is Jean Depardieux," said Markham as he rose and shook hands with Henri Charlemagne and his colleague.

"It is I and the French people who are indebted to you for bringing this tragedy to our attention, Monsieur Markham," said Charlemagne who in French fashion embraced Markham with a kiss on both cheeks.

Markham called De Gaulle International Airport and learned that no aircraft were leaving for JFK airport in New York until the following day, and the earliest flight was 8:00 a.m. After he made reservations at the InterContinental Paris-le-Grand hotel in the center of Paris, where he had previously stayed with Teri, Markham decided that a good dinner at one of his favorite restaurants was in order.

After a delightful meal at the Boeuf Soigne Restaurant, Markham, with time to kill, sat at a sidewalk café table sipping a glass of Scotch and became absorbed in the parade of colorful pedestrians. It wasn't long before his presence elicited the attention of a mademoiselle which in his younger days would have flattered him possibly into action, but now he was satisfied with the role of spectator in a city that had no equal in excitement.

At first he did not hear the ring of his cell phone due to the street noise but then before the last ring he picked up the call and it was from Alex.

"Alex, I'm sitting in a café sipping scotch while watching the fascinating life in the streets of Paris. Can't get any better than that," said Markham.

"I'm glad you're enjoying yourself, Jim," replied Alex. "When are you catching a flight to New York?"

"Tomorrow morning at 0800 hours," replied Markham.

"Well, I've got some news for you," said Alex.

"Is it good or bad?" asked Markham.

"I'll let you decide that," replied Alex. "When the FBI went to the Defense Academy for Credibility Assessment at Fort Jackson, South Carolina, to serve Peter Loefler with a search warrant and inform him of the charges, Loefler went into the bathroom and blew his brains out. I guess he figured that the jig was up."

"Good grief, Alex," said Markham, "I didn't expect that."

"The good news is that the taxpayers are spared the expense of a trial," said Alex.

"I still feel sorry for his family though. They have to pay for the sins of the father."

"Amen brother," replied Alex. "See you tomorrow, hopefully."

No more than an hour had passed when Markham received another overseas telephone call, this time from Jean Galian in Montreal.

"My goodness, Jean, that's two overseas calls within the hour," said Markham.

"Oh, yeah! Who was the other call from?" asked Jean.

"From Alex," said Markham. "He just informed me that Peter Loefler committed suicide when he was served with a search warrant by the FBI."

"No kidding," replied Jean. "How did he kill himself?"

"While the FBI was searching his office, Loefler went into the bathroom, locked himself in a stall and shot himself in the head," said Markham.

"Well, my friend, this is the night for shootings, 'cause I just learned from a police detective friend of mine in Quebec that late this afternoon when Henri Marceaux stepped out of his office building he was shot several times by two gunmen in a car parked in front of the building entrance. Coincidentally an unmarked police car driven by detectives from the Provincial Police happened to be driving on that street when the shots were fired. They gave chase at high speed that led onto the highway and apparently the gunman at the wheel lost control of the car, went off the highway and into a cement divider that flipped the car killing the passenger gunman. The driver, who was wearing his seat belt, miraculously survived the accident with minor injuries and was arrested for murder. I was told by my friend that during the interrogation they learned that the gunmen were from Paris, France. The surviving gunman named Jules Carpentier insisted he was only the driver and his associate Yves Calumet was the boss who did the shooting. He said that Calumet became incensed when Henri Marceaux refused to pay him his fee of one hundred thousand euros for the Bucelli murder because they had not killed James Markham who was also at the scene of the shooting," said Jean.

"Did Carpentier admit being the driver in the Bucelli murder?" asked Markham.

"I don't know, Jim, I didn't ask, it was a brief conversation," said Jean, "but it doesn't matter because he's being charged with Marceaux's murder."

"You'd think that being a lawyer, Henri Marceaux would have known better than to stiff hired killers," said Markham. "Well, that takes care of the loose ends doesn't it?"

"It sure does. Now you can rest easy, Jim," replied Jean.

"You live by the sword, you die by the sword," said Markham.

"Those old clichés usually turn out to be true, don't they," said Jean. "So where are you now and what are you doing?"

"I'm sitting at a sidewalk café in Paris admiring the scenery," said Markham.

"Huh! Huh! Just be careful that the scenery doesn't blind you into doing something I wouldn't do," said Jean laughing.

"Don't worry, Jean, I've got a plane to catch early tomorrow morning for New York City to attend Teri's funeral," said Markham.

"Oh, yeah! That's right. I'm so sorry, Jim," said Jean apologetically. "Michelle and I send you our condolences."

"Thanks Jean. Give my best to Michelle, au revoir mon ami," said Markham.

After that last conversation, Markham decided it was time to go back to the hotel and retire for the night. *Paris,* he thought, *is not the same without Teri.*

The next day, Markham boarded the Air France jet aircraft as a first class passenger and after factoring in the five hour gain, estimated his time of arrival at JFK to be 0900 Eastern Standard Time. He planned to rent a car with global positioning system and drive directly to the Hilton Garden Inn in Riverhead, New York which should put him in Riverhead at about 11:00 a.m., a reasonable time to attend any of the funeral services.

The flight across the Atlantic Ocean was pleasant and uneventful and the rented car's GPS functioned most accurately in getting him to the Hilton Garden Inn at 11:50 a.m.. While checking in, Markham inquired about Alex Petrov and there was no answer from his room telephone. Markham then called his cell phone and Alex answered.

"Alex, this is Jim, I'm at the Hilton Garden Inn" said Markham.

"I'm riding in the funeral procession which is heading to Saint Isidore's Cemetery. Ask the desk clerk for directions if it's not on your car's GPS," said Alex.

"OK! See you soon," replied Markham.

After getting directions from the Inn's desk clerk, Markham proceeded in his rented car to Saint Isidore's Cemetery and once inside he observed a large group of people in the distance gathered around an ornamental coffin, that rested on a lowering device over an empty grave, with a priest reciting prayers. Markham drove by a black limousine parked on the street near the ceremony but continued driving until he found a nearby parking lot full of cars, no doubt for mourners. Markham, wearing his dark suit, white shirt and blue tie because he didn't have time to buy a black one, slowly walked through the circle of relatives and friends of Theresa Brenner, whom he knew better by her cover name of Teri Flanigan. He found Alex Petrov standing across the grave from the immediate family, seated at the edge of the grave. "Glad you could make it," Alex whispered to Markham in order not to interrupt the Priest who was praying for the repose of the soul of Theresa Brenner and for the consolation of the family. As the Father started reciting scriptures from the old and new testaments, Markham's attention was drawn to the woman in center stage who appeared to be in her mid fifties and most likely Teri's sister Jennifer. She was flanked by a young man in his mid twenties and a woman of the same age, probably his wife. Jennifer had her head bent down listening to the priest praying for Theresa's salvation. The priest then recited a psalm with the mourners joining him, and then he asked everyone to join him in the Lord's Prayer. The priest sprinkled holy water over the coffin which caused Jennifer to raise her head in full view of Markham who almost went into shock when he saw the face of Teri Flanigan. He stared at her in disbelief, looking for an explanation. *How could this be*, he thought, *who is in the coffin?* Markham's forehead broke into a cold sweat thinking that perhaps he was having a nervous breakdown.

"Alex," whispered Markham, "What in God's name is going on?"

"What do you mean?" whispered Alex.

"I'm staring at Teri Flanigan across from her grave," whispered Markham.

"That is Teri's identical twin sister Jennifer," whispered Alex.

"Good God, I need a stiff drink," whispered Markham.

"You'll get your chance at the wake," whispered Alex.

The priest then offered petitions for the repose of Theresa Brenner's soul and invited the mourners to respond to each petition with "Lord have mercy." He then sprinkled holy water and threw a handful of dirt on the coffin ending the ceremony with a blessing.

As the coffin of Theresa Brenner was being lowered, Markham stared at Jennifer with continued disbelief at her uncanny resemblance to Theresa. He had an irresistible urge to talk to her to see if her voice and accent were also similar. With the ceremony ended, people started paying their respects to Jennifer and what turned out to be her son and his wife. Alex took that opportunity to introduce Markham to her.

"This is Jim Markham, Mrs. Templeton," said Alex. "He is the man I told you about who was with Teri when she died."

Jennifer stood up and held out her hand which Markham held tenderly as he looked into her vivid green eyes reminiscent of her sister.

"I'm so glad you were able to come to my sister's funeral Jim," said Jennifer whose soft voice made Markham's heart tremble with memories.

"Teri never told me she had an identical twin sister. For a moment I thought I was seeing a ghost," said Markham. "I can't get over the resemblance."

Jennifer could see from Markham's demeanor the remarkable impact she had on him which brought the first smile she had displayed since the news of her sister's death.

"You must come to my house for the wake, Jim," said Jennifer. "I would like to talk to you about my sister who wrote to me about you."

"I will be there Mrs. Templeton," replied Markham.

"Please call me Jennifer. I've been a widow for twenty years."

Jennifer then excused herself and joined her son and his wife in the walk to the awaiting limousine.

Markham and Alex started walking in the direction of the parking lot where they had parked their rented cars.

"You looked like you were struck with a bolt of lightening, Jim," said Alex.

Markham remained silent, still evaluating his encounter with Jennifer.

"You know, Jim, Jennifer is the spitting image of Theresa, but she's not Teri."

"That, Alex, is for me to find out," replied Markham.

"Oh, boy! Here we go again," said Alex.

Had they looked up into the sky above, they would have seen two large winged seagulls circling overhead in witness to the death and resurrection of a lost love.

The End

REFERENCES

Ball, P. (28 January 2005). To Know a Veil. *Nature online* (http://www.nature.com/news/205/050124/full/news050124-17 html

Bennett, J. (2009). Sacred Blood, Sacred Image – The Sudarium of Oviedo. Fort Collins, Colorado: Roman Catholic Books.

Damon, P. E., D. J., Donahue, B. H., Gore, A. L., Hatheway, A. J. T., Jull, T. W., Linick, P. J., Sercel, L. J., Toolin, C. R., Bronk, E. T., Hall, R. E. M., Hedges, R., Housley, J. A., Law, C., Perry, G., Bonani, S., Trumbore, W., Woelfli, J. C., Ambers, S. G. E., Bowman, M. N., Leese, M. S. (1989-2002). Radiocarbon dating of the Shroud of Turin. *Nature,* 337 (6208): 611-615.

Gardiner, P. (2007). *The Ark, the Shroud, and Mary: The untold truths about the relics of the Bible.* Franklin Lakes, New Jersey: The Career Press, Inc.

Gove, H. E. (1996). *Relic, Icon or Hoax? Carbon Dating the Turin Shroud.* Boca Raton, Florida: Taylor and Francis Group.

Heller, J. H. (1983). *Report on the Shroud of Turin.* Boston, Massachusetts: Houghton Mifflin Company

Humber, T. (1980). *The Sacred Shroud.* New York: Pocket Books.

Iannone, J. C. (1998). *New Scientific Evidence: The Mystery of the Shroud of Turin.*

Staten Island, New York: Fathers and Brothers of the Society of St. Paul.

Marino, J. G., Benford, M. S. (2000). Evidence for the skewing of the C-14 Dating of the Shroud of Turin due to Repairs. *Sindone 2000 Conference*, Orvieto, Italy.

Meacham, W. (2005). *The Rape of the Turin Shroud.* Swindon, Wiltshire, UK: W. H. Smith. Co. United Kingdom.

Mills, A. A. (1995). Image formation on the Shroud of Turin. *Interdisciplinary Science Reviews*, Vol. 20.

Picknett, L., Prince, C. (2000). Turin Shroud. London, England: Corgi Books.

Rogers, R. N. (January 20, 2005). Studies on the radiocarbon sample from the Shroud of Turin. *Thermochimica Acta*, Vol. 425, Nr. 1-2; 189-194.

Rogers, R. N., Arnoldi, A. (2003). "The Shroud of Turin: an amino-carbonyl reaction (Maillard reaction) may explain the image formation" in Ames, J. M. (Ed.): *Melanoidins in Food and Health*, Publication of European Communities, Vol. 4: 106-113.

Ruffin, B., Ruffin, C.B. (1999). *The Shroud of Turin.* Huntington, Indiana: Our Sunday Visitor Publishing Division, Our Sunday Visitor, Inc.

Shroud of Turin. Wikipedia, The free encyclopedia. en,wikipedia. org/wiki/shroud_of_turin.

Silverton, J. (2005). *Decoding the Past: The Shroud of Turin.* History Channel video Documentary produced by John Joseph.

Wilson, I. (1998). *The Blood and the Shroud.* New York: Free Press.

Made in the USA
Charleston, SC
15 July 2010